BLACK FOREVER

VICTORIA QUINN

KMA

4-2018

This is a work of fiction. All the characters and events portrayed in this novel are fictitious or used fictitiously. All rights reserved. No part of this book may be reproduced in any form or by any electronic or mechanical means, including information storage and retrieval systems, without written permission from the publisher or author, except in the case of a reviewer, who may quote brief passages in a review.

C alloway
The sound of the whip was amplified in my ear, sounding three times as loud and three times as powerful. My fingers gripped the leather handle like it might slip away at any moment. I lashed it across her back and her ass, making her moan and cry at the exact same time.

I finally felt like myself again.

When I told Isabella what to do, she obeyed. Having that unfaltering obedience gave me an adrenaline rush like no other. I had the power once more, the absolute control. I got what I wanted and was respected as the strong Dom that I was.

Her back was marked extensively, and I had my fill. I

replaced the whip on the stand and took a seat on the leather sofa against the wall. My heart was still beating a million miles a minute, throbbing inside my chest like I'd just won a marathon.

Isabella remained on her knees, not moving despite the uncomfortable position. She didn't raise her head or lift her gaze. She stayed still like a statue, fulfilling her role as a sub beautifully.

I propped my fingers across my mouth, letting my fingertips rest against my bottom lip. I stared at where she waited, enjoying the silent power I had over her. Jackson left long ago, retreating to his office so I could have privacy to be the man I truly was.

After making her sit just like that for nearly ten minutes, I allowed her to move. "You can relax."

She immediately pulled her legs from underneath her because she was uncomfortable. She felt the marks along her back then turned her gaze on me.

"Eyes on the floor," I barked. "I never gave you permission to look at me."

She snapped her neck and stared at the floor, making up for the error by being still.

My body tightened in approval at her reaction, overwhelmed by the high her obedience gave me. My fingers moved over the stubble of my chin while the other hand made a fist. I couldn't combat the joy that coursed through my veins. I felt more alive than I had in nearly a year. Instead of feeling guilty or ashamed, I felt free. "You're not to touch me. Do you understand?" My own voice echoed back at me, amplified by the four solid walls surrounding us. It was amazing how quickly I fell back into place. It was like my true self had never left in the first place. This was the man I was all along— underneath my mask.

Isabella's eyes didn't move.

"You may speak."

Like the good submissive she was, she didn't do anything unless I specifically allowed it. "Yes."

I growled in response, telling her that wasn't the right answer.

"Yes, Sir," she said quickly, her breathing deep and erratic. She fell right back into our dance, her arousal obvious in the way she licked her lips. There would be no touching, and certainly, no fucking. But it would get her aroused for the man she chose to sleep with.

"You will do as I say, when I command it."

"Yes, Sir."

"We're not monogamous. You're free to be with any Dom you want. But when I walk in here, you're mine. Do you understand?"

"Yes, Sir."

I felt like a king in that moment, a man with more

power than a superhero. I was a Dom again, the darker version of myself. The fact that it felt so natural only convinced me what I was doing was necessary, not wrong. "Get on the bed. Ass in the air."

She nearly ran to the bed because she was so excited, probably hoping I would fuck her like a dog in heat.

"One hand on your left cheek." I didn't get up from my spot on the couch. My hands came together and rested in my lap.

She balanced herself on her knees and one arm before she placed her left hand on her ass cheek.

"Spank yourself, Isabella. Hard."

I'd never asked her to do anything like this, so she hesitated.

"What did I say, Isabella?" My voice turned threatening all on its own.

She smacked her palm against her left cheek, making a loud clapping noise.

"You can do better than that."

She did it harder, this time leaving a handprint.

I stared at her with satisfaction. "We're going to do ten of those. You're going to count with me. Understand?"

"Yes, Sir."

"Go."

She pulled her hand back before she slapped it hard against her left cheek, making it turn red along with the whip marks I already gave her. Her breath came out shaky, her words a whisper. "One..."

"That wasn't good enough, Isabella. Start over."

Her hand shook before she obeyed, slapping herself harder. This time, her word came out loud. "One..."

2

Rome

I didn't know when Calloway would be home, so I had dinner and put the leftovers in the fridge. I had some laundry to do along with other chores, and without him there to distract me, I got things done pretty quickly.

For some reason, I loved taking out his collared shirts from the hamper and putting them in the wash. They were infused with his smell, a mixture of his cologne, masculinity, and the aftershave he slapped on his face and neck after he shaved in the morning. I always pulled the shirts to my chest and smelled them before they were washed on cold. Tom was the one who dropped off his suits from the dry cleaners, and they were usually hanging in the hallway right when we got home. I pulled the plastic wrap from them and placed them on his side of the closet. Calloway's shoes were shined too, looking just as nice as the day he purchased them.

After vacuuming the floors and doing the dishes, I suddenly felt light-headed. A sensation started deep inside my stomach, and I needed to sit just for balance. I pulled out one of the dining chairs and took a seat, feeling my heart swell three times in size.

I was happy.

I loved sharing a house with Calloway. I'd never lived with a man before, but I also fantasized it would be this way. His presence would linger even when he was no longer in the house. I wouldn't care about picking up after him because it was just another way to be close to him. I had a connection with his personal things, knowing they complemented who he was as a man.

I knew I wanted this forever.

Calloway still hadn't told me he loved me, but he showed it every single day. I saw it in the way he looked at me, the way he touched me, and certainly the way he loved me. I wore the black ring he gave me every day, and I couldn't recall a time when I didn't see him wearing his. It felt like we were married already—for the most part.

But I still wanted the real thing.

In time, I knew we would get there. Calloway still struggled to let go of his old ways. He would have to make peace with that on his own. But whenever he was ready, I would be ready too.

The front door opened, and I heard his footsteps against the hardwood floor.

Once I knew he was home, I left the chair and circled from the kitchen to the living room since it opened to the entryway. "How'd it go—" I stopped when I saw the intense look on his face, the unexplained ferocity in his blue eyes. I'd seen that look countless times. He gave it to me right before he fucked me so hard I screamed in ecstasy. The scorching stare didn't suggest he was simply horny or in the mood for sex.

He just wanted me.

"Take. Off. Your. Dress." His arms remained by his sides, but he suffocated me with his violent stare. "Now."

If he bossed me around in any other context, he'd get a good slap across the face. But when he looked so sexy as he made his demands, I didn't care about my pride. My pussy was already humming to life, beginning to soak for this man.

My fingers moved behind me, and I unzipped my dress from top to bottom. Once it was loose, it started to fall down my figure. Slowly, it moved to the floor until it landed at my feet.

Calloway's eyes swept over my body, violating me with his piercing stare. "Now the bra."

I unclasped it and let it fall. My tits immediately felt cold when they weren't pressed against his chest. The nipples hardened and turned a deeper shade of pink.

"The thong." Even though he didn't raise his voice, his words reached every corner of the room.

I pulled it down my legs and let it fall on top of the rest of my clothes. The only thing left was my shoes, but since he didn't tell me to take them off, I left them on. I was suddenly in a responsive mood, waiting for direction rather than making the decisions for myself.

He walked to me, taking his time even though his legs gave him a long stride. When he stopped in front of me, he didn't touch me as I hoped he would. He removed his jacket without taking his eyes off of me. Then he unbuttoned his collared shirt, undoing one button at a time. He seemed to be taking forever on purpose, teasing me for as long as possible. "I'm hungry."

I hoped he wasn't hungry for food.

"Get on the dining table." He undid his belt, his hands working at their own discretion.

I moved to the large table made of cherry then waited for more direction, unsure what position he wanted me in.

The belt zipped out of the loops then hit the tile floor. "On your back."

I turned around and pulled myself up, my legs dangling over the side.

Calloway grabbed my hips then adjusted me on the table, my ass barely hanging off the edge. He pulled up a chair then took a seat right at my opening, his shirt wide open. He gripped the backs of my thighs then spread me wide apart as he moved his face in and pressed a kiss to my lips.

Wow.

I closed my eyes as I felt his lips caress me gently, moving between my folds then around my clitoris. He worked slowly and gave me purposeful kisses, stimulating my entire body as well as my mind.

My hands glided over my tits then crawled into his scalp. I dug my fingers into his thick hair and held on to his head, my hips slowly rocking with his mouth to heighten the pleasure. "Calloway…" I was already in heaven, being adored by the man I loved. He was the only man who could make me crumble like this, and I couldn't keep from saying his name the second his mouth was on my pussy.

He ate me out for fifteen minutes, making me come twice in the meantime. I just got to lie there and enjoy it, feeling Calloway love me with his tongue. I touched my tits and played with my nipples, still rocking with him.

Calloway moved farther south and suddenly kissed me in a place he never had before. His tongue stroked me until my opening could finally relax. Then he slipped his tongue inside my asshole, wetting it with his saliva.

I wasn't sure what to think. I liked it, but in a different way.

He continued for a few minutes before he stood up and dropped his slacks and boxers. He grabbed my hand and shoved two fingers inside his mouth, sucking on them until they were slightly pruned. Then he placed them at my back entrance. "Finger yourself, sweetheart."

The only reason why I did it was because Calloway told me to. He'd never led me wrong before, so I slipped one finger inside then two.

"Good." He pointed his cock inside my pussy then shoved himself inside, stretching me with his huge dick. A dark gleam settled in his eyes as he thrust into me on the table. He gripped the backs of my knees as his cock impaled me over and over, moving through my slippery slickness.

It felt so good that I didn't care what my fingers were doing.

Calloway didn't give me any expression of affection, not like he usually did when we made love. Now he looked angry, his jaw tense and his eyes unforgiving. It looked like he just wanted to fuck me—plain and simple.

Not that I minded.

He grabbed my wrist and pulled my fingers out

before he grabbed his cock and pressed it at my other entrance.

Goddamn.

He'd fucked me in the ass before, and it was definitely an experience I'd never forget. It felt like he was going to rip me in half because his length was so large inside me. I tried to get used to it but was never successful. What turned me on was how much Calloway enjoyed it.

He pressed his head into my tight little hole and pushed. My body struggled to accommodate him because his entrance was so intrusive. I tried to relax, but the pressure only made me tighten up more.

Calloway pushed until he got his dick inside. Then he slowly entered until he was he nearly covered to the hilt. He gripped both of my hips then adjusted me on the table, my ass hanging over the edge. He started to thrust inside me, ramming into my tight channel like he owned it as much as every other part of my body.

It was painful at first, but I got used to it. With every thrust, I felt so full, like I could explode at any moment. I watched Calloway, six feet and three inches of all man, as he fucked me on the kitchen table.

His right hand migrated between my legs, and he pressed his thumb to my clit, rubbing it aggressively as he thrust harder into my ass.

My head rolled back, and I released an involuntary moan. Being touched in both places made my body hum to life. My nerve endings were firing all over the place, sensory overload. He'd already made me come twice, but I knew another one was just over the horizon.

Calloway's gaze was glued to mine as his thrusts turned aggressive. He fucked me harder and faster, ramming his enormous cock inside me. A quiet grunt escaped his lips from time to time. "You." He thrust harder. "Are." His hand moved around my neck. "Mine." The muscles of his stomach tightened with every movement he made. The sweat that dripped down his body gave it a sheen that reflected the light from the chandelier above me. His thumb worked my clitoris harder, trying to bring me to home plate before he finished.

The dark arousal in his eyes was what made me snap. I loved it when he possessed me like this, took complete ownership of me the second he walked in the door. He couldn't wait a minute, not even a second, to have me. He did things with me I would never allow any other man to do—because he was special.

His cock thickened noticeably inside my ass, and I knew what was coming next. "Come. Now."

I didn't dare disobey him when he was like this. My body heeded his command like it had a mind of its own, and I was swept away by the ecstasy that took my body to a heavenly place. I lay my head back and stared at the ceiling, my vision becoming blurry because the explosion was so powerful.

He gripped me tighter and thrust himself harder into me, coming with a loud moan as he filled me with his hot seed. "Fuck." His hand tightened around my neck, but he forced himself to release his hand, knowing he was taking it too far. He inserted himself to the hilt and released everything he had inside me.

I could feel the heat deep inside me, the weight of his come as it filled my passage. Now that my orgasm was over, I was aware of how much he was stretching me, the innate pain that came from his massive cock.

Calloway didn't pull out of me until he was ready. He slowly slid his dick out then stared at my asshole. "Show me."

I tightened my lower muscles and pushed his come to my entrance. I heard a splash when some of it hit the floor.

Calloway's expression didn't change, remaining as dark as it had been when he'd fucked me. He pressed his fingers to my entrance and felt his come cover his fingertips. His look intensified, like we hadn't just had sex at all. He leaned over me and stared me down, his lips close but no kiss in sight. "You are mine. Say it."

His arms moved against the table on either side of my head as he stared me down. My nipples hardened as I was both intimidated and aroused again. When it came to our sexual relationship, I didn't hesitate to give him what he wanted. I simply obeyed, lost in the moment with him. "I am yours."

The second I woke up the following morning, Calloway was on top of me. He spread my knees with his thighs and positioned himself between my legs. His warm chest was pressed to mine, and a sleepy look was in his eyes, mixed with arousal. He inserted himself inside me and slowly began to move.

My ankles automatically locked around his waist, and my arms circled his neck. I pressed my forehead to his and breathed with him, our bodies moving together like gentle waves against the shore.

Calloway was much gentler with me compared to last night. He slowly rocked into me then pressed a soft kiss against my lips, loving me just the way I liked. He cherished me with his restraint and his patience.

He made love to me.

Our alarm clock was about to go off, but he didn't speed up his pace. It wasn't a quickie before work. It was a long session, one where we both wanted to take our time. Every time he moved within me, he rubbed his pelvic bone against my clit and heightened my arousal. His smell enveloped me, delicious and masculine. Sex was always good, but when it was first thing in the morning, it was the best.

He made me come a moment later. Then he followed me immediately afterward, making another deposit between my legs so I would carry his seed all day long. A quiet moan escaped his lips as he finished then he kissed me on the lips.

Now I didn't want to go to work.

He pulled out of me then immediately got into the shower. He didn't say a single word to me, not like he usually did. He normally asked how I'd slept the night before. Or he made a comment about how I looked first thing in the morning. But words were unnecessary because he said everything he needed to say with his body.

We both got ready for work then sat in the back seat of his car. Tom drove us to the office while we remained silent in the back. Calloway stared out the window, his hand propped underneath his chin. His expression was unreadable, stoic.

He seemed different in some way, but I couldn't put my finger on it. He seemed more intense than usual, his authority ringing in the air even during the quietest of times. It almost seemed like he was angry, but the affection he showed me disproved that theory.

We walked into the building and took the elevator to our floor.

Calloway stood with his hands in his pockets, staring straight ahead like he was sharing the elevator with a stranger.

I checked emails on my phone just so I had something to do.

He walked me to my office then stepped inside with me. Both of his hands immediately went to my face as he cupped my cheeks and kissed me on the mouth. His kiss was slow but full of passion, telling me he would miss me while he remained down the hall for the rest of the day. He sucked my bottom lip before we broke apart.

His fingers brushed a strand of hair from my face, grazing my cheek with the same gentleness he showed me that morning. He gave me a final look of longing, as if he wanted to stay in that tiny little office with me for the rest of the day. Without saying another word, he walked out and left me standing there, weak in the knees for the man who made me tremble with just a single kiss.

I sat at my desk and stared at the black computer screen, still thinking about that final kiss before he left. Something was different between us. His feelings seemed to intensity, to amplify. I didn't know what the difference was, but I knew I liked it.

Calloway and I left the office at the end of the day and got into the back seat of Tom's car.

"Do you want to stop by and see your mom?"

Calloway stared out the window like he hadn't heard me. His five-o'clock shadow was already starting to come in now that the evening drew near. In his black suit, his frame looked powerful and prominent. Despite the fact that every inch of his frame was covered, it was obvious he was a muscular man. "Sure."

Tom headed for the assisted-living facility at the edge of the city once he heard Calloway's response.

I stared out the window and enjoyed the silence between us. Calloway and I didn't always need to talk to fill the emptiness that emerged through lack of conversation. Just being together seemed to be enough for both of us. Since we were together all the time, there wasn't anything new to discuss.

The quiet was fine with me, but I missed his affection. I hadn't received any since this morning, so I reached across the seat between us and grabbed his hand. My palm was much smaller than his, nothing comparable. I felt the thick veins across the top of his hand and wished those powerful hands were all over my body.

Calloway stared at my hand before he brought it to his lips and gave it a kiss. His mouth was warm against my cold hand, his lips wet and soft. He locked eyes with me as he kissed me, the intensity powerful and scorching at the same time.

He lowered my hand and rested it on his thigh, his hand positioned on top. He turned his gaze back to the window, his fingertips over his lips as he returned to his thoughts.

"Calloway?"

"Hmm?" His eyes didn't shift back to me.

"What are you thinking about?"

The corner of his mouth rose in a smile. "That I wish Tom weren't around."

We arrived at the nursing home then walked inside. Calloway didn't have a book with him, so he pulled out his phone and downloaded the book. Sometimes, his mother wasn't in the mood to be read to, but most of the time, she was.

We walked into her room then the balcony, where she sat in her rocking chair. We introduced ourselves as usual then took a seat.

Theresa stared at Calloway hard, giving him an expression neither one of us had seen before. It was similar to the look Calloway gave me when he was angry. But her expression was much softer.

Calloway held her look, waiting for her to say something.

I didn't want to get my hopes up, but every time I came to visit, I hoped his mother would have a revelation. Something about me stimulated her memory once, and I hoped Calloway's presence would somehow remind her that he was her son. I knew it hurt Calloway that my appearance had more of an impact on her than his ever did, despite the fact that he'd been diligently visiting her for years.

A pained look stretched across her face, a stress that couldn't be quantified based on her expression alone. "Have we met before?"

My lungs immediately stopped working because my body could no longer function. I'd always known a mother's love for her children would outweigh any illness. There was no way she could look at Calloway and ignore those crystal blue eyes that she shared. She couldn't look at him and not see the same visage her husband once possessed.

Calloway's expression didn't change as he held her look. Sometimes it was impossible to tell what he was thinking because he didn't give anything away. I could usually detect his moods, and when he was really transparent, his thoughts. But right now, the thoughts behind that handsome face were a mystery. "Yes. I've been visiting you every week for the past three years. You've met me many times."

"I have?" she whispered.

Calloway nodded. "I've read the first half of Harry Potter to you over three hundred times. It's your favorite book."

The pained expression returned to her face. She pressed her thin lips tightly together in distress. "I feel like... Were you just here?"

Maybe this was going somewhere. Maybe seeing her so often had given her memory a positive push.

"Yes." Calloway's voice grew stronger, filling with hope. "I was here two days ago. And I was here the day before that."

Theresa turned her gaze on me, studying my face like she recognized it. "There was another young man with you...I think."

Now I could hardly breathe.

Calloway's chest stilled in reaction, floored by what he just heard. "Yes. That was my brother."

"I think I remember him..." Her hand immediately went to the necklace around her throat, feeling the gold chain. "Very handsome...very nice."

"Yeah," Calloway said in agreement. "Do you remember anything else?"

She stared at the wood floor beneath her feet, her

fingertips still stroking the chain. "No...just that he was a fine young man."

I turned my face to Calloway, silently asking him what we should do. I wondered if Calloway would ever tell her that he was her son, that she lost her memory due to illness, but he was still there for her. Would that just upset her? Frighten her? There was no way to know.

Calloway pulled his phone out of his pocket and handed it to me. "Call him."

I followed his instructions immediately and returned to the lobby where I would have privacy.

Jackson answered almost immediately. "See? I told you that you would feel better. You're a new man."

I didn't have a clue what he was talking about, but I didn't care to find out. "We need you to come down here to see your mother."

Jackson paused over the line. "Rome?"

"Yes," I said in frustration. "Now can you come down here?"

"Why? Is she okay?" Alarm shot into his voice, turning protective just like Calloway.

"She's fine, but she claims to remember you. If you come down here, maybe it'll help her memory even more."

Another pause. "She remembers me...?"

"Yes. Could you please come down here?"

Jackson's hesitation was obvious over the phone, even in his silence.

"Get down here, or I'll come get you. What's it gonna be?" Jackson was twice my size and a much bigger pain in the ass, but I would make it work somehow.

Jackson probably didn't take my threat seriously, but he must have realized he would have to deal with Calloway if he didn't come down there. "Alright. Give me five minutes."

"Thank you."

"And by the way, stop calling me from Calloway's phone. Don't wanna say something I shouldn't."

"Maybe you should just say hi first instead of blabbing everything that comes to mind." I hung up and crossed my arms over my chest. I was furious with Jackson even though he'd done nothing to deserve my wrath. I was anxious about Theresa and wanted Jackson there as quickly as possible. Every moment wasted was a moment we may never get back. She might lose her train of thought and forget what she said altogether.

I needed this to work for Calloway. I knew what it was like not to have a single parent. Christopher and I did just fine, but it was still a lonely existence. Calloway's father was an asshole, but his mother contained the innocence of an angel. I wanted Calloway to have this, to have something to counteract all the bullshit in his life.

I would do anything to make it happen.

Jackson walked inside an eternity later. He wore a blue suit with a gray tie, showing distinct similarities to his brother. They were both tall and muscular, being the definition of masculinity.

"Alright, I'm here." He adjusted his cuff links like he was about to walk into a business meeting. "What do I do?"

"Just walk in there and be normal."

"How can I be normal when my mother has no memory of me?" he snapped. Without waiting for further instruction, he headed to her room.

I followed behind him until we reached the balcony. Calloway was sitting in the exact same position as he was before, gazing at his mother with a hopeless expression.

Jackson took the seat directly beside him and rested his hands on his knees. He stared at his mother blankly, not having a clue what to say. He took a deep breath and opened his mouth to speak, but he quickly shut it again.

I sat beside Jackson and waited for something to happen.

Calloway took the reins. "Theresa, this is my brother Jackson."

Theresa stared at him with the same empty expression. Slowly, recognition spread across her face. "Yes...I remember you."

My hands moved together, and my fingers interlocked just to remain steady.

Jackson held her stare, no longer the macho man I heard over the phone. When Jackson was faced with his mother, he turned into a vulnerable and compassionate man, something I didn't think was possible. "It's nice to see you again. Your hair...looks nice."

"Thank you." A smile spread across her face. "I remember your face, but I can't remember what we talked about."

"That's okay," Jackson said. "There's always time to get to know one another again."

I wished I were sitting by Calloway so I could rest my hand on his thigh, give him some sort of affection so he would understand he wasn't alone in this. But it seemed like we were a mile apart with Jackson between us.

"Do you have a woman in your life?" Theresa asked.

Jackson chuckled. "No, not really."

"What's with the laugh?" she asked.

Jackson shrugged. "I'm not really looking to settle down. Not a one-woman kind of guy."

Theresa and Jackson talked about his love life, almost like mother and son. I turned to Calloway to make eye contact with him, but he wouldn't meet my look. He stared at his mother, his eyes glazed over with pure nothingness.

I kept waiting for something big to happen, for Theresa to realize her flesh and blood was staring right back at her. But the connection never came. She talked about knitting and asked Jackson about his work. It seemed like she was having a conversation with a friend rather than a family member. Maybe she remembered his face from the other day, but she certainly didn't remember anything else.

I couldn't hide my disappointment.

After visiting for a few hours, we said goodnight and headed on our way.

Jackson walked with his hands in his pockets as we reached the lobby. "Well...I guess that went well."

Calloway was silent, his brooding energy seeping into the skin of everyone around him.

"Maybe if we keep visiting her, we could help her create new memories," I said. "If she can continue remembering us, then we can eventually tell her she's your mother."

Calloway shook his head. "She said she recognizes faces but can't remember the conversation. I don't think that's promising. For all we know, she might think she remembers us but has no memory at all."

I hated his pessimistic attitude, but I couldn't argue

with him. Maybe we weren't moving forward at all. Maybe we were just wasting our time altogether. "It's worth a try, right?"

"I don't know," Jackson said. "I hate seeing her like this...not fun."

"I don't like it either," Calloway said. "I'm starting to believe there's no hope. She's stuck in a prison in her mind, and there's nothing we can do to break her out."

"That's not true..." Even if it was true, I didn't want to believe it.

Calloway didn't look at me.

"This is too hard for me, man," Jackson said. "I want to be there for her. I really do. But I can't keep staring at the blank look on her face. She has no idea who I am. And she'll never know who I am. She'll never know you visit her several times a week. She'll never know we even exist. So what does all this work matter? If it were me, I'd want my kids to enjoy their lives and not worry about me. I wouldn't want them to waste their time reading to me when I'm gonna forget them the second they leave. Not worth it..." Jackson walked away without further comment. He walked through the front doors then disappeared from our sight.

Calloway didn't go after him and try to change his mind. He accepted his brother's feelings completely. But he still wouldn't look at me, probably not interested in the sadness on my face.

"Whatever you decide, I'll support you." I had no right to tell Calloway what to do in this regard. He was the one carrying the emotional burden of his mother's illness, something I would never understand since I hadn't experienced it. Even if I didn't agree with his decision, it would be wrong for me to steer him in a different direction.

Calloway finally looked at me, his blue eyes dark with despair. "I know."

3

Calloway

It amazed me how suddenly I regressed back to the man I was before I met Rome. My exterior had suddenly callused, and now I was hard as steel once more. My jaw was always tight with fury, and I couldn't stop my hands from constantly forming fists. My need to dominate, to exert my authority and power into every room I walked into, was overwhelming.

But I liked it.

I got what I needed from Isabella. I hurt her—a lot. And every time she cried, it gave me immense satisfaction. I was a sadist, and I knew I would always be a sadist. I never had the intention or desire to hurt Rome because I focused all my efforts on a different person entirely.

And that allowed me to cherish her.

I enjoyed our lovemaking even more now that my other needs were fulfilled. I could concentrate on her and all the thing she loved. To my surprise, I loved it too. The gentle touching, the soft caresses, everything revved my engine.

But sometimes I found myself wanting to dominate her even though she made it clear she didn't want to be treated like a sub. When I walked in the door after being with Isabella, I wanted to fuck Rome hard—and the way I liked.

But to my surprise, she always did what I asked without giving me lip about it. Normally, she ran that sassy little mouth of hers until she pissed me off and got her way. But she hadn't been doing that lately.

Because she liked it.

I knew she did—deep down inside. If she really kept an open mind and gave it a chance, she would love it. But I knew she was too stubborn to let me spank her with my belt. I'd have to accept her the way she was.

And she would have to accept me.

I sat at my desk and finished a meeting I had over Skype with a prominent donor. Unfortunately, most people only made donations to my nonprofit for the credit, so they called and requested new ways for their contribution to be announced, either with plaques, banners, or trophies.

Fucking annoying.

When I finished that, my assistant buzzed me over the intercom. "Mr. Owens, Isabella is here to see you. Should I send her in?"

The mention of her name immediately set my teeth on edge. If I wanted to be her Dom, I would go down to Ruin and make it happen. She had no right to come here and expect to get what she wanted. That wasn't how it worked. "Yes, send her in." I hit the button so hard I nearly broke it.

"Yes, sir."

A moment later, Isabella walked inside. She wore a trench coat, and that told me everything I needed to know about her visit. She approached the desk with her gaze averted, not looking me in the eye because she hadn't been given permission.

I was livid.

"Kneel."

She did as I asked immediately, bending her knees and declining to the hardwood floor.

I stared at her, grinding my teeth together.

Isabella returned to her position as a sub perfectly. Despite how silent I was, she still didn't ask me a single question. She took steady breaths, remaining as still as possible. She did her job, and she did it well.

"Did I command you to come here?"

"No, Sir," she whispered.

"Then you had no right coming here. I never want you to come here again. Do you understand?" I leaned forward over the desk, my elbows resting on the surface.

"Yes, Sir."

"Tell me why you're here."

She rested her hands on her thighs, her head still tilted to the floor. "I missed you."

Not good enough. "Don't ever miss me again, Isabella. I'm not yours to miss. When I want to rule you, I will. You have no say in the matter."

"I'm sorry, Sir."

"Don't apologize," I barked. "Just don't do it."

"Yes, Sir," she whispered.

Now I wanted to punish her for disobeying me. I wanted to hurt her for coming here. I wanted to break her for crossing the line. "On your feet."

She rose to her full height, standing perfectly straight in her heels.

"What are you wearing underneath the coat?" I came around the desk and yanked my belt from the loops.

"Black teddy with garters." Her voice picked up a notch, full of hope.

"Drop it."

She undid her jacket and let it fall off her shoulders and to the ground.

"Bend over. Now." I slapped the belt hard into my hand, feeling the bite of the metal against my own skin.

She bent over with her cheek pressed to the wood. Her hair was sprawled out across the desk, reaching over the papers I'd just been reading.

"Don't make a sound. Do you understand me?"

"Yes, Sir."

"I'm gonna punish you for what you've done. There'll be tears in your eyes before you walk out of here."

Her breathing hitched. "Yes, Sir."

I pulled the belt back and swung hard, striking her hard against the ass cheek and making a dull clap echo around my office.

She clamped her teeth together to avoid letting out a whimper. Her hands dragged across the wood as she searched for something to hold on to.

I wasn't letting her walk out of there until her skin was red and weathered. "Count to ten, Isabella."

She swallowed hard. "One…"

Did I feel guilty for what I was doing?

That was a complicated question.

With a more complicated answer.

Yes, a part of me did feel bad for what I was doing. I was using another woman to satisfy my urges. But I didn't touch her, fuck her, or let her go anywhere near me. I wasn't even hard as I whipped her. Instead, I felt a surge of relief, an abundance of satisfaction. I felt alive in the moment, doing what I loved to do.

Then the other part of me didn't give a damn what I was doing.

I resented Rome for not giving me what I wanted, and it was ridiculous to think I wouldn't end up getting it somewhere else. She wouldn't allow me to spank her, to chain her to the headboard and whip her bare ass. She wouldn't allow me to make her cry, to let me get off to the sounds of her tears.

So what did she expect me to do?

I needed this.

The second Jackson put that whip in my hand, I fell back into the abyss Rome dragged me out of. I was a little out of my mind, a little insane. Blood lust had taken over, and now I couldn't think straight.

Rome didn't realize it at the moment, but this was the best thing for our relationship. I got to relieve my urges with someone who enjoyed being hurt. I got it out of my system so when I was with Rome, the dark desires were gone. I could kiss her and appreciate the softness of our embrace. I could make love to her and enjoy the closeness without wanting something more.

I didn't have to jerk off in the shower while she was downstairs.

I didn't have to touch myself in the office as I pictured hurting her.

All of those fantasies were gone.

Now I could just live in the moment with her.

After the workday ended, I went to her office and watched her type an email at her desk. Her back was to me, and I appreciated the way she positioned her shoulders back as she held herself with impeccable posture. No matter what the circumstance was, she always carried herself with complete grace. She could be a queen if she wanted.

She must have picked up on my presence because she glanced over her shoulder and spotted me. "Do you ever say hi?"

"No." I placed my hands in my pockets and leaned against the doorframe, my head nearly hitting the top of it. "I don't need to. You know when I'm here."

She turned back to her computer and finished her email. After she sent it off, she turned off her computer and grabbed her purse from under the desk. "I only know that because I can feel you." She rose out of the chair and joined me in the doorway.

"Where exactly can you feel me?" I stepped forward and pressed my body into hers. Without any regard to passersby in the hallway, I kissed her as my hand moved under her dress and between her legs. I found her clit through her panties, and I brushed my thumb against it with restrained aggression.

She immediately took a deep breath, her following words drowned out with a quiet moan.

I kept rubbing her, fascinated by the sexy expression she made. It was easy for me to tell when she was aroused because she practically wore it as a billboard. I was tempted to press her inside the office and kick the door behind me. I could fuck her on her desk and not give a damn what the rest of the staff thought. I owned this desk.

I owned this woman.

But Rome cut it short when she grabbed my wrist and pushed it down. "Calloway..." She stepped back and pressed her lips tightly together as she composed herself, her eyes still full of arousal and her desperation for my hand to return between her legs.

"You never answered my question."

"You know where I can feel you, Calloway," she said, her gaze fiery. "And it's not there."

"Then where?" I leaned in again, my eyes on her lips.

She grabbed my hand and placed it over her heart. "You know exactly where."

I felt her heartbeat under my palm, beating strongly and powerfully. I knew the quick pace was caused by me and my hand, eliciting her desires from her body. Instead of focusing on the luscious curve of her tit, I focused on the warmth of her body. This woman had given herself to me in more ways than one. I had her body, but I also had her heart and soul. "I can feel you too."

When we came home, I wasn't interested in dinner.

I was interested in Rome.

Once we crossed the threshold, I scooped her up in my arms and carried her upstairs to the bedroom we shared on the third floor. I laid her down on the bed and immediately slipped off her heels. She wore a gentle smile, aroused and playful at the same time. She pressed her bare feet against my chest as she pulled down the straps of her dress.

I got my clothes off then pulled her panties from her long legs. They fell on top of my slacks where they belonged. I lifted up her dress to her waist then returned her feet to my chest. I loved having her pinned underneath me like this, like she was only mine to enjoy.

I directed my cock to her entrance and wasn't surprised to feel the wetness that greeted me. I couldn't recall a time when I was inside her and she wasn't soaked. It didn't matter if she just woke up first thing in the morning or if it was in the middle of the night. She was always ready to go—for me.

I inserted myself completely inside her, pushing until the base of my cock hit her entrance. She looked incredible underneath me, her plump lips utterly kissable and delicious. Her soft strands were spread out across the sheets, perfect for me to grip.

Her mouth widened as she panted, growing used to my enormous size. "God, your dick is big."

My cock automatically twitched in response, still buried deep inside her warm pussy. "That's your fault, sweetheart. You make him bigger than he's ever been before." I slowly rocked into her, sliding through the lubrication her body produced for me. I would never get tired of knowing I was the only man to be inside her, to feel her tight pussy for the first time. I hadn't broken her in because it was impossible. She was simply a petite woman with small parts.

But I loved that.

I rocked into her quicker but never became aggressive. Right now, I just wanted to feel her. I wanted to feel her pulse through her feet and let her feel my heartbeat in return. I wanted to conquer the woman I adored beyond reason. She was my world—my everything. Without her, I wouldn't know what to do with myself.

"Calloway..." She cupped my neck with her hands and pressed her face to mine, still rocking with me slightly by pushing against my chest. "I...I love you so much."

Those words went straight into my chest, making me feel warm and alive. If any other woman had said that to me, I would have tossed her out on her ass. But when it came to Rome, I loved her affection. I loved her devotion. I wanted her to cherish me the way I cherished her.

But I still couldn't say it back.

I didn't know what stopped me. She already knew how I felt. I already told her a dozen times without actually saying the words. She knew wasn't just my world, but my stars and my moon. She knew my entire existence revolved around her happiness. I would gladly shorten my life so hers would be longer. I would gladly do anything so her smile never faltered. "Rome..." The words never left my lips, but the emotion was in my voice.

That seemed to be enough for her because she came, her lips trembling against mine. Her fingers tugged on the strands of my hair as she moaned through the sensation, her pussy unbelievably tight around my dick.

Her passion always cut me to the bone. I loved her desperation, the way she clung to me even when her orgasm was over. I was the only man she allowed herself to rely on. She allowed me to take care of her, to protect her, and to provide for her. The fact that I was the only man who earned the honor made me feel worthy of her.

The final thought pushed me over the edge, causing me to spasm as I released inside her. I gave her all of my come, every last drop of it, and I wanted to do it every night for the rest of my life.

The rest of my life.

Shit, that was heavy.

Her fingers softened against my skull, and she gently ran them through my hair, treating me delicately after the violent way she gripped me before. Her tits were caged behind her knees, and the sweat accumulated on her neck.

Instead of being angry with my reluctance, she adored me just as much as she did before. She craned her neck so she could press her lips against mine for one final embrace. She closed her eyes and savored the touch like my lips were made of honey.

The only reason she wasn't mad was because she knew how I felt.

She had to know.

Christopher texted me. *Hey.*

What's up? It wasn't like him to beat around the bush. He usually came out and said whatever he needed to say.

Do you know of any hot ladies you can set me up with?

Rome mentioned he was looking for something serious. I was the worst person to ask. All my life, I'd only dealt with the erotic art of fucking. Not relationships. Rome was the first woman who walked into my life that I couldn't let slip away. *I know a lot of hot ladies. But not sure if they're the relationship type.*

Every woman is a relationship type.

Not the ones I was familiar with. *What exactly are you looking for?*

You know, smart, beautiful, funny.

So, the perfect woman? I couldn't stop myself from smiling. I sat at my desk in my office with my phone held between my hands.

Exactly! Do you know of anyone?

Just one. *No. Sorry, man.*

My phone suddenly started to ring, Christopher's name on the screen.

I took the call. "Why didn't you just call in the first place?"

"I didn't realize you were going to be so difficult. I thought you were just gonna spit out a name and number."

"Like a vending machine?" I asked incredulously.

"Yeah, kinda. You're a ladies' man."

Not really. I just preferred women with specific tastes. And they preferred me because I could give them what they wanted. "Well, I don't know anyone who fits your description."

"Really? Not a single person?"

"Except Rome. But I doubt you're interested in that."

"Yuck." He gagged into the phone. "I'm not into incest."

"You aren't related."

"She's my sister, in my eyes."

"I'm surprised you haven't met anyone on your own."

"Oh, I can meet women just fine," he said with a laugh. "But they're too skanky, you know?"

"Too skanky?" I asked with a laugh.

"Yeah. I tell them I'm looking for something serious, and they immediately jump into bed with me, get all clingy, and then it's just uncomfortable. It's basically the worst pickup line ever invented."

"There are worse problems then getting too much pussy." I didn't care how I spoke to Christopher. He knew what kind of guy I was before Rome came along.

"I tried doing the online thing, but that didn't pan out."

"Why not?"

"Some serious catfishing going on," he said. "A girl posts a picture of herself from high school, and then I meet her and she looks nothing like that. It's creepy."

"That's too bad."

"So, I want you to come out with me tonight."

Now I'd lost his train of thought. "What?"

"Hot chicks are always in pairs. I need a second guy to help me corner the good one. You feel me?"

I laughed because the suggestion was outrageous. "I'm gonna pass. I like not being single."

"You don't have to do anything with them," he argued. "Just distract one girl while I go for the other."

"Rome is definitely not going to be down with that. And don't you have any other friends?"

"They aren't as good-looking as the two of us. You and I would be unstoppable."

Rome would never let this fly, and honestly, I'd be offended if she didn't care. If she did this same thing with a girlfriend, I'd be livid. "You know who you should go with?"

"Hmm?"

"My brother, Jackson. He's a serious ladies' man, and he's always looking for pussy."

"Good-looking guy?" he asked.

"He looks a lot like me. Just less attractive."

"Sure," he said. "Text me his digits, and I'll give him a call."

"Alright. I'm glad I set you up on a playdate." I hung up then turned my attention back to work.

A moment later, my assistant's voice came through the phone. "Ms. Moretti has asked to speak with you."

Ms. Moretti.

I never called her that. Just like how I hated it when she called me Mr. Owens. "Send her in." I was immediately irritated because I specifically told Rome she didn't have to check in with anybody. She could walk in here like she owned the damn place.

The door cracked, and Rome stepped inside in nude heels and a pink dress. I saw her this morning when we left for work, but anytime I saw her after a long break, her appearance got me hard.

And I was hard right now.

She carried a stack of papers, probably her progress report for the past month. "Sorry this is late, but I—"

"Rome, I said you don't need to check in with my assistant. You need something from me, you walk in."

She held the papers at her waist and stared me down, her gaze suddenly turning cold. "Calloway, we're at work. We have to have some sort of professionalism—"

"Exactly. I'm your boss—and you do what I say."

Now her eyes were on fire.

"Everyone knows we're fucking, Rome. So just walk in. My woman doesn't wait for anybody—not even me."

Her anger dimmed, but only slightly. "We both know I'm not doing that, so let's just drop it."

My anger immediately came to the surface at her disobedience. I was used to unwavering loyalty from Isabella, and I didn't like my woman questioning me. This wasn't news. Rome had always been her own woman. But that never quenched my need to be in control. I suspected it would never be quenched, even with Isabella there to fulfill my needs. "And we both know I always get my way. So next time, just come in here." I rose to my full height, staring her down with my arms by my sides. I pressed my hands against the wood of my desk and leaned forward, staring her down like prey.

Rome pressed her lips tightly together, either because she was ticked or aroused. At the moment, it wasn't easy to see the distinction. She suddenly threw the papers on my desk where they slid across the surface and fell at my feet. "Let me know when you're done being an asshole. Maybe then we can have a mature conversation." She walked out with her head held high. She probably wanted to slam the door shut, but she found the restraint not to do it. When the door shut behind her, I was alone with my thoughts.

And I knew I fucked up.

When I arrived at her office later that afternoon, she wasn't there.

Her computer was shut down, her purse was gone, and the lights were out.

Fuck.

I immediately walked to the elevator and did my best to appear calm to my employees. I wanted to sprint to the elevator but forced myself to walk. I itched to grab my phone and call her right then and there, but that wouldn't be smart either.

Once I was in the elevator with the doors closed, I called her.

No answer.

"Fuck." I called her again, feeling the terror form inside my stomach. I didn't care that she was pissed at me. Once I got my hands on her, I'd kiss her and fuck her until she forgave me.

But I was worried about her.

Anytime I wasn't with her, she was vulnerable. Hank could make a move at any moment, possibly preparing for the instant she and I let our guards down. And if something happened to her because of my stupidity, I'd literally murder him.

I called her again, but there was no answer so I left a message.

I texted her. *Just tell me you're safe.*

I stared at the phone and waited for the three dots to appear. But nothing came on the screen.

Goddammit, Rome. Just tell me if you're home or not. The elevator hit the bottom floor, and I walked out, flustered and furious.

The three dots lit up.

Thank fucking god.

I'm home. I suggest you find somewhere else to go because you aren't coming here.

I never thought I would be so happy to hear her sass me like that. Relief flooded through me like incoming waves from the ocean. *Thank you.* I'd never meant those two words so sincerely before. Knowing she was safe made up for the terror I felt in my heart.

Of course, I went home anyway. Even though she was safe inside the house, the only thing that could truly make her safe was me. I was the single barrier that nobody could cross. It didn't matter if Hank had a knife or gun. None of that shit could get through me.

Tom dropped me off at the house, and I used my key to get inside.

"What did I say?" She sat on the couch with her legs crossed, her Kindle sitting on her lap.

"You shouldn't have taken off like that." My relief at her safety quickly wore off when I remembered the little number she pulled. "Something could have happened to you."

"What?" she snapped. "Trip on the sidewalk?"

My eyes narrowed. "Don't be a smartass right now."

"Don't be a jackass right now."

I wanted to fuck her so hard. I was pissed, but my cock was at full mast at the exact same time. "Whatever happens between us, taking off on your own isn't the solution. Hank could have done something."

"Hank is no longer a problem, and you know it."

"We'll never know that until he's fucking dead." I walked farther into the living room, feeling my hands form into fists. My need for control was outweighing my need for logic. I was thinking emotionally, not objectively. When it came to Rome, I couldn't see straight. "So don't pull that stunt again. I mean it."

"I can do whatever the hell I want, Calloway. You aren't the boss of me."

I'd give anything to be the boss of her. I wanted to flip her over and spank the shit out of her. Now it was all I could think about, making her cheeks rosy red and inflamed. My fists tightened until my knuckles turned white.

I knew I should apologize, but I couldn't bring myself to do it. I knew exactly why I acted the way I did earlier, not that the reason justified the action. But the second she took off, she sucked away all my sympathy. "I mean it, Rome. Don't ever do that again. You can be mad all you want, but don't put yourself in jeopardy."

"Don't be a bitch-face, and I won't take off."

"A bitch-face?" I snapped. "What the hell is that?"

"You." She threw her Kindle down, showing her small rampage. "Why did you make a big scene like that at work?"

"How can it be a scene if no one is around?"

"Your assistant could have heard you."

"Who gives a shit if she did?" I threw my arm down. "It's my building. It's my office. And you're my woman. I do what I want—no questions asked."

She rolled her eyes. "Get over yourself, Calloway. You aren't the king of the world."

I wanted to pin her down right on the couch. "All I wanted was for you to know that you're the most important woman in my life. If you need something, you walk in there. I don't give a shit what I'm doing or who I'm speaking to. You're my priority, and you always come first. Sorry if that's so offensive, but I fucking love you, and that's how I goddamn show it." I barely got a glimpse of her before I turned around and stormed out of the house. I slammed the door so hard the hinges nearly broke off. I hadn't changed out of my suit or even taken off my watch. I knew exactly where I was going, and nothing was going to stop me.

I was going to Ruin.

I turned my phone off so I didn't have to feel it vibrate in my pocket. Rome would call me all night long, wanting to work this out and subdue my anger.

But it was too late for that.

I walked into the underworld, the dark place I considered home, and I found Isabella as if I had a GPS on her. She was at the bar talking to some guy who was clearly interested in putting a collar around her neck.

Not an ounce of jealousy.

I felt nothing for her.

If I asked her to be my sub for the evening and she said no, I still wouldn't care.

I walked up to her and locked my gaze with hers, silently telling her what I wanted. The guy sitting beside her was irrelevant at that point. Couldn't care less about him.

She held my gaze with the same dark expression. She finally gave a slight nod.

That was the gesture I was looking for, so I walked off and headed to the playrooms upstairs, not concerned if she was standing behind me or not. I knew she would follow me—because she always followed me.

Once she joined me in the playroom, I locked the door and finally felt myself come undone. I was out of my mind with rage. I was so livid I couldn't see straight. Rome ticked me off, pushed me to the edge, and now I needed to release the frustration deep inside me. I grabbed the shackles and secured them around Isabella's wrists. After a tug on the rope, she was lifted from the floor, her feet dangling inches from the ground.

"Make me hurt, Sir," she whispered. "Make it hurt so good."

I went to the display case and looked through the selections of whips and floggers. I found a particularly brutal one, with a big knot at the end that would mark her for days. "I will, Isabella. Don't you worry about that."

4

R ome
    This day just kept getting worse.

    He pissed me off.

Then I pissed him off.

Then he pissed me off again.

And then he told me he loved me.

He finally said those words to me, and instead of making me happy, they made me feel like shit. Sometimes Calloway turned possessive and controlling, and I knew I needed to be more sensitive to his behaviors. He didn't know how to express himself like most people. He showed me he loved me in ways that weren't completely transparent.

Love meant something different to him than it did to me.

And I chased him away after he finally confessed his feelings.

I called his phone a hundred times throughout the night, but every time I tried to reach him, his phone was off.

That was like a punch to the stomach.

At two in the morning, I couldn't stay awake any longer. I lay on the couch with a thin blanket and hoped I would hear the door once he came inside, if he came home at all. I was dead asleep when I heard his heavy footfalls against the hardwood floor in the entryway.

I sat upright and pulled the hair from my face, relieved that he was home and no longer out on the town.

He immediately stripped off his jacket and tossed it on the coatrack. He undid his watch and threw it on the table, not caring about protecting it from scratches. He stepped farther into the room as he unbuttoned his collared shirt.

His eyes settled on me, just as frightening as they were when he stormed out.

I kicked the blanket aside and left the couch. I hadn't changed since I came home, and I was still in the dress I wore to work. My makeup was probably smeared because I shed a few tears after I got his voice mail.

The lights were off, but I could still make out his hard features, full of unbridled anger.

Now that I was face-to-face with him, I didn't know what to say. Words left me at that moment. I didn't know how to express myself, not after the roller coaster of emotions we experienced throughout the day.

I finally found something to say, but it felt hollow in comparison to how I felt. "I'm sorry…"

He didn't drop his arctic glare. He stepped closer to me then cupped my face, both of his hands pressed against my cheeks. He forced my head back then kissed me, an embrace that was just as aggressive as he was angry. His tongue darted into my mouth, and he pressed me up against the wall, kissing me harder and groping my body everywhere. He yanked up my dress then pulled my panties down my thighs. When he couldn't get them past my knees, he ripped them with his bare hands instead.

I yelped when I heard the tear of the fabric, desperate to get him inside me now that I knew how much he wanted me. My hands went to his slacks, and I yanked them off as well as his boxers. The second he was free, he lifted me into the air and pressed my back against the wall.

Then he shoved himself inside me.

Instead of the tender lovemaking we should have had after he first told me he loved me, he fucked me so hard I screamed. I dragged my nails down his back and panted into his ear. I was still angry, but so grateful he was home. "Fuck me harder."

His eyes locked to mine before he did what I asked. He thrust his hips and pushed me against the wall, making my back thud against the solid material as he moved hard and fast. He gripped me by the ass and the thighs, groping me hard like this was a one-night stand rather than lust between two committed people. "I'll make sure you can't walk tomorrow, sweetheart." He dug one hand into my hair and yanked my head back as he shoved his massive dick inside me, stretching me over and over.

"Fuck…" I felt the explosion between my legs and had no time to prepare for it. It came suddenly and without warning. Calloway made me melt right into the floor, turning me into a puddle of desire.

When he felt my pussy tighten around his length, he released with a grunt, keeping me pinned to the wall. We were a sea of tangled limbs, our bodies wrapped around one another so tightly it didn't seem like we could ever be free.

He pumped his seed inside me, claiming me as his once again. He rested his face in the crook of my neck as he finished, breathing through the exhilaration. His lips sealed over my skin, and he gave me a sexy kiss before he pulled away from the wall, his cock still inside me. He carried me up the stairs to the bedroom then lay me flat on the bed, his throbbing cock slipping out of me.

He kicked off his jeans and boxers then climbed on top of me, his powerful body making the bed sink under his impressive weight. He looked down at me like he was nowhere near finished. "I know I'm an asshole sometimes. But I don't know how to be anything else besides an asshole. It's all I've ever known."

I knew that was as close to an apology as I was going to get.

"I don't know how to deal with these feelings I have for you. Ever since you walked into my life, it's been chaos. When you were a virgin, I was patient with you. I'm a virgin too, but in a different way. Please be patient with me."

That was even better than an apology. All the anger I felt toward him disappeared in that moment. Somehow, I felt deeper in love with him. He was the one, the man I was going to spend the rest of my life with. It might take us a while to get to a place where we were both comfortable, but we would make it there eventually.

We just had to try. "I'll wait forever for you, Calloway."

His eyes softened before he leaned in and kissed me. "I knew you were going to say that. But I wanted to hear it anyway."

Calloway and I didn't talk much after our fight. He returned to his silent brooding, his face a mask of impenetrable stoicism. He didn't seem angry with me, but he wasn't as easy to read as he used to be.

Something seemed different.

Maybe it was his mother. His hostility seemed to come from nowhere, emerging from somewhere deep inside him. Maybe her well-being and lack of memory elicited this change in him. Now he was a bomb that had just gone off, but the aftershocks were still rolling in.

I wanted to ask him about it, but I feared it would only make it worse.

We had dinner together at the table in silence. Calloway wasn't much of a talker, but he had less to say than usual. His eyes were either on his food or out the window, never on me. His mind was weighed down with thoughts. I could he see the cogs turning deep inside his mind. His mood reflected in his eyes like mirrors.

When we finished, I carried the plates to the sink and started the dishes.

"No." Calloway came up beside me and scooted me over with his size. "I'll take care of this."

"Calloway, you really don't have to—"

He silenced me with a threatening look. "I said I would take care of it. Now go sit down."

I dropped the argument because I knew I wouldn't win. I sat on the couch in the living room and listened to the dishes tap against the sink as the water ran out of the faucet. He rinsed everything before he placed the dishes in the dishwasher and turned it on. He washed his hands then walked into the living room, looking hot as hell in the black sweatpants that hung low on his hips. His tight ass was defined, even in the loose clothing. He wore a black V-neck that showed his chiseled chest and his thick arms. He took the seat beside me then grabbed the book he'd been reading off the end table. He opened it and picked up where he left off.

"Calloway?"

He left the book open on his lap and faced me, his jaw stern and his eyes dark. Whether he was happy or angry, he still wore the same hard expression. Right now, I had no idea what was going on behind that beautiful face. Verbal responses from him were few and far between.

"You've been different lately. Is everything okay?"

He continued to stare at me, his eyes empty. His jaw was lined with a thick appearance of hair, highlighting the distinct angles of his face and his obvious masculinity. "Different in what way?"

"I don't know…short, angry, hostile."

He turned his head away and looked at the fireplace. The flames burned down to simmering coals, crackling once every few minutes. "I'm not angry with you, if that's what you're asking."

"Then are you angry at someone else?"

He took a deep breath like he was about to give a lengthy answer. But instead, he had very little to say. "No, not particularly. I'm just…this is who I am."

"Yes, sometimes. But not all the time." Lately, this was the only version of Calloway I'd seen. He was dark and brooding, seeming constantly displeased about something. Even though he didn't issue threats or do anything to suggest he was unhappy with me, he still exuded this aura of threat. "Are you upset about your mother?"

"No. She's lost her mind, and she'll never get it back. There's nothing to be angry about."

Even if he was being sincere, I didn't believe him. She wasn't even my mother, and I was angry about it. "You know you can talk to me, Calloway. Whatever it is, you know I'll listen and understand."

He turned his head back my way, searching my expression. For a moment, his features seemed to soften, he seemed to become more human. But like a light switch, he immediately returned to his former darkness.

His silence ended the conversation, shutting me out like it had never happened.

Now I suspected something really was wrong, but he didn't want to tell me what it was. The only person he would confide in besides me was Jackson. So maybe I would need to speak to him alone.

If I could figure out how to do that.

When Calloway was in the shower, I made my move.

Guilt flooded my heart when I grabbed his phone off the dresser and opened it. I felt like I was snooping around when I had no right to. It made me look like a jealous girlfriend who didn't trust the man she loved. If he went through my things, he'd get an earful about it. I quickly found Jackson's number then copied it into my phone so I could call him later. Just when I finished, the water in the shower turned off.

I panicked and abandoned the phone on the dresser. Then I hightailed it out of there and returned downstairs where I would normally be. The food was still on the stove, and I did the best I could to stop it from burning.

A moment later, he joined me in the kitchen in his sweatpants and t-shirt. He leaned against the counter and stared me down, his eyes cold. He crossed his arms over his chest and stood in silence.

I felt the sweat collect on the back of my neck, the

adrenaline powerful. Did he know? Was that why he was looking at me the way? Or was I just being paranoid? Since he was constantly inhospitable, I never knew what Calloway was thinking. "Dinner's almost ready."

He continued to eye me in the exact same fashion, accusation heavy in his stare.

I finally turned to him when I couldn't handle the look any longer. "What?"

He moved toward me and wrapped his arm around my waist as he stood behind me. His lips found my neck, and he kissed me slowly, showing me love when he'd just shown me displeasure. "You're the only woman in my heart." He kissed the shell of my ear before he walked to the kitchen table, leaving me standing at the stove.

I was frozen in place, holding the spatula in my hand but unsure what to do with it. My heart was beating so fast it was painful inside my chest. My rib cage vibrated from the force of my beating heart. I could feel my entire frame shake. Did he know I looked at his phone? Or was that just a coincidence? It sounded like something he would say for no reason. But it was also a huge coincidence.

I kept my cool and served dinner, doing my best to mask the terror gripping me by the throat.

Calloway stared at me across the table, his gaze piercing. Like he could see right through me, he stared me down. For an inexplicable reason, my neck felt hot, and I squeezed my thighs together. Seeing him look at me like that made me both turned on and terrified. Something about his power, his natural authority when he entered the room, made me turn into a woman with carnal desires.

I couldn't explain it.

Calloway continued to gaze at me with more intensity than ever before. He interrogated me with just his look. I already knew I was the only woman in his life. I wasn't worried what Calloway was doing when we weren't together. He was absolutely loyal to me, his hands reserved for my body alone.

But I could never tell him what I was really doing.

I dropped my napkin onto the table and came around the side, heading straight for him. I hiked up my dress the second he yanked down his sweatpants and boxers to reveal his large and pulsing cock.

I straddled him as I pulled my underwear to the side, sheathing his cock the instant I lowered myself onto his lap. I gripped his shoulder for balance and breathed through both the pain and the pleasure.

He pressed his face to mine, the thick hair from his jaw gently scratching me. He breathed into my ear as he enjoyed my warm, tight pussy. His hands moved to my hips, and he moved me up and down his length, impaling me the second he was inside me. "Rome…"

My arms locked around his neck, and I rode his cock like I needed it to survive. "Calloway…"

I waited until I knew Calloway had a meeting with the vice president of one of the biggest banks in the city before I called Jackson. Calloway rarely ventured to my office during the workday. The only time we crossed paths was during meetings or when I went to his office to discuss figures.

The phone rang a few times before Jackson answered in a tired voice. "Hmm?"

"Hello to you too."

His voice immediately perked up. "Hey, baby. Who's this?"

I cringed. "Baby?"

"Yeah. You sound hot. What's your name, sweetheart?"

"Uh, Rome. Your brother's girlfriend."

"Oh…" His voice flattened again. "Sorry. You have a sexy voice. Thought you were one of my ladies."

"Did you just wake up?" It was one in the afternoon.

"Yeah. So?"

"It's after lunchtime."

"You know me," he said. "I'm a creature of the night. So why are you calling me? I think you're hot, but I wouldn't cross my brother like that. And not just because he's my brother, but because that guy is batshit crazy."

I rolled my eyes. "That's not why I'm calling."

"Then what's up?"

"I wanted to talk to you about Calloway."

"Well, I'm not a good person to ask. I hardly know the guy."

"That's completely untrue."

"I disagree," he said. "We keep our conversation to a minimum. We talk about work most of the time, sometimes Mom. But we don't have deep conversations about the meaning of the universe."

"Well, I don't want to talk about the universe, so I think we're okay."

"Then what's on your mind, baby?"

My hand immediately tightened into a fist. "Call me baby again, and I'll kick you in the nuts the next time I see you."

"Jesus," he said with a laugh. "You want me to call you ma'am?"

"Rome would be just fine."

"Whatever," he said. "What do you want to know, *Rome*? See, it doesn't roll off the tongue."

I ignored the last thing he said. "I'm worried about Calloway."

"Worried about him in what way?" he asked. "He's

usually Mr. Grumpy Pants, so that's pretty normal for him."

"Jackson." I needed him to be serious right now because I was genuinely concerned.

He sighed into the phone. "What's the problem?"

"He's been really different lately. Quiet. Stern. Moody. He's just not himself. I asked if something was on his mind, but he said he everything is fine. He just seems...cold. He seems distant. I can tell his feelings for me haven't changed. I don't think our relationship is at risk. But something seems off."

Jackson remained silent over the line.

I waited for him to say something, but nothing seemed to be forthcoming. "Have you noticed that too?"

"Well...I don't know."

"You don't know?" I asked. "Does he seem the same to you?"

"Calloway is just complicated. I wouldn't read too much into it."

Something in my gut told me Jackson knew more than he let on. I could feel it all the way to my bones. "Jackson?"

"Hmm?"

"Why do I feel like you aren't telling me something?" Since he was Calloway's brother, I understood his loyalty. But I was genuinely worried something serious was happening with Calloway.

"I really don't want to get involved in this. I suggest you talk to Calloway, not me."

So there was something wrong. "Jackson, please. I'm not above begging."

He sighed into the phone again. "It's not my place, Rome. Confront him. Talk to him the right way, and he'll open up."

"Jackson, I'm actually scared right now." I stopped my voice from shaking, but barely. "My mind is running wild. At least, tell me what this is about. Tell me that he's okay, that he's not sick or something—"

"Nothing like that," he said quickly. "Calloway is fine. He's just struggling with a few things."

"Like what?" I demanded.

"Goddammit, Rome…" He paused over the line.

I waited on the edge of my seat.

"He still struggles with dominance. That's all."

"So…he still wants me to be his sub."

"Rome, he's always gonna want you to be his sub. He struggles to be what you want sometimes. I think he's acting this way because it's the only form of control he can attain."

The air left my lungs. I was both relieved and overwhelmed. I thought we'd put this in the past, but I suspected it would never go away. Calloway would always be a Dom no matter how hard he tried to fight it. "Thanks for telling me."

"Yeah, sure."

I dragged my hand down my face and closed my eyes.

"I know you don't want my advice, but I'm gonna give it to you anyway."

"Okay."

"Just do it, Rome. Be his sub."

I didn't want to have this conversation with Jackson. It was my personal life, not his. "No. I'm not lowering myself to that level."

"Then you're gonna lose him," he said matter-of-factly. "Not today or tomorrow. But one day, you will. I can promise you."

My blood went cold. "Calloway loves me. We'll make it work."

"I have no doubt he loves you. But he can't change who he is, Rome. He's tried a million times, and he keeps going back to his roots. Maybe he can control it for a while longer. But eventually, he's gonna realize he has to choose. And he'll choose dominance."

I didn't want to believe it because the idea was too heartbreaking. I couldn't lose Calloway. The last time we went our separate ways, I was completely lost. I put on a brave face and did my best to stay strong, but I was absolutely miserable.

"I'm sorry, Rome. I know you don't want to hear this, but it's true. I suggest you reconsider your beliefs.

Because when it comes down to it, you're going to have to choose between Calloway and what you stand for. So make sure your beliefs are really strong enough to sacrifice the love of your life. Because that's exactly what's going to happen."

5

Calloway

Jackson asked me to come to Ruin to help him with something. I wasn't sure if Isabella was behind it, trying to get me alone so I could dominate her. But if that was the case, I didn't mind.

I desperately needed to control someone.

I wanted to watch someone obey my every command, not to flinch when I made an outrageous request. I could picture Rome in my mind while staring at Isabella. I'd done it more times than I could count.

I walked into his office, the same office I used to occupy every night. "Do you actually need me? Or was Isabella working your strings?" I sauntered to the armchair then fell into the cushions. I crossed my legs then rested my cheek against my hand.

Jackson looked up from his phone. He seemed to be typing a message. "I wanted to get you away from Rome."

"Why?"

"Because she called me yesterday." He tossed his phone to the side, finished with his message.

I stopped breathing the instant I heard what he said. "Why? What did she say?"

"She said you've been acting different lately. Wanted to know if I knew something about it."

I lowered my hand to my lap, shocked she took it that far. "When I got out of the shower the other day, I could tell she'd looked through my phone. Thought she was paranoid I was cheating on her."

"She was probably getting my number."

I was a little relieved. I didn't want her to think I was sneaking around behind her back. She was the only woman who brought me to my knees. It was ludicrous to think there could ever be someone else. What I did with Isabella was simply about primal instincts. I didn't lay a hand on her sexually, so it didn't count. "What did you tell her?" I knew Jackson would never throw me under the bus, no matter how much he pretended to hate me.

"Everything besides Isabella."

"Which is?"

"That you're a Dom, and you're always going to be a Dom. She needs to be a sub, or it's not gonna work out."

I felt my heart race in my chest like I just ran a mile. "And what did she say to that?" Excitement burned through my veins at the prospect of her changing her mind. Maybe Jackson said the right words to make her realize she needed to submit to me—not just because it was one of my desires, but because it was one of my needs.

"Same ol' bullshit, man," he said with a sigh. "That she couldn't do it."

I shouldn't be surprised by that answer, but I was still disappointed. "Goddammit."

"I didn't mention Isabella," he said. "But I told her she needed to change her mind. Otherwise, she's going to lose you."

I would always struggle with my dominance, and that was a fate I accepted as long as I got to keep her. "She's never going to lose me. I get what I need from Isabella. It'll be fine."

"And when Rome finds out, you think she's just going to be okay with that?"

I shrugged. "She's gonna have to be. It's either that or..." I couldn't finish the sentence. I couldn't picture my life without Rome. But I couldn't picture my life without being a Dom. If only Rome would reconsider, my life would be much simpler.

Jackson gave me a look full of pity, something that didn't happen very often. "What are you going to do?"

I didn't have a clue. "No idea." I rose out of the chair and walked to the door. "Let me know if she calls you again."

"Alright."

I walked over the bridge then looked down at the bar. Sure enough, I spotted Isabella there. She sat alone with a drink in front of her, her jet-black hair hanging down her back. She wore a black, backless dress with a matching choker. Her eyes were tilted to the counter, uninterested in anyone else around her.

Even if what I was doing was wrong, I couldn't stop myself. Every time Rome defied me, it just made me angrier. I couldn't control her, and that made me lose my mind. It made me doubt who I was as a man. If only she would just do as I asked, I could have everything I'd ever wanted.

But she wouldn't listen to me.

I walked downstairs and approached Isabella from the side. I pushed her drink away because I didn't like a drunk sub.

She met my look then quickly turned away, becoming submissive instantly.

"Upstairs," I commanded. "Now."

"Yes, Sir." She abandoned her drink and slid off the stool, her heels tall and her dress short. She walked up the stairs and across the landing as I walked behind her, exerting my presence without her being able to see me.

We entered a playroom and immediately got down to business. I intended to take Isabella even further tonight, to push her into a new realm of pleasure and pain. I needed to exert all my frustration, all my longing for the woman I couldn't have. "Take off your dress." I needed to see that bare skin before I slashed it. "Now."

I sat on the couch as Isabella got dressed. My eyes were averted because I wasn't interested in her physique. Her curves used to drive me wild, her pale skin used to make me excited. But now I didn't feel anything. All I cared about was her obedience, having the power to make her strike herself with force.

That satisfied my craving.

I drank my brandy and stared at the opposite wall, feeling so relaxed I could do this all night. The itch I'd felt had been relieved. The pain in my gut had been removed. Now I could return to Rome without wanting to grab her by the neck and force her to her knees. I could be the boyfriend I promised myself I would be.

Isabella slipped on her heels then approached the couch. She was about to sit right beside me and have a drink herself.

"No." I didn't want her anywhere near me. She wanted me to fuck her, and that was never going to happen. I didn't want her skin to come into contact with mine. We had a strict no-touching policy.

She stilled at my command.

"Sit on the floor."

She didn't hesitate before she got comfortable on the dark hardwood floor.

I poured her a glass and handed it over, careful not to touch even her fingers.

She stared at me like she wanted to speak.

Since playtime was over, I gave her some freedom. "You can speak freely."

"Good," she said quietly. "Because there's something I'd like to say."

I flicked my hand, telling her to spit it out.

"I want Rome out of the picture. I want you and me to be what we were before." Confidence shone in her eyes like she might actually get what she wanted. What was more concerning, she spoke like she thought she deserved it.

"No." I didn't bother with an explanation. I didn't need to tell her that Rome was the only woman I wanted in my bed. Isabella was just a toy, something I used to satisfy my sinister urges. She didn't mean a damn thing to me. I wasn't going to be so cold as to remind her of that reality.

"Yes." Her words came out with a bite, a sharp ring. "Calloway, leave her or else."

My eyes narrowed on her face, my body tensing at the threat. "Or what, Isabella?" What could this woman possibly do to me?

"I'll tell her."

I didn't react to her words because I needed a few extra seconds for them to sink in. "And what will that accomplish?"

"She'll leave you."

"And even if she does, I'll never be your Dom again."

She tilted her head, attitude in her eyes. "What are we doing now?"

"I'm using you. You know that."

"And if Rome weren't around, you'd bend me over the bed and fuck me."

Maybe I would. Maybe I wouldn't. With Rome in my life, I couldn't picture myself with anyone else. It was difficult to determine what I would really do since it was impossible for me even to get hard for her. "Who knows?" I drank my brandy and let the alcohol burn down my throat.

"I mean it, Calloway."

"And I'm calling your bluff."

"You really think I won't do it?" she asked coldly. "Think again. Leave her, and she never has to hear about these nightly sessions. Or do nothing, and I'll tell her the truth myself. What's it gonna be?"

"Do whatever you want, Isabella." I finished the brandy and left the glass on the table. "But in either scenario, you aren't going to get what you want."

6

R ome

Calloway came home that night in the same mood he'd been in for weeks. He was cold and distant, hardly acknowledging my presence when he walked into the bedroom. He stripped off his t-shirt and jeans until he was only in his boxers. His watch came off next, but his ring stayed in place.

I sat on my side of the bed in one of his t-shirts. I was reading on my Kindle and trying to watch him out of the corner of my eye at the same time. I hadn't confronted him about what Jackson told me because I didn't know how to approach it. And now that he'd spent the evening with Jackson, I was sure he knew about the phone conversation.

Calloway got into bed beside me and snatched the Kindle out of my hand.

"Uh, do you mind—"

He crawled on top of me and pinned me down, my hands stuck to the mattress on either side of my head. His knees spread my thighs until his cock pressed against my pussy through our underwear. He stared me down with the kind of intensity that burned right through my skin. "If you want to know something, just ask me."

I knew exactly what he was talking about. "I did. You didn't give me an answer."

"I didn't give you the answer you wanted to hear." His hands tightened around mine. "What do you want me to say, Rome? I need more than what you're giving me. That's the truth, and that's always been the truth. Unless it's gonna change, why talk about it?"

"Does it really bother you that much...?"

His eyes shifted back and forth between mine. "Sometimes. Some days, I'm fine. Some days, I'm not."

"Are you saying you aren't happy with me?" It was difficult to ask these questions because I couldn't bear it if he gave an answer I didn't want to hear.

"You're my world, Rome. You know that."

"You didn't answer the question."

He pulled the front of his boxers down so his cock could be free. Then he dragged my panties off until the apex of my thighs was available to him. He positioned himself between my legs and pressed his hard cock against my lips, rubbing through them and across my opening. "I wouldn't be here if I weren't happy, sweetheart. Sometimes I struggle to control myself when I'm around you. That's when I go dark." He tilted his hips and slid the head of his cock inside me, pushing through my tightness.

Like always, I moaned.

"But make no mistake." He kissed me hard on the mouth before he spoke into my mouth. "You're the only woman I want to be with." He rocked his hips harder until he shook the bed.

When he was inside me and we were connected like this, I didn't think about anything else. My hands broke free of his hold, and I gripped his shoulders, my nails almost piercing the skin. I rocked my hips and took his length quicker, wanting more of that huge cock.

I should be concerned about what he'd just said. I should use logic to understand that this relationship was in jeopardy. After the year we'd been together, we still weren't perfect. He hadn't walked away from his old lifestyle because he still needed it. I wasn't willing to sacrifice what I wanted, and neither was he. What kind of future could we have under these conditions? Would we be husband and wife someday, but still unhappy?

Would Calloway resent me the way he was resenting me now?

But I loved this man so much that I didn't care. I turned off my brain and let my heart guide me, because what we had was too beautiful to walk away from. I'd rather keep working on this broken relationship than find a normal man who didn't need to hit me to feel good. I would rather cry a million times with Calloway than smile with another man.

***

Calloway joined me in the shower the next morning, his perfectly chiseled body flawless under the warm water. He grabbed the bar of soap from the shelf then rubbed it against my chest, lathering my tits and stomach with the suds. His eyes met mine with the same intensity he had last night. "You have the most beautiful body." Both of his hands grabbed my tits and gave them a gentle squeeze. His hands were large enough to cover my breasts completely.

"I think you do, actually." I reached out and grabbed his hard cock, lubricating it with the soap from my hand. My thumb flicked over the tip and brushed away the bead of pre-come that formed there.

"I guess that means we're beautiful together." He cupped my face then leaned in and kissed me, giving me a soft kiss that made me tingle everywhere. It wasn't a sexy embrace, the kind he gave right before he fucked me hard against the mattress. It was a gentle greeting, a good morning kiss.

It was the sweetest affection I'd gotten from him in a long time.

He pulled away then stood under the shower, letting his short hair get wet. He looked sexy no matter what he did, but he looked particularly gorgeous in that moment.

So I got on my knees and gripped him by the thighs.

He looked down at me, his eyes darkening.

I pointed his head into my mouth then pushed him deep inside my throat, nearly making myself gag right from the beginning.

"Fuck..." He gripped the back of my neck and thrust his hips, burying his cock inside my mouth. "You have no idea how sexy you look right now."

And he had no idea how sexy he looked to me.

<hr />

He walked me to my office door then kissed me in the hallway, ignoring Chad as he walked by. Calloway's arm was tight around my wrist, and he smothered me with affection that wasn't appropriate for any public place.

I had to force myself to step away. "I'll see you after work."

"I have a feeling you're going to see me sooner than that." He gave my ass a gentle squeeze before he finally walked away.

Once he was gone, I felt the blush move into my cheeks. When he came inside my mouth that morning, he seemed immensely satisfied. It was like our conversation from the previous night never happened. Maybe I was just trying to ignore it as much as possible because nothing good would come from it, but that didn't matter to me.

I sat down and got to work.

No one in the office had an assistant except Calloway, so we handled everything on our own. We all agreed it was better to save that money and give it back to the communities we were trying to help rather than making our jobs more convenient.

So when someone came to my office, I had to deal with it right away instead of hiding behind an assistant.

"Rome Moretti?" The woman was immediately hostile, her jet-black hair long even though it was pulled into a high ponytail. She wore a short dress and heels that only a supermodel could pull off.

"Yes." I didn't recognize her from anywhere in the office, and she didn't look like she was from the mail room either. "Do I know you?"

"No." She held up a large orange envelope and invited herself into my office. She tossed the packet on the desk like she owned the damn place.

"Uh, did you skip the manners section in kindergarten?"

She stepped back and crossed her arms over her chest, unaffected by the insult. I knew this woman didn't like me the second she walked in the door, and I had no idea what I could have done to a stranger to elicit this kind of disrespectful behavior. She looked down at my hands, and a quick reaction shook her body. She automatically stepped back as she took a deep breath, like she saw a spider on me.

When she looked me in the eye again, it really seemed like she wanted to kill me.

"Who are you?" I demanded.

"I can't believe he gave that to you." Her rage was mixed with despair. Her voice nearly broke when she spoke, so full of anguish.

"Who gave me what?"

She eyed my hand again. "That ring."

I looked down and spotted the black diamond Calloway gave me so long ago. He asked me to take him back in exchange for walking away from Ruin. But he asked me to wear this anyway, his only request. "How did you know...?" My mind worked quicker than my mouth, and I suspected I found the answer.

She was one of his subs.

Probably his most recent one.

And I was repulsed. The fact that he ever touched this woman, kissed this woman, made me more jealous than I'd ever been in my life. Without knowing a single thing about her, I wanted to strangle her.

"All those nights that Calloway has been at Ruin, he's been with me. He takes me in his playroom and spanks me, whips me, and does many more unspeakable things —because you won't give it to him. I'm his sub. I've been his sub for a very long time. Just thought you should know." She nodded to the envelope. "All the proof you need." She gave me another threatening glare before she stormed out of my office, shaking her ass like a model on the runway.

I wanted to scream.

Her confession immediately sent me into a spiral of panic. Calloway had been acting strange because he was sneaking around behind my back. When I couldn't give him what he needed, he went to someone else.

How could he do this to me?

I eyed the envelope sitting on the table then ripped the seal open, needing to see the proof that was sitting inside.

But then I stopped myself.

Calloway would never do that to me. He was loyal to me, devoted to me. He told me he loved me and showed it every single day. Maybe we had our problems, but he would never hurt me like that.

I gripped the envelope by the edges but didn't open it. I didn't need to see what was inside. It had to be Photoshopped images that she threw together. None of the contents had any basis in reality.

I knew Calloway.

And I trusted him.

I left my office with the envelope tucked under my arm and headed to his office on the other side of the building. This time, I took his request seriously and walked right inside without checking in with his assistant.

She stared at me with surprise but didn't dare try to stop me.

Calloway was on the phone when I walked inside. "Of course, Greg." He listened to him over the line as his eyes locked to mine. When he saw the concern on my face, he finished up the call. "Greg, I've gotta go. I'll see you on Tuesday, alright? Talk to you then." He placed the phone on the base. "Sweetheart, what's wrong?" He rose to a stand and came around the desk, buttoning the front of his suit on instinct.

I held up the envelope. "One of your old subs stopped by my office just now."

Calloway's concern immediately melted away. He stiffened at the subject and released a quiet sigh. He eyed the envelope but didn't take it. Like he'd done over the past few weeks, he became unreadable once more.

"She told me you've been sneaking off with her at Ruin, that she's your sub because I can't give you what you need. Then she handed me this for proof." I shook the envelope.

Calloway placed his hands in his pockets and tilted his head to the floor.

"What a psychopath. I didn't realize she was still obsessed with you."

Calloway slowly raised his head and looked at me, his eyebrows slightly raised.

"She barged into my office like she owned the damn place. And she expects me to believe this bullshit?" I wanted to throw the envelope against the damn well. Better yet, I wanted to light it on fire and watch it burn to ash. That woman had a lot of nerve trying to come between Calloway and me. It would take a lot more than a filthy lie to get me to think twice.

His face suddenly softened in a way it never had before. His eyes crinkled in the corners, and he swallowed hard. He placed his hand underneath his chin and rubbed the scruff along his jaw. His eyes closed like he suddenly needed a moment to recuperate. It wasn't clear if he was touched by what I said or repulsed.

"What?" I asked, unable to read him the way I used to.

He returned his hand to his pocket and opened his eyes again, this time meeting my gaze head on. "Rome... she wasn't lying. Everything she said is true." He swallowed hard again, his Adam's apple moving slightly.

I heard what he said, but I couldn't conceive of it. It was a fact, a confession, but it still didn't sink into my brain. "What...?" There was no way this really happened. There was no way Calloway would sneak around behind my back. There was no way he would touch another woman. "I...what?" I immediately stepped back because I suddenly wasn't getting enough air. I needed to breathe. Otherwise, I would collapse.

A slight look of remorse was in his eyes, but the rest of his body remained strong. "She has been my sub for a few months. When I go to Ruin, I hit her. I strike her with my belt or hit her with my whip. I give her a command, and she obeys. She does what I ask, gives me the control. She gives me what I need..."

I took another step back, my eyes filling with tears. "Calloway..."

"I didn't sleep with her. I didn't kiss her. I never touched her, actually. I've been faithful to you in every way imaginable. But...she does the one thing you won't do. I wish I could have walked away that night when I had my breakdown but I couldn't. I needed it."

My heart finally relaxed when I heard what he said, that he didn't fuck her while I slept in the bed I shared with him. It was such a relief I considered sitting on the floor and enjoying that fact.

But then the pain returned.

The heartbreak.

The devastation.

"How could you do this...?" Now I couldn't stop the tears from coming. They bubbled at the corners of my eyes before they streaked down my face. I didn't bother wiping them away, wanting Calloway to hurt the way I was hurting.

His eyes cringed slightly, pained by what he saw. "I don't know what to say... I needed it."

"That's your excuse?" I hissed. "That's what justifies it?"

"I'm just explaining—"

"So if I needed sex because you were working late, I'd have every right to screw some other guy?"

His jaw clenched at the suggestion. "Not the same thing and you know it."

"It is the same goddamn thing, Calloway."

"I told you I didn't touch her. I meant that. I just bossed her around, and she obeyed. That's all I wanted from you, but you refused to give it to me."

"Because I refuse to disrespect myself like that?" I hissed. "Because I refuse to bow to a man? Wasn't that the reason you were attracted to me in the first place?"

"Yes. But I wanted to break you. I've always wanted to break you."

"Well, I don't break for anyone, Calloway. Not even you." I headed to the door, determined to get the hell away from him once and for all. We were officially done. I could deal with his strange desires and the rough way he took me from time to time, but I could never deal with this. It didn't matter that he didn't touch her. It didn't matter that he didn't fuck her. He still shared a sexual experience with someone else.

I got the door opened and marched out, waiting for him to grab me by the wrist or the arm.

But the touch never came.

I turned around to shut the door and spotted him on the other side of the room, looking out the window of his office. His hands rested in his pockets as he examined the city below him. There was no fight in him. He had no intention of doing whatever he could to keep me.

He was letting me go.

7

Calloway

I had Tom follow her to make sure she was okay. He followed her all the way to the house then waited outside for her to finish packing her things.

I assumed that's what she was doing.

I stayed at work until the end of the day, knowing she probably wouldn't be there when I got home.

But there was nothing I could do about that.

I expected to feel more pain for what I'd done. I expected to feel more guilt. When those tears streaked down her cheeks, I felt terrible. But when she walked out of my office, I didn't bother chasing her down.

I knew we were done.

In the back of my mind, I knew this was going to

happen. The moment I whipped Isabella, I knew Rome and I wouldn't last. No matter how much I tried to avoid who I really was, it never worked. The man I was deep inside would never change. I would always need domination and control. And I would always be a sadist.

It was time to accept that.

I walked home once the day was over, taking my time because there was nothing waiting for me when I arrived. I didn't call Rome or send her a text message. I didn't waste my time trying to talk to her.

She had every right to leave.

She should leave.

When I arrived at the house, Tom's car was waiting at the curb. That had to mean she was still inside, gathering the rest of her things. I was surprised it was taking her so long. I hoped I'd be spared the pain of watching her leave the house one last time.

But I knew I deserved that agony.

I stepped inside and saw her bags piled in the entryway. She wasn't in the living room, so she must have been upstairs, grabbing the rest of her things. I took a seat on the couch and waited for her to return, refusing to crowd her when she was still upset.

Fifteen minutes later, she came to the bottom of the stairs with two more bags. She didn't notice me right away, her face stained with old tears and her eyes still puffy.

"Tom is waiting outside for you."

She grabbed her chest and nearly jumped out of her shoes. "Shit, you scared me."

I turned my gaze to the floor and massaged one of my knuckles. "Tom will take you wherever you want to go. I suggest you go to Christopher's. You'll be safe there. And if not there, I have no problem buying you something nice. It would give me peace of mind."

She remained in the entryway, her lower body in my peripheral. "That's it?"

I raised my head and turned back to her, not certain what she meant. "Do you want more?" She'd never been the kind of person to ask anything of me. Any time I'd tried to give her money, she was extremely offended.

"You're just going to let me go?" Her voice cracked as more tears emerged. "I mean...is this what you wanted the entire time? Is this your way out of this relationship?"

The sound of her tears was as painful as dragging knives down my back. Knowing I was the reason behind her agony just made me feel worse. I got off the couch and walked toward her, keeping my hands in my pockets so I wouldn't be tempted to grab her.

She wiped her tears away, but more spilled out. "I wish you'd just told me you didn't want to do this anymore. I wish you were man enough to tell me the truth. I wish...I wish for a lot of things."

"Rome." The second I said her name, I realized she was really leaving. It hit me harder then, that the one woman I ever gave a damn about was walking out on me. "I don't want this to end. I don't want to lose you. You know that."

"I really don't," she whispered. "You wouldn't have gone to her if you felt otherwise."

"She doesn't mean anything to me," I said quietly. "I just needed what she gave me. I was never even hard for her. Any time I was with her, she relieved my stress and fulfilled my needs. Then I came home to you, and I was better. I felt better." I turned my gaze and stared at the stairs. "And then I could be what you needed me to be. That's all."

She shook her head like that answer wasn't enough.

"I love you." My voice didn't shake when I spoke. It was steady as a rock. "I've loved you far longer than you've loved me."

Her eyes met mine, and her chest froze in place because she stopped breathing.

"But...this is who I am. I've tried fighting it, and it hasn't worked. I've tried just being a boyfriend to you, but that hasn't worked either. As much as I love you, as much as I want to make this work, I can't do this anymore." The pain started in my heart then circulated everywhere else. Soon every muscle in my body tensed with the imminent pain. Just like the last time she left me, I would be utterly heartbroken. But I would have to ride out the sorrow until I was finally better. And then one day, I would be back to where I was.

She crossed her arms over her chest and forced herself to stop crying. She was never the kind of woman to show pain or fear, so she tried to box everything up and hide it as much as possible.

"I know I shouldn't have been with Isabella. I just thought if she gave me what I needed, it could make *our* relationship better. Now I know that was wrong. When things got really bad...I should have ended this."

Her breathing picked up again as she tried to combat another round of tears.

"I don't want to be with anyone else," I whispered. "I want to spend my life with you." I knew I would never have the chance to say this to her again, so I needed to say it now. "I'd ask you to marry me if things were different. I'd do the whole father thing and grow old with you. I'd make any sacrifice that you wanted. But if you can't give me what I need...it'll never work. I wish I were normal. I wish I weren't so fucked up in the head. But I am...and that will never change."

Rome stepped back like my final words just made things worse.

A part of me still hoped she would change her mind, that she would forget her past and really trust me. That she would trust me to take her to a place she'd never been before. I'd done everything possible to make this relationship work. Now I hoped she would make the ultimate sacrifice to save us.

But she didn't. "I should go..." She turned to her bags, probably to cover her face more than anything else.

I felt the rush of pain at her response, knowing there really was no hope for us. Rome was walking out of my life for good, and I would have to spend years trying to truly get over her. I'd fall into a life of meaningless sex and booze to fill the hole she just carved in my chest. "Let me help you." I grabbed two of her suitcases.

I knew the only reason why she allowed me to do anything was because she was trying to get out of there as quickly as possible. She didn't object to using Tom to get to Christopher's apartment. She was in flight mode, and there was no time for pride.

I put her things in the trunk and watched her get into the back seat. She shut the door and locked it, her appearance invisible due to the dark tint over the windows. I stood on the sidewalk and stared at the place where I imagined she would be, her face covered in a waterfall of tears.

The car pulled away from the curb and onto the street. It faded farther into the distance as it drove away. I inserted my hands in my pockets and stared at the taillights as the car drove down the road. Eventually, it came to a stoplight, where it turned right.

When the car was gone from my sight, I knew she was really gone.

And gone forever.

8

R ome
     When I reached Christopher's door, I was on the verge of sobbing.

I just lost the love of my life.

It hurt so much I couldn't handle it. My throat was tight, my heart was weak, my knees could barely hold me up.

I hardly had the energy just to knock on the door.

Christopher opened it a moment later, and when he saw the look on my face, he didn't ask any questions. He did something he rarely did, only during the most extreme cases. He wrapped his arms around me and held me on the doorstep.

And I cried.

I cried into his chest, soaking his t-shirt until it was

damp. I shouldn't cry over a man, whether I loved him or not, but now I was falling apart at the seams.

Christopher ran his hand up and down my back, comforting me in a way only my brother could do. When it went on for over ten minutes, he guided me inside and grabbed the bags Tom helped me carry to the door. He piled them in the kitchen then came back to me, concern written all over his face. "Rome, talk to me." He grabbed a handful of tissues then placed them in my hand.

I told him what happened, taking time between sentences to stop myself from shedding more tears. "So I left...and now I'm here."

He grabbed my shoulder and massaged it, his eyes crinkled with sadness. "I'm so sorry, Rome."

"I know you are..."

"You're welcome to stay here as long as you want. I was a little lonely without you anyway."

I forced a chuckle even though I wasn't in the mood to laugh. "You're just saying that."

"I'm really not." He grabbed my bags and carried them into the room I used to occupy.

I drifted behind him, unsure what to do with myself. Now that Calloway was gone, I wasn't even sure how to live anymore. Spending every day playing house with him was a dream. Having that taken away so suddenly was jarring. I wasn't sure if I would ever recover.

Christopher sat on the edge of the bed and patted the space beside him. "Do you want to be alone right now?"

I moved to the spot next to him, feeling the bed sink just the way it used to. "Honestly...I don't know what I want right now."

"I'm always here if you want to talk."

"There's not much to say... I can't believe he did that to me."

He nodded.

I crossed my arms over my chest and stared at the floor.

"Now what?" he whispered.

"What do you mean?" I wasn't even sure how I was going to get through the next day.

"Do you have anything else left at the house that you need?"

I shook my head. "Nothing that I care about."

"What about your job?"

Could I really work for the man who broke my heart? "I don't know. I would find something else, but I'm never gonna find anything that pays me nearly as well. With my salary, I can afford to live on my own...and food."

"Yeah, that's true."

"But...I'll never move on if I run into Calloway."

"How often do you see him?"

"Very seldom."

"Well, you can stay there for now and look for something else in the meantime. I'm sure Calloway will do his best to avoid you."

I pulled my knees to my chest and stared at the floor.

Christopher remained silent beside me, unsure what else to say. There was nothing that could cure this pain, could erase the loss I felt in my heart. The entire day had been chaotic. Calloway's former lover confronted me at the office, and he confirmed everything she said was correct. And then he told me he had his doubts that we would ever work...so it was best if went our separate ways.

It was catastrophic.

It was hard to believe the morning started so beautifully. He kissed me in the shower and held me under the warm water. He walked me to my office and kissed me again like he couldn't get enough of me.

And then later that day, he let me go.

I think that hurt worst of all.

He was no longer fighting for me. He'd come to accept our doom. He told me he was willing to sacrifice his former life to make this work. But in the end, the happiness he got from me didn't outweigh what he was missing.

I wasn't enough for him.

Now I wanted to cry again.

Christopher must have noticed my change in

breathing because he started to rub my back. "I know things are tough right now. I know you're heartbroken. But remember who you are. You're Rome, and you're gonna get through this. We were both locked in that basement for a week, and you didn't give up. And you wouldn't let me give up either."

Being locked in a basement was far less painful than this.

"I'm not gonna let you give up. You're gonna hold your head high and get through this. And some day, you're gonna find the right guy who treats you the way you want to be treated. This will all seem like a bad memory then."

It was hard to imagine ever moving on to a different guy. I suspected I would always love Calloway. It was the kind of love that never faded. It was solid like a statue, standing through the ages of mankind. Like a scar that would never heal, his presence would always be visible on the surface of my heart.

But I nodded anyway to make Christopher feel like he was helping. "Yeah…hopefully."

———

Later that night, Calloway texted me. I was surprised to see his name light up on my screen since he was the one who admitted he didn't see our relationship working out. Even though I'd walked out, he was the one who dumped me.

I'm not gonna bother you again after this. But there are a few things I'd like to say.

My heart was beating so fast as I saw the dots light up on the screen.

Stay with Humanitarians United. You're perfect for the job and the community. Whenever you have to deal with me, I'll always be professional. I'll never mention anything about our relationship.

The dots lit up again as he kept writing.

If you ever need anything from me, I'll always be there. Even if it's five years down the road, there's nothing I won't give you. I'll keep a close eye on Hank and know his whereabouts at all times so you'll never be in danger. I'm not just doing this for your protection, but so I can get some sleep at night.

The dots lit up again.

I want you to know that everything I felt for you was real. I'll love you until the day I die, no matter what happens in the meantime. I wish things could have turned out differently for the two of us. I just wanted you to know that. Goodbye, Rome.

The dots disappeared.

I knew that was the last thing I would ever get from Calloway. Now we were officially strangers on this earth. I would run into him at work from time to time, but we would never have a real conversation. We would always be aware of one another, but distant at the same time.

Like a shooting star, our relationship was brilliant and beautiful, but it happened so fast that it didn't seem to last very long. We only had a year together—the best year of my life. The ring he gave me was still on my finger, the black diamond that Isabella recognized. I knew I should take it off, but I'd grown used to the weight. I loved the way it was snug around my finger, just the way Calloway's love used to be. I couldn't part with it so suddenly, so I would take it off first thing in the morning.

But not a moment sooner.

A week passed, and I didn't see Calloway. He probably didn't come into the office at all just to give me space. If he really wanted to, he could work from home. There was nothing pressing that kept him physically in the office. I suspected he was there most of the time just because I was down the hall.

I kept glancing at my phone, waiting for a text message to appear. But I wasn't sure why because I didn't want him to text me anyway.

I could never forgive him.

Even if Calloway said he could conquer his demons,

I couldn't give him another chance. Knowing he had erotic moments with Isabella, even if there was no touching, still made me sick to my stomach.

It was an act of betrayal.

Christopher was particularly nice to me all week. He was the one who made dinner and cleaned the apartment. My laundry was always done and folded on the bed by the time I got home.

I appreciated the gesture, but nothing could fix my broken heart.

Christopher didn't mention Calloway. He always picked a random subject to talk about, like work or whatever was on TV. The second things became too quiet, he would pull out a game, anything that could distract me.

But there wasn't a distraction in the world powerful enough.

"You wanna go for a jog in the park?" Christopher asked when I came home from work.

"A jog?" I couldn't remember the last time I jogged. It was probably in Calloway's personal gym in the garage, the one he made so he wouldn't have to leave me alone. The memory of his protectiveness suddenly made me feel weak all over again.

"Or a walk. Whatever. I just think I would be good to get some fresh air."

I had no energy to do anything. "I walk around all

day at work. I don't need any exercise."

"Come on, don't be lazy. You know I'm gonna bug you until you change your mind."

That part was true. "Okay, fine."

"Great."

We pulled on our gym clothes and running shoes then walked to the park just a block away. We joined a trail and walked briskly as the summer sun slowly faded behind the trees. We passed a few ice cream stands, but neither one of us was interested in the frozen treats.

Christopher talked about work even though he'd already told me most of his stories. It was obvious he was just looking for something to say to keep me distracted.

He was doing his best to make me feel better, and it was incredibly sweet. "Thanks for trying to cheer me up, Christopher. I appreciate it."

He shrugged as he walked, with his hands in the pockets of his shorts. "What are brothers for?"

"But you don't need to bend over backward for me. I understand you have a life."

"Yeah, I know. But I know you would do the same for me if I were crushed like you are."

Absolutely.

"Staying busy always helps me when I'm down. Going for a walk. Playing a game. All those sorts of things."

"Yeah…"

Christopher was so absorbed in me he didn't even check out the pair of beautiful women who walked by in their leggings and t-shirts. He stared straight ahead, focused on me and our conversation. "Have you seen him at work?"

"No."

"Has he tried contacting you?"

I didn't want to mention the text messages the night we broke up. "No."

He nodded like he was agreeing with me, when there was nothing to agree on.

"Don't tell him off like you did last time, okay?"

"I wasn't planning on it."

That was surprising. I eyed him as we walked side by side. "I thought you might want to kill him."

He shrugged.

That reaction was even odder coming from a guy as vocal as Christopher. He always wanted to give his two cents on everything, making sure his voice and his fury were heard. His calm reaction to all of this was strange. "There's something you aren't telling me."

"Like what?" he asked.

"Why aren't you angrier with Calloway?"

"What am I supposed to do, Rome?" he asked. "You aren't the kind of woman who expects someone to fight your battles."

"And I don't expect you to do that. I guess I'm just surprised that you aren't more upset."

He stared at the black asphalt and walked around a snail that was right in his path. "I guess...never mind."

"You guess what?" I pressed.

"It doesn't matter," he said quickly. "This is your relationship, not mine. My opinion is irrelevant."

"Why do you take that stance now, when you've always stuck your nose in my business? Now tell me."

"You really wanna know?" His eyes found mine as he searched for affirmation.

"Yes." I could handle anything he said.

"I told you this might happen."

"That Calloway would cheat."

"He didn't really cheat," Christopher corrected. "He told you what he was into, and you wouldn't do it. So he found someone else who would. I mean, I can't say that I'm surprised. If I met a fabulous woman, and she said she would never give me a blow job, I'd probably leave too. I know it's not the same thing, but I couldn't be in a long-lasting relationship with a woman who wouldn't give me what I wanted. Would you stay with Calloway if he wouldn't do vanilla sex every now and then?"

I stared straight ahead because my answer was obvious.

"See?" he said. "I think the relationship was doomed

to fail. I can tell the guy really loves you, but he just needs more. I can't say I blame him."

The fact that my own brother agreed with my ex didn't make me feel any better. "After what Hank did to me—"

"You don't have to explain yourself to me," he said quickly. "I totally understand your point of view. I respect it, and I'm sure Calloway does too. But I still don't blame Calloway for what he did. He did his best but collapsed under the pressure. It happens to the best of us."

Now I was just as depressed as I had been at the start of the week, not that I'd made much progress to begin with.

"I think if you really can't live without Calloway, you should give him what he wants. Because he's gonna find some other woman to do it in a heartbeat."

"I'm aware."

"So that's off the table?" he asked.

"Yeah."

Christopher finally dropped the subject. "You wanna get some ice cream? My treat."

The last thing I wanted was food in my stomach. The only reason why I usually ate was because Christopher was force-feeding it to me. But after the admission that he sided with Calloway, I felt too stick to consume anything. "Thanks, but no thanks."

9

Calloway

Instead of being distraught, I was numb.

In the back of my mind, I'd been expecting this relationship to crash and burn. That was probably why I wasn't as devastated as last time. I'd anticipated the ending long before it actually happened.

Not that it made this any easier.

I worked from home for the first week, wanting to give Rome as much as space as possible. Having Isabella storm into her office like that must have been scarring. Having to listen to me correct and confess what I'd really done must have been worse.

I felt like shit.

Sometimes I questioned if I was doing the right thing. I knew how I felt about Rome, and I understood I would never feel this way for another woman as long as I lived. But I was walking away from her because my urges were too powerful. I'd been willing to compromise with her, to go half-and-half, but she wouldn't meet me in the middle.

So I had to walk away.

Right now, I wasn't ready to be with another woman. Isabella pissed me off, so I definitely wouldn't be joining her in the playroom. I would have to let my heart bleed until there was nothing left. Once I had nothing left to give, perhaps I could start over and return to my previous life.

Even if it was lonely.

In the end, I chose sex and control over the woman I loved. It made her seem insignificant, unimportant. But that wasn't how I felt. I just couldn't control my urges any longer. If she didn't give me what I needed, I would resent her and find it in some other way.

So it would never work.

My house felt more like a prison than a home. Her presence was everywhere. I smelled her scent from the cushions on the couch. A load of her laundry was still in the dryer because she forgot about it in her haste. A strand of hair sat in the bottom of the shower drain. A pair of her panties were still tucked in my drawer because she must have put them there by mistake.

Normally, I'd probably jerk off with them, but even that was too painful.

Where did I go from here?

I drank a lot. I drank during work and all through the night. I was always on the verge of being completely drunk, the perfect amount to where I was in control of my faculties and I was numb from the pain.

It was the only way I could exist.

Jackson called me at the end of the week, probably catching wind of what happened from Isabella. "Hmm?" I didn't give him a warm greeting. Right now, I had nothing to live for.

"I should have known you would be drunk."

"Any time I'm not drunk is a waste of time, if you ask me." I was sitting at the kitchen table with the bottle of scotch right beside me. I didn't even bother with a glass, even though I liked ice cubes in my drink.

"I guess I shouldn't bother asking if you're okay. It seems pretty clear."

"You catch on quick," I said sarcastically.

"So, she packed her things and left when Isabella threw you under the bus?"

"Not exactly." I stared at the amber liquid right in front of me, feeling the smooth burn even though I didn't take a drink. "Rome actually assumed Isabella was lying…because I would never do something like that. I corrected her."

"Damn."

"Her loyalty hurt more than anything else. I earned it, and then I lost it."

"Yeah…but you could have lied."

I wasn't the lying type. "Not my style."

"It almost seems like you wanted her to know."

I dragged my hand down my face, grateful the migraine I had earlier finally disappeared. Every illness could be cured with a quality glass of scotch. "Yeah…I think I did too." I wanted her to catch me, to understand how much I needed what she wouldn't give me. I thought she would finally give me what I wanted when she knew she would lose me.

But that didn't happen.

"You want Ruin back?" Jackson asked.

"I gave it to you, Jackson. The place is yours."

"Come on, we both know I do a piss-poor job. I'm not cut out for it."

Jackson had always slacked off when we were growing up. He never had the patience to sit and listen to instruction. I was never a big fan of school either, but his concentration was worse than mine. "Give it time."

"No, man. I want you to take it back. I miss fucking around all the time. I hate sitting in the office, away from the festivities."

"You're being serious?" Hope surged in my heart because I knew I wanted it. I missed being in the dark with the rest of the devils. It was where I belonged. In fact, I belonged in hell.

"Absolutely. Come in and sign the papers."

"You're sure?" Running Ruin would get my mind off the brunette who stole my heart. I needed anything to distract me right now—anything at all.

"Yes," he said with a sigh. "Stop making me repeat myself. I miss getting paid to do nothing. It was a lot easier back then."

I wanted to laugh, but I couldn't bring myself to do it. "Alright. You convinced me."

"Awesome. I'm behind on bills and everything else... so you have that to look forward to."

I rolled my eyes, still surprised by Jackson's inadequacy. "You can pay most of that shit online."

"But I always forget the password..."

"You can't just not pay bills," I argued. "That's how businesses go under."

"I know, I know. That's why you need to get back in here."

"Apparently." I grabbed the large bottle and brought it back to my lips, taking a large drink that I would probably regret later.

"So...now what?"

"What do you mean?"

"You're just going to go back to what you were before?"

The idea sounded so unappealing. I wanted to be a Dom again, but I didn't want another sub besides Rome. I would never feel that exquisite passion again. I would never come so hard my heart nearly gave out.

I would never feel alive again.

But at least I would be in control. "Eventually. Right now, I just need some time."

"Well, I'm here if you need anything."

"I know, Jackson." Jackson was an ass most of the time, but I couldn't recall a time when he wasn't there for me. No matter what tension existed between us, we put it aside when it came to each other's well-being. "I'll talk to you later."

"Alright. You know I'm just a phone call away."

"Yeah, I know." I hung up and tossed the phone on the table. The screen was lit up for a few seconds before it turned black again. I hadn't changed my wallpaper yet because it was too difficult. It still had a picture of Rome sleeping on my chest, her hair a mess from where I'd fisted it just minutes previously. I should take the photo off because it was painful to look at. It reminded me of the fact that I would never sleep well again as long as I lived—not without her.

But I still couldn't do it.

And I had a feeling I never would.

I finally went back to work the following week. I knew I couldn't avoid Rome forever, and I had to get it over with. Perhaps seeing her on a regular basis would make me less affected by her.

But I doubted it.

I stayed in my office and concentrated on work as much as possible. If I stopped, even for a second, my mind returned back to the fiery brunette on the other side of the building. And since I wasn't drunk, it was even more difficult for me to keep steady with my emotions.

Was she as devastated?

That was a stupid question. Of course, she was. She didn't have any time to prepare for the heartbreaking end to our relationship. At least I knew the end was coming before it finally arrived.

Because I was an ass.

I tried to finish a report, but I kept thinking about her, missing the way her body felt underneath my fingertips. I tried sleeping last night, but that didn't get me anywhere. I just lay in bed the entire night. When I did fall asleep, I had a nightmare about losing her.

But then I realized that wasn't a dream.

Unable to stop myself, I called Christopher.

He was probably at work, but he worked in his own office so he usually answered the phone. I hoped he would because I really need to speak to him.

When he answered, his voice was emotionless. It wasn't clear whether he hated me or didn't give a damn about me at all. "How can I help you?"

I wasn't naïve enough to expect a different reaction from him. "You know why I'm calling."

Christopher sighed into the phone before the sound of typing entered the background. He was probably sitting at his desk, finishing up an email. "She's a complete mess. But you already knew that, Calloway."

"For what it's worth, I'm just as fucked up."

"No offense, but I don't really care how you feel. Whatever my personal opinion is on the matter, I'm on her side. You broke her heart, and that's all I need to know."

I was glad he was loyal to her. That was exactly how family should be. "Is she eating? Sleeping?"

"No. And no."

I'd hoped this conversation would make me feel better, but it just made me feel worse.

"It's gonna be a while before she's back on her feet. She's a strong woman, but I've never seen her struggle like this before. Last time, she put on a good front. This time, she's not even bothering."

I fucking hated myself.

"What's the deal with Hank? Do I need to get a gun?"

I was relieved to say I wasn't worried about that asshole. "No. I have guys tailing him wherever he goes.

If he comes with a mile radius of Rome, they'll let me know. If I can't get there in time, they've been instructed to intervene."

Christopher sighed in relief. "Well, that's something to be grateful for. Now I can shut my door at night."

I turned in my chair and looked out the window, noting how dark the sky looked now that Rome wasn't mine anymore. The sky wasn't any different, blue as ever, but to me, it was just a blanket of gray. "I wish it didn't have to be this way. Honestly."

"I know you love her," he said quietly. "I can tell."

"Thanks…" That meant a lot to me that he recognized my sincerity. I'd never doubted my feelings for Rome, just my restraint.

"I tried to explain your actions to her, but it didn't make a difference."

"What do you mean?"

"Basically, that all people have certain needs, and it's not outrageous for them to leave if they don't get what they want. I told her I would never be with a woman who was against blow jobs. Blow jobs aren't the center of my universe, but could I really settle down with a woman who refused to give me one once in a while? No. I know it's not the same thing, but I tried to get my point across to her. She didn't take the bait."

I stared at the black ring that still sat on my right hand. I didn't have the strength to take it off. My heart was still committed to that woman. "She didn't understand either?"

"No. She's not gonna change her mind about the whole thing. Sorry."

I appreciated him trying. And I appreciated him being so understanding. "Thanks for saying something."

"I hate seeing her hurt like this. But I think she's being a little unreasonable. I know she's been through a lot. No one knows that better than I do. But it's in the past, and we need to move forward. If she really gave it a chance, I think she would understand it's not abusive. But she's a stubborn woman...as you know."

Just as stubborn as I was. "I miss her." I didn't know what possessed me to say that. When I felt the emotion, I just admitted it out loud. Right now, I had nothing else to lose. It didn't matter if Christopher thought less of me for wearing my heart on my sleeve. I didn't give a shit what anyone thought of me.

"She misses you too."

I rested the back of my head against the leather chair and closed my eyes, trying to fight off the crippling sensation that just swept through me. "Keep me posted, okay?"

"Sure, man. Take care."

It felt like I was saying goodbye to him too. In the past year of my relationship with Rome, Christopher had become a friend. In fact, he seemed like more than just a friend—more like family. Being his brother-in-law actually sounded appealing. Since that was an impossible future, I pushed the thought out of my head. "You too." I hung up and let the phone fall to my lap, my eyes still closed like that would somehow protect me.

But nothing would protect me.

———

I walked to the elevator at the end of the day and was relieved I didn't see Rome once. She was nowhere in sight now, so I didn't have to suffer through an awkward elevator ride down to the bottom floor.

But just when I reached the elevator, Rome appeared from the right, having taken a different route to the elevator.

Fuck.

She stopped when she spotted me, obviously just as disappointed at seeing me as I was at seeing her. Her face looked pale like she'd lost most of her blood. That sexy fire wasn't in her eyes anymore. Anytime she looked at me, there had always been a hint of desire. But now she stared at me like I was the grim reaper.

Despite her sickly appearance, I immediately got hard.

It was the first boner I'd had in over a week.

My fascination with this woman would never die, clearly.

The doors to the elevator opened, and I stuck my arm inside. "I'll catch the next one." I couldn't stand inside that elevator with her. I couldn't make small talk about work or the weather. It was too soon to be normal, to act like a typical boss with one of his employees.

She didn't think twice before she walked into the elevator, her bag tight over her shoulder.

I pulled my arm back and returned my hands to my pockets, waiting for the doors to shut. I knew I shouldn't look at her, but the temptation became too much. I lifted my gaze and met hers, looking into the green eyes that I used to stare at when we made love. A sense of longing overcame me, and I desperately wanted to hold her.

When she'd left me, I didn't get to hug her. I didn't get to kiss her goodbye. I had to keep my hands to myself and watch her walk out of my life. Now I had to do it again as I waited for the doors to shut.

She held my gaze, the heartbreak obvious in her eyes. Instead of being angry with me like she should, she was only devastated. When the doors finally began to close, she looked away, unable to see the intensity in my eyes.

I never thought I would be so grateful to have a solid barrier between us.

But I was utterly relieved.

———

"The Humanitarian Gala is next Saturday. Should I tell the senator you'll be attending?" My assistant placed my messages on my desk then stared at me with expectation.

My mind drifted away, thinking about that beautiful creature with the green eyes. "Sorry, Cynthia. What did you say?"

"The Humanitarian Gala is next week. You've been nominated as Humanitarian of the year. This is the fourth time you've won it. That's so exciting." Her curly black hair was pulled back into a tight ponytail, and gold hoops hung from her lobes. She set a few packets on my desk and organized them by priority. "Shall I tell the office it's mandatory they intend?"

Rome won that award last year for her small company. I remember sitting at the table when she joined me. We spoke for nearly an hour before I took her home and kissed her on the doorstep.

It seemed like a lifetime ago now.

"Yes, tell the staff they're expected to attend."

"Of course, Mr. Owens." Cynthia walked out and left me alone with my thoughts.

It had officially been a year since I made Rome mine. Instead of celebrating our time together, we were living separate lives. The last time I saw her, she got into the elevator and didn't say a word to me. She looked just as devastated as the day she walked out on me.

I'd give anything to go back in time and relive that happiness.

When I thought about the gala next Saturday, I realized I had a huge problem on my hands.

Hank.

He would definitely be there. And when he realized I was no longer in the picture, he would strike.

No doubt about it.

Shit.

I had men tailing Hank wherever he went so he couldn't touch Rome again. But I really didn't want to give him the impression that she was unguarded. If he made a move, it would only scare her. She put on a brave face for me when she was scared, but I'd seen her become vulnerable and honest.

She was terrified of him.

And she knew I was the only thing saving her.

That would mean I'd have to talk to Rome about it, to get her to agree to be my date for the evening. We'd have to pretend we were still together, put on a show for anyone who was watching—especially Hank.

But would she go for it?

The act would be difficult for both of us. It would be difficult for me to touch her without taking it further. It would be hard for me to walk away from her when she was so close to me.

It would break us all over again.

But I didn't know what else to do. I couldn't let Hank know she was an easy target. But I didn't want us to get close to one another if we were both trying to move on. Either way, I lost. I could live with letting Rome go, but I couldn't live with knowing something terrible might happen to her.

So I made my decision.

I stared at my phone for another minute before I finally grabbed it and called her. I'd been drinking all night so I wasn't at my finest, but I would make do. I held the phone to my ear and listened to it ring over and over, waiting for her beautiful voice to answer.

But it continued to ring.

Maybe she wouldn't answer at all.

Finally, the click sounded as she picked up. Instead of answering with a spoken word, she announced her presence with her silence. Her light breathing could barely be heard, distant and far away.

My words died in my throat because I just wanted to

listen to her. If I closed my eyes, it seemed like she was right beside me. I could picture us lying together in my bed, our bodies tangled together after a good session of lovemaking.

"You told me you wouldn't bother me."

Acid formed in my stomach, making me feel sick. I wasn't sure what I expected her to say, but that wasn't it. The hopefulness inside me imagined her telling me that she missed me, that she still loved me.

Not that I deserved that affection. "I know. That's not why I'm calling."

"Oh…"

"That Humanitarian Gala is next week. I'm getting an award, so I have to be there. I suspect Hank will be there too."

Her breathing increased, blowing into the phone.

"I think we should give him the impression we're still together. If he suspects we're broken up, he might come after you again. I've got guys tailing him, so don't worry. But I'd rather not give him any hope that he can get to you."

She was still quiet, her breathing exactly the same.

"Sweetheart?" I cringed the second I uttered the endearment, knowing I should only call her by her first name from now on.

"Yeah, I think that would be best."

I knew she wanted to reject my offer because being

close to me would be difficult. But her fear for her safety was still paramount. I suspected she had trouble sleeping not just from our breakup, but because I wasn't around to protect her anymore. "Okay. I'll pick you up an hour before."

"Okay." She didn't say another word.

I listened to the silence and knew it was time to hang up. I wouldn't talk to her again for another week. It would be seven days of pure loneliness.

"Calloway?"

I missed hearing her say my name. "Yes?"

"Are you... Never mind. Good night."

I didn't just want to know what she was going to ask. I needed to know every thought that passed through that pretty little head of hers. "Ask me whatever you want, Rome."

"I'm not sure if I want to know the answer."

That could only mean one thing. "I haven't been with anyone, Rome. I won't be with anyone for a very long time. You don't need to worry about that." I might find a new sub to whip, but I certainly wouldn't touch anyone sexually. The idea of fucking someone wasn't the least bit arousing.

"I can't picture myself with anyone but you..."

I shouldn't love hearing those words, but I did. They made my chest relax. "Neither can I."

10

R ome
As time went on, life didn't get easier.

I still hardly slept at night, unable to handle ice-cold sheets now that Calloway's body wasn't there to keep them warm. His rhythmic heartbeat used to soothe me like a lullaby. His strong arms were always around my body, keeping all the demons away.

Including Hank.

I didn't think Hank was a problem anymore because it seemed like Calloway truly scared him off. But Calloway was right. Without him around, Hank would probably find the courage to pursue me again.

As much as I hated to admit it, I was scared.

One of my biggest fears was getting raped, a fear all women must have. I didn't think Hank would ever kill me, but being used like that was just as bad, if you asked me. And now I was faced with the reality that I truly relied on Calloway for a lot of things, not just my happiness.

But there was nothing I could do about it.

"I think I'm going to buy a gun."

Christopher was eating on the other couch, and he stopped in mid-bite to look at me. "What?"

"I need a handgun, something small. Maybe a Glock."

He put down his bowl of rice and chicken. "You aren't serious, right?"

"I think it'll be good to have."

"Is this about Hank?"

Who else would it be about? "Yeah."

"Honestly, I think guns are dangerous. You're more likely to hurt yourself."

"Not if I take some gun safety courses and truly learn how to handle a deadly weapon." I wasn't ignorant enough to think I could learn everything in a day. There were a lot of precautions when it came to carrying a firearm.

He ran his hand through his hair as he shook his head. "Calloway said he has men keeping an eye on Hank. I don't think you need to resort to that. Plus, I'm right across the hall from you."

"Calloway won't protect me forever," I reminded him. "One day, he'll move on and protect someone else."

It was painful to imagine him being as attentive to someone else as he was to me, but that was a fact I would have to accept. "And Christopher, you're going to have your own life too. Having a gun will make me feel safe when I have no one to rely on but myself."

"I think you should think about it for a while, do some research. Because people accidentally kill themselves with their own weapons all the time. That's a fact. I'm not just pulling that out of my ass."

"I know." I ignored his growing hostility. Whenever he was concerned about me, he usually grew protective and angry. "You know I don't take anything lightly."

He grabbed his bowl and started eating again, his eyes glued to the TV despite the red tint to his face. He knew he should combat his anger when he was around me. When it came to arguments, I usually won. And Christopher knew I was too stubborn to change my mind about most things.

Hank grabbed me by the throat and squeezed my windpipe so hard I couldn't breathe.

"Let go of me!" I fought back, kicking and throwing my arms down.

He hiked up my dress and separated my thighs with

his knees. "I'm gonna fuck you until you cry, sweetheart."

"Stop!" I threw my arms forward and pushed as hard as I could.

I jumped upright in bed and opened my eyes, seeing my dark and empty bedroom. The door was shut and locked, and the faint sound of traffic could be heard in the distance. I clutched my chest as I breathed through the agony. "Just a dream...just a dream." The hot tears were warm on my face, and I snatched my phone off the nightstand and called the first person who came to mind.

Calloway answered immediately. "Sweetheart, everything alright?"

I couldn't slow down my breathing, couldn't stop the panic inside my chest. "I had a nightmare... Hank... he..." I didn't want to say the words out loud. Once I did, they would become even more true.

Calloway shuffled in the background like he was moving. "It's okay. He's at his apartment. One of my guys just checked in with me." The sound of moving keys and then the door opening and closing came to my ear. "You're safe."

I pulled my knees to my chest as I sat alone in the dark, clinging to Calloway's strong voice for comfort. "Where are you?"

"I was at home. I just left."

I knew exactly where he was going, but I didn't object. I was still upset, still terrified. Ten minutes of silence passed. I didn't want to go into details about my dream because they were irrelevant. They would just work me up even more. I hadn't had a dream like that in a really long time. Now I realized how much I took for granted. When I slept with Calloway every night, I never had a restless night of sleep. I always slept like a baby.

"I'm outside."

I stared at my bedroom door before I got up and walked to the front of the apartment, the phone still pressed to my ear. I checked the peephole just in case, even though that seemed pointless. The memories of the nightmare were still fresh in mind, and I couldn't shake the feeling of terror.

I unlocked the door and opened it.

Calloway hung up and placed the phone in the pocket of his jeans. Instead of a hard expression that I couldn't read, his features were as easy to decipher as the words of a children's book.

He stepped inside without waiting to be invited and circled his arms around my body. The second his powerful body was wrapped around mine, I felt absolutely safe. Nothing could touch me, nothing could hurt me.

I buried my face in his chest and closed my eyes,

realizing how much I missed the way he smelled. It was such a simple trait, but I definitely took it for granted. My hands bundled together against his stomach, and I concentrated on the way he breathed, doing my best to match it.

Calloway held me that way for a few minutes before he shut the door and locked it behind him. He took my hand and guided me to my bedroom where my mattress sat, the sheets a mess from the way I'd convulsed during my nightmare.

He pulled his shirt over his head and dropped his jeans, his powerful body just as strong as I remembered. His pecs were large, and his tight stomach led to a V at his hips. He was still the sexiest man I'd ever seen in my life.

He got into bed and pulled me with him, cuddling with me like no time had passed. One arm sat around my waist, while the other rested in the crook of my neck. My leg was pulled over his hip and across his waist. He was soft underneath his boxers, not interested in sex. His chin was thick with hair since he hadn't shaved in a week. The usual brightness in his eyes was no longer there either. "As long as I'm breathing, no one can hurt you, sweetheart." Although his face was just inches from mine, he didn't lean in to kiss me.

And I wanted him to kiss me. "I know."

He leaned in and pressed his lips to my forehead,

giving me the kind of embrace I didn't want. It was soothing and warm, full of love and affection. It gave me shivers and left me wanting more. "Good night."

I moved farther into his body, fighting back tears. I'd never been so happy and sad at the exact same time. I was grateful he was there to chase away my demons, but I was miserable that he would be gone the next day.

And we would be back to normal.

* * *

My alarm woke both of us up the following morning.

I leaned over his chest and smacked my hand down on the button, silencing the ringing sound before it had a chance to annoy me any further. Sleep was heavy in my eyes, but I actually felt rested for the first time in weeks.

Thanks to Calloway.

He opened his eyes, the same sleepy look on his face that I wore on mine. Except he looked naturally sexy, his hair messed up from the way I ran my fingers through it. His beard was even thicker, but it looked great on him. "Morning."

"Morning." I was so happy to see his face first thing in the morning. I had gotten to do it every single day until he broke my heart. Even after the way he hurt me, I still found him to be the most incredible man I'd ever known.

I didn't want him to leave.

His momentary joy disappeared once he realized we were in the exact same position we were last night. We were still apart—for good. He moved to the edge of the bed then pulled his shirt over his head, hiding the prominent muscles of his back. Then he stood and pulled on his jeans, his knees and phone rattling as he pulled his pants over his long legs.

I hated watching him get dressed. I hated watching him prepare to leave.

I left the sheets that were now saturated with his smell and stood beside him, in my gray sweatpants and an old t-shirt. I didn't bother changing because he'd already seen me this way. I didn't look much worse than I usually did anyway.

Calloway walked out, and I followed him to the door.

Christopher was already awake, wearing slacks and a collared shirt as he ate a bowl of cereal over the sink. He was in the middle of chewing when he spotted Calloway come around the corner. He stopped eating, his eyes popping wide open.

Calloway gave him a quick nod before he walked out the front door.

I followed him even though there wasn't much point.

It's not like we would have an amazing kiss before we went to work. We were back to exactly what we were before—old lovers. "Thanks for coming over..." I shut the door behind me so Christopher couldn't overhear us.

"I'll always be here for you." He held my gaze with his arms resting by my sides, his jaw tight like he was trying to stop himself from kissing me. He slid his hands into his pockets then stepped away. "See you later."

I couldn't bring myself to say goodbye. I never wanted it to be goodbye. "See you later..." I watched him walk all the way down the hallway until he reached the elevator. Instead of waiting for it to rise to this floor, he turned and took the stairs.

I walked back inside, even more heartbroken than I was when we first broke up.

Christopher leaned against the counter with his arms across his chest. His half-empty bowl of cereal sat on the counter. He never wasted food, but he'd obviously made an exception this time. "Uh...what's going on?"

He had the right to ask since this was his apartment. I wouldn't make a fuss about it. "I had a nightmare last night. Calloway came over to make me feel better."

"Oh...are you back together?"

I swallowed hard and couldn't meet his look. "No."

"Oh…" Christopher rubbed his chin and stared at the floor. "I was hoping that you two worked it out."

We could never work it out. "Unfortunately, no."

He rubbed his chin again, having nothing to say. "I need to get to work, but I can be a little late if you want to talk about it." He eyed his Rolex on his wrist.

"No, that won't be necessary." I walked past him and headed back to my room. "I'll be okay, Christopher. Don't worry about me."

"Just a few days ago, you told me you were going to buy a gun." He turned his body toward the counter and grabbed his mug of coffee from the surface. "So, no, I'm not going to stop worrying about you."

11

Calloway

Now that I'd spent the night with her, held her, comforted her, I was horny as hell. I missed being inside her, making love to her right before we both went to sleep. Even the vanilla stuff was incredible.

I missed her so much I almost didn't care about my needs.

But then I was reminded that nothing had changed. I would always crave Rome, but I would always need my darker fix. Going over there the other night wasn't a smart idea. It only set me back in terms of heartbreak. But when she called me and needed me, I didn't hesitate.

I was there for her—in a heartbeat.

But my desire for her was clouding my judgment. I

couldn't think clearly because I hadn't had sex in three weeks. Maybe that wasn't long for some people—but that was an eternity for me.

I needed her.

I'd been drinking all night when I opened my top drawer and spotted the black thong she'd left behind. It was right on top of my socks, an erotic piece of fabric that had been soaked with her arousal more times than I could count.

I pulled it out of the drawer and brought it to my face, taking a deep breath to smell her scent. I couldn't make anything out because it was clean and had been stuffed inside my drawer with my own clothes. Unfortunately, it smelled like me more than it smelled like her.

But that didn't stop me from getting rock-hard.

I carried her panties to the bed and got undressed. I lay back on the mattress, squirted lube in my hand, and then went to town on myself. I wrapped her thong around my dick and used it to jerk off, feeling the fabric rub against my skin with every pump of my hand.

It wasn't as good as her pussy—but it was good enough.

I pictured her bent over my bed, her hands tied together behind her back with my tie. Her ankles were secured together in chains so she couldn't run away from me. I placed my hand on the steep curve of her back and pushed her down, squishing her into the mattress. My hips worked furiously to fuck her harder, driving into that warm pussy that I owned.

"Fuck."

I came in record time, shooting toward the sky then splashing across my chest. Her panties still rubbed against my cock and my hand, soaked in a mixture of lube and come. It was a powerful orgasm despite the fact that she wasn't really there with me. But her thong was strong enough to do the trick.

Now I felt a little better.

***

I didn't see her for the rest of the week.

Days came and went, and she didn't contact me again. Hopefully, her nightmares stopped altogether. Christopher was right across the hall from her, and I knew where Hank was every second of the day, so she had no reason to be scared.

Maybe she didn't have a nightmare at all. Maybe it was just an excuse to see me.

I wished that were true. If it were, I wouldn't have slept with her all night. I would have done a lot more than that.

The gala was the following night, but I hadn't spoken to Rome about it. She and I avoided each other like we hadn't shared an affectionate night together. Fortunately, we didn't have any conference calls or meetings, so there was no reason for us to interact. The only sign of her presence was a short email she sent me the other day, which was so professional it annoyed me.

At the end of the day, I wanted to walk down to her office and talk to her about our plans for the following night. But coming face-to-face with her seemed too intimate. Last time we were close to each other, I almost pushed her up against the wall and crushed her mouth with mine.

When I headed to the elevator, I texted her. *I'll pick you up at 7.*

The three dots appeared on the screen. *Okay.*

Do you need help picking out a dress?

I'll manage.

I don't mind getting you something. She had a nice salary but not enough to pick out something fancy. I didn't mind buying her anything she wanted—even the Hope Diamond.

Calloway, I'm fine. I'll see you tomorrow.

I got inside the elevator and watched the doors close. When her dots faded and she went radio silent, I suddenly felt lonely. When I walked through my front door, I would step inside an empty house. She wouldn't make dinner while I showered upstairs. We wouldn't share a bottle of wine over our meal. We wouldn't relax on the couch and read while we stared at the fire.

The thought was so depressing that I decided not to go there.

I decided to go to Ruin instead.

The bass from the music thudded against my ears. To a novice, the beat would be uncomfortable against the eardrum. But I enjoyed the loudness. It was much better than the silence of my empty house.

I moved through the crowd and watched the couples dance under the strobe lights. Flashes of blue and green moved across the dance floor and the walls. Men wore dark masks, while the woman adorned themselves in chains. Some women didn't wear tops at all, showing off their nipple piercings.

I moved farther into the club and approached the bar. The bartender noticed my presence immediately and ignored the customers who were there before me. He poured me a scotch then tended to the others, treating me like royalty.

A light hand rested on my arm, her nails painted blood-red. "Hello, Calloway."

I looked into the face of a beautiful woman I'd never seen before. Judging from her skintight black corset and dark jeans, she was looking for a Dom to beat her into submission for the night. "Call me Cal. Pleasure to meet you." I patted my hand on hers before I pulled away, not wanting to be touched.

She didn't make another move. "I would love to call you Master for the night, if you'll have me."

I swirled my glass before I took a drink. I swallowed the amber liquid hard and felt it burn all the way down my throat. It baffled me that beautiful women wanted me to dominate them, begged me to do it, but Rome wouldn't even give me a chance. I could change her life, but she wouldn't give me the trust I deserved.

No matter how much I resented her, I wasn't ready to fuck someone yet. I would think about her the entire time, and the connection with this woman would feel forced and unsatisfactory. "Maybe some other time."

She pouted her lips, her lipstick just as red as her nails. "My girlfriend will be disappointed."

I turned back to her, an eyebrow raised.

She glanced over her shoulder to another beautiful woman, a brunette with humongous tits that actually looked real. She held up her hand and gave me a seductive wave with her fingertips.

The woman standing next to me continued on. "That's Amanda. I'm Ribbon."

"Ribbon?" I asked.

"Yeah," she said. "Or whatever you want to call me. So how about the three of us?"

I had to admit, I was intrigued. I could command one to whip the other. I could control both of them, have them do things with my authority alone. I could have Ribbon spank Amanda until she screamed. Then I could make her eat her pussy. It sounded perfect because I wouldn't get my hands dirty. "Let's go."

I sat in the back of the car at the curb of Christopher's apartment. I hadn't left the back seat and walked upstairs just yet, choosing to waste time by stalling. It was unusual for me to feel nervous, but I felt uneasy about seeing Rome.

Because I missed her so fucking much.

I would hold her waist and pretend to be her date for the evening, but I would be back here dropping her off again. I was just torturing myself—torturing her. I had been a Dom for the evening, commanding two women to carry out whatever command I issued. They touched each other, kissed each other, spanked each other—but I still wanted Rome.

I wished Hank hadn't fucked her up so much.

When I'd wasted enough time, I finally went to her apartment and knocked.

Christopher answered the door in jeans and a red t-shirt. He obviously had no intention of going out tonight. "Hey." He stepped away so I could walk inside. "Rome, he's here," he called down the hall.

"I'm coming." Rome appeared a moment later, wearing a backless dress with five-inch heels. Two thin straps crisscrossed over the top part of her back, but the rest was bare to the top of her ass. It was short, stopping a few inches above the knee. And it was skintight, highlighting every curve she possessed under the thin fabric.

So. Fucking. Hard.

Shit, I wanted to come in my slacks right then and there.

What the fuck was she doing to me?

Was this intentional?

She held her clutch under her arm, champagne pink and subtle. Her hair was pulled back in a gentle updo, some of her strands coming loose and falling around her face. I loved her long hair and running my fingers through it, but I also loved it when she showed off her face like that. She was far too beautiful to hide her attributes.

I wasn't going to last the night without kissing her.

No fucking way.

I looked her up and down and felt my mouth go dry. I didn't even care that Christopher was standing there and I was eye-fucking his sister. As far as I was concerned, she was mine. This woman would always be mine.

I tried to think of something to say that was appropriate for the occasion. Christopher's presence had no impact on my words; only the state of our relationship did. "You look beautiful." It was a very tame compliment. In fact, it wasn't even honest. I certainly thought she was more than just beautiful.

She was absolutely perfect.

"Thank you. You look handsome...but you always look handsome."

This was dangerous territory, complimenting one another like this. But I didn't have the strength to downplay my feelings, and she obviously didn't either. "Ready?"

She nodded. "I'll see you later, Christopher."

"Night." Christopher walked into the living room, finally giving us some privacy.

Rome and I left and got into the back seat of the car. I quickly adjusted myself without caring if she noticed. My hard cock was painfully uncomfortable against the zipper in my pants. My cock wanted to break free and bury himself inside that warm pussy I missed so much.

We didn't speak on the drive, but I could feel the tension between us. I'd fucked her in this back seat before, her legs straddled across my hips, and I would love to do that right now. I wanted to drive my cock so deep inside her that she screamed loud enough for Tom to hear. I wanted to touch the smooth skin of her back with my callused hands, feeling her bare skin and gripping her petite frame.

I kept my gaze out the window and tried to keep my arousal contained. But I was doing a piss-poor job.

"How was your day?" She broke the silence first, being political with a meaningless question.

I woke up at two in the afternoon because I didn't go to bed until nine. I was out late with Amanda and Ribbon, watching their asses turn red from spanking each other so much. "Good. You?"

"It was okay. Christopher and I got breakfast this morning."

I was probably still at Ruin at the time. "Let me guess, you guys split a waffle and one egg." I raised the corner of my mouth so she would know I was kidding.

"Something like that," she said with a light chuckle.

We spent another ten minutes in silence. We were almost to the hotel, but traffic was congested on the weekends.

Rome spoke again when the car pulled up to the curb. "You know he's gonna be here?"

"I'm sure he will be. Was he here last year?"

"Actually, no."

"Well, it's better to be safe than sorry." Tom opened

my door, and I got out first. I extended my hand to Rome and nearly shivered when she grabbed it. The electricity I felt any time we touched was just as strong as ever.

But that only made this harder.

I gripped her hand and escorted her inside, fully aware of the fact that I had the most beautiful woman right by my side. I couldn't get angry at the men who looked at her. If I were them, I'd be doing the exact same thing.

My hand moved around her waist, and I touched her bare skin, which was warm. I pictured my chest pressed against her back, warm and covered in sweat. I'd give anything to take her from behind right now, to feel that passion I never got from anyone else.

We entered the ballroom to a swarm of people. Men and women immediately greeted me, congratulating me on my award that I had yet to receive. I made a small talk and remained as polite as ever, but I didn't really care about a single conversation that I had.

All I cared about was the woman right beside me.

I pulled her away and returned my hand around her waist, the place I preferred to touch her. I could bring her closer into my side, let her feel my warmth since she must be chilly wearing nearly nothing. "Champagne?"

"Sure."

I grabbed two glasses from the bar and handed one over.

As if she was nervous, she brought it to her lips and drank nearly all of it right on the spot.

I wondered if she was anxious because of me or because of someone else. "Want another?"

"No, I'm good." She set the empty glass on a passing tray that a waiter carried.

I scanned the crowd and didn't see Hank anywhere nearby. "I haven't seen him. And even if he is here, there's no reason to be scared."

"I'm not worried about him, Calloway."

"Then what are you worried about?" I pulled her closer, the champagne still in my other hand.

She stared at my chest, her head nearly a foot shorter than mine, even in heels. "It's just hard for me to be around you...because I miss you."

My fingers slackened on the glass I was holding. The room turned quiet, the conversations fading away. Her eyes were averted, just like a submissive. I knew that wasn't what the gesture meant, but that was all I could think of.

My fingers moved under her chin, and I tilted her head upward, looking into the beautiful face I saw every night in my dreams. I didn't care about crossing the line. I didn't care about breaking the rules. I kissed her because I needed to kiss her. I kissed her because she was the woman I loved.

She kissed me back, her lips trembling with need. Her hands moved up my chest the way they did when we were alone together, hungry for my physique. Her lips were soft against mine, warm and tasting just like champagne.

I inhaled deeply the second we touched, my heart beating so fast I felt it slam against my rib cage. My fingertips felt numb since all the blood was traveling elsewhere. Even though the room was filled with people, I didn't care about anyone else except the two of us.

She was the one who broke away first, her lips still parted like she wanted more. "I'm sorry..."

My arm tightened around her waist. "Don't be. I miss you more than you can comprehend."

She held my gaze with affection, the longing and love deep in her eyes. She cleared her throat and suddenly turned away, like the connection between us was too much to handle. "I need to use the restroom..." She slid out of my fingertips and left me standing there. She walked across the room, moving with perfect grace. Her shoulders were back and her head was held high, but the sadness was in her eyes. I could spot it a mile away.

My eyes turned to a different corner of the room and landed on the man I despised. Hank stood in a circle of men, social elites and public figures. They were chatting away, but he wasn't listening. His entire focus was on the woman I adored.

I wanted to snap his neck.

I set my glass down then maneuvered across the room. His attention was so focused on Rome that he didn't spot me approaching him from the left. He stood right beside one of the senators from New York, but that didn't stop me from making fists with both of my hands. I had no idea what I would do once I got there, but I definitely wanted Hank to know that I watched every move he made.

I closed in on him and stared at his profile, his cleanly shaven jaw and his broad shoulders. He was a good-looking man, so the only reason he preyed on Rome like he did was because he was a psychopath. He could get laid whenever he wanted, especially as the DA of New York.

But he chose to torture women instead.

How could Rome ever compare me to him? How could she ever think I would treat her the way Hank did? It was ridiculous. "Eyes on me, asshole." I spoke so only Hank could hear what I said. The rest of the guys were chatting away about the new election cycle, so they didn't seem to mind the two of us.

Hank stiffened where he stood and dropped his gaze, losing his view of Rome. His breathing increased slightly as the adrenaline kicked in. He knew it was me standing beside him even if he didn't look.

"What did I just say?" The only reason why I hadn't murdered him was because I couldn't get away with it. He was too well-known, and after interviewing a few witnesses, people would realize I had serious beef with him. If I mutilated him in a dark alley, Hank was a powerful lawyer who could throw me in the slammer for six months. Who would protect Rome then?

So I had to scare the shit out of him with just my words. He didn't know what I was capable of. That gave me the advantage.

Hank cleared his throat then finally turned to me, his flute of champagne held in his right hand. As much as he tried to cover it up, the fear still thudded in his eyes.

It was difficult for me to stand so close to him and not rip his throat out. "Don't look at my woman." I stepped closer to him, my face nearly touching his. I didn't care if people saw our hostile interaction. I needed to keep this asshole in his place as long as I could. Hopefully, he would settle down with a wife and kids and forget about her.

He clenched his jaw.

"Did you hear me?" I moved forward, causing him to step back like a pussy.

Hank faltered slightly, spilling some of his champagne on the front of his tuxedo.

I spoke louder. "Did you fucking hear me, asshole?"

Hank flinched again, like the little girl he was. "Okay."

"Okay, what?" I said with a growl. "You harassed her, and now I'm gonna harass you for the rest of my life. You've made yourself a very powerful enemy, Hank. Make sure you look over your shoulder—because I'll always be watching you."

He couldn't back up any more because he was pressing against Senator Swanson. He opened his mouth to speak, but nothing came out. Immediately, he darted his eyes to the floor, unable to put his money where his mouth was.

Senator Swanson noticed the commotion. "Gentlemen, is everything alright?"

I glared at Hank and forced him to answer.

"We're fine." He cleared his throat. "Just talking about the Mets…gets a little heated."

"I'm a Yankees fan," I lied.

Senator Swanson shook my hand once he recognized me. "Mr. Owens, how nice to see you this evening. Congratulations."

"Thank you, sir." I gave him a firm shake. "It's an honor."

"It certainly is." He dropped his hand and eyed Hank. "Are the two of you friends?"

"Yep," I said. "We've known each other for years. But he used to bully me in grade school."

"You guys went to school together?" Swanson asked with a laugh. "So you go way back."

"We do," I said in agreement.

"Looks like your bullying days are over." Swanson patted Hank on the shoulder. "Mr. Owens isn't the kind of man you can push around." He drifted back to the men he was speaking to, leaving the two of us alone together.

I stared Hank down with an expression that would terrify anyone. "Look at Rome again, and I'll kill you. Do you understand me?"

Hank gave a curt nod.

"I didn't hear you, bitch."

Irritation flooded his eyes at the insult, more offended by that than by being called an asshole. "Yeah… I understand you."

"Good." I patted his cheek, insulting him in the most fundamental way possible. "Enjoy your evening." I turned away and headed to the entryway toward the restrooms. Rome was already standing there, her arms across her chest and her eyes on me. She must have witnessed the whole thing because her face was pale as milk.

When I reached her, my arms circled her waist, and I immediately kissed her, not caring if that crossed the line. I recognized it and what it meant. She needed me. She needed my mouth on hers and my strong hands on her body.

Her lips moved with mine, treasuring the comfort I gave her. Her mouth was plump and sexy, feeling so good against my mouth. I'd wanted to kiss her to make her feel safe, but now I kissed her because I couldn't stop. All I wanted to do was take her home and make love to her, bury myself inside her so we would both feel happy—even if it didn't last long.

She pulled away and leaned her forehead against my chin. Her arms rested in the crooks of mine, and some of her strands of hair had come loose. The dark makeup around her eyes brought out the beautiful green color of her irises. Her lashes were long and thick, making her look like a collectible doll. I thought she looked perfect first thing in the morning, when her face was relaxed after a good night of sleep. But right now, I thought she looked more beautiful than I'd ever seen her.

I could barely hear her speak since the chatter in the ballroom was so loud. "What happened?"

"I threatened him—just to keep him on his toes." I didn't tell her he'd been staring at her. It would probably make her uncomfortable, make her feel violated from his look.

"And what did he say?"

"He backed up like a pussy. He's terrified of me. You don't need to worry about him."

"Then why did you confront him?"

I didn't like to lie, but I thought it would hurt her more if she knew the truth. "I want him to know I'll always be his enemy. If he even thinks about trying something, I'll know about it. Instilling fear will make him too scared to do anything, even in the brief moments he feels safe. It's psychological warfare." And I was the master of psychological warfare.

She nodded, her eyes still downcast.

"Rome." I placed my fingertips under her chin and forced her to meet my gaze.

"Hmm?"

"Where's the strong woman I met when she slapped me in that bar? I miss her." I loved her fire and her strength. She commanded respect the instant she walked into a room. But now, she was rigid and scared. I loved protecting her. I love having her rely on me. But I missed the woman she used to be. "Every time he tried something, you got away. You defended yourself because you're strong. Don't lower your head in fear. Raise it up high and show him you aren't scared. That's the woman I know."

Her eyes brightened and softened at the same time. She nodded her head in agreement. "You're right."

"Damn right, I am." I kissed the corner of her mouth

and felt incredible joy at just the small affection. She made me burn white-hot at the most innocent touch. "Now let's have dinner."

We got into the back seat of the car, and Tom pulled away from the curb. I sat on one side, and Rome sat on the other. We were far apart just as we had been at the beginning of the evening. But the distance between us had no effect on the closeness of our minds.

Tom headed back to the apartment she shared with Christopher with the divider up between us. It gave us privacy, not that we needed it.

I looked out the window and tried to keep my desperation in check. I wanted to tell Tom to drive back to my place so I could roll around with her on my sheets. I didn't even want to fuck her. I wanted to kiss her everywhere, take my time, and make love all night. There were no whips and chains on my mind.

Just Rome.

But I couldn't do that. It would give me immediate satisfaction, but when she left the following morning, it would be painful all over again.

So fucking painful.

Rome's hand snaked across the leather seat and grabbed mine. Her soft fingers interlocked between my digits, and she brushed her thumb over my hard knuckles.

I eyed our adjoined hands, losing my train of thought.

"Calloway."

I looked into her beautiful eyes and knew exactly what she was going to say next.

"Let's go to your place."

I'd just told myself it wasn't a good idea, but I didn't have the strength to say no to her now. My heart would be broken all over again, but I would worry about that later. For now, I just wanted to enjoy her one last time, to tell her I loved her while I made love to her.

I hit the button on the ceiling. "Tom, change of plans. Let's go to my place."

"Yes, sir."

I undid my safety belt and scooted across the seat until we were pushed together against the other door. I wrapped my arm around her shoulder and pulled her close to me, smelling her perfume and recognizing it from my sheets. Just a hint of the smell remained, but it wouldn't last much longer. Now she could freshen it up and extend it.

My hand slid up her thigh and under her dress, feeling the smooth skin of her perfect legs. I couldn't wait to feel them wrapped around my waist, her ankles locked together as I thrust into that warm pussy I adored.

She pressed a sexy kiss to my neck then my ear, her breathing deep and aroused.

Now I wasn't sure if I could wait until we got to my house.

"Calloway?"

"Yes, sweetheart?" I pressed a kiss to her hairline, loving the feeling of her hair against my lips.

"Have you...still been seeing Isabella?"

Isabella was the last thing I wanted to talk about right now. She was nowhere on my mind. "No."

She couldn't hide the relief that swept across her face. "Have you been with anyone else? Have you... dominated anyone else?" Her voice shook slightly, like she didn't want to hear my answer.

Just the night before, I'd had my fun with two women. It would be easy for me to lie since I was so close to getting laid. But I couldn't lie to Rome about something that could change her feelings. "Yes."

"Oh..." Her body suddenly went cold.

"I didn't touch them."

"Them?" Her voice picked up in alarm.

"I met these two women at Ruin last night. They wanted me to be their Dom, so I made them do things to each other. But I didn't touch them." When I told one woman to slap the other, she did it. When I asked one to whip the other, she didn't hesitate. It fulfilled my urges perfectly. Rome and I weren't together so I was free to do whatever I wanted, but I still felt terrible for hurting her.

"Oh..."

"I didn't touch them," I reminded her for the third time. "I haven't been with a woman besides you." My need to dominate wasn't necessarily sexual all the time. What I did with Isabella was strictly to control my anger and need for domination. Fucking her never crossed my mind. But I didn't expect Rome to understand that.

She pulled her hand from mine, pushing away my affection. She swallowed hard, loud enough for me to hear. With every passing second, she drew away from me. She closed off her heart, her body, and everything else.

I knew I wasn't getting laid tonight.

She hit the button on the ceiling. "Tom, take me home." She looked out the window so she wouldn't have to look at me.

"Yes, ma'am," Tom said through the intercom.

I stared at the side of her face, both angry and indifferent. "Rome, I don't want to do these things with other women. I only want to do them with you."

She kept her gaze focused through the glass like I wasn't even there. "While I sleep alone in my bed, heartbroken, you're out having a good time."

"I'm out having a terrible time because I wish I were with you."

She pressed her lips tightly together and shook her head.

"You really can't even consider doing this for me?" I asked incredulously. "You're willing to let me go and end up with somebody else because you're that closed-minded?"

She turned back to me, fire in her gaze. "Excuse me? Calloway, you have no idea what I've been through."

"Exactly," I barked. "Because I know you changed your name and you're running from something, but you never had the balls to tell me."

Shock crept into her features.

"At least I was man enough to be honest with you. Yes, I'm into some kinky shit. But that's who I am. You keep comparing me to these abusive men from your past, when I'm nothing like that. You don't trust me."

"Fuck you, Calloway." She turned back to the window. "You had one of your men look into my file?"

"Yeah, I did." I knew that made me lose the argument, but I didn't care. "Only because you wouldn't tell me anything yourself."

"Maybe I just wasn't ready to say anything."

"If you love me, you should be ready," I snapped. "You've never really let me in me, Rome. You can blame me for the downfall of this relationship, but you're the one at fault."

"Wow." She shot me a glare. "You have a lot of nerve."

"I don't have enough nerve, actually. I'm the one who's changed. I'm the one who's pushed the boundaries and made sacrifices to be what you need. I've never done the boyfriend thing before. I've never had a woman live with me. I've never loved someone, let alone told them that. I've grown, Rome. I've sacrificed everything I possibly can to make this work. What sacrifices have you made?"

Her lips were pressed together, clearly having no rebuttal.

"You haven't made any, Rome. If you really trusted me, really loved me, we could make this work. You would be my sub with the same perfection that I've been your boyfriend. You want to keep me away from Ruin? Then do this for me. You can't blame me for getting my needs met elsewhere. If I weren't willing to give you what you needed, you would have left a long time ago. So stop treating me like a monster. Stop treating me like I'm some kind of asshole. I'm more than just a Dom. If you don't see that, then you obviously don't know me very well."

She threw the door open so she could get out.

I yanked on her arm and pulled her back inside. We were at a red light, and the car was about to move.

"Don't bother. I'll go." I practically broke the door off its hinges as I got out. Then I slammed the door so hard the car shook.

I stepped onto the sidewalk and didn't look back. No one was out on this side of town because they were on the main streets. It was dangerous and stupid for a woman to be walking around here at night. No way in hell was I going to let Rome walk in that dress. She wouldn't last ten minutes.

I walked back to my house with my hands in my pockets, my jaw tight with anger. I was so livid I could barely see straight. The woman I loved was sitting in the back seat of my car. I'd given her the world, but she wouldn't give me something so minor.

She wouldn't give me anything.

This was probably just the anger talking, but I needed to move on and forget about her. I'd always been man enough for her, but she'd never been woman enough for me. She didn't bend over backward for me, not the way I did for her. I admit what I did with Isabella was wrong, but Rome forced my hand.

Now I was officially over it.

I was over her.

R ome
Now I was a hollow shell.
I wasn't sure what possessed me to ask a question when I didn't want the answer. I wasn't sure what my expectations were. Calloway made his feelings about our relationship very clear. He needed more than what I was willing to give him.

After everything he said to me, I knew there was no hope for us now.

And not ever.

I kept thinking about what he said, that I hadn't sacrificed as much as he had to keep this relationship going. I didn't agree with that initially, but the more I thought about it, the more I realized how much he'd changed.

He gave up his ownership of Ruin for me.

He asked me to move in with him.

He told me he loved me.

He introduced me to his mother.

All the things he refused to do with anyone, he did them for me. He even tried to give up his lifestyle in the pursuit of vanilla with me. It was all he'd ever known, and he tried to walk away from it.

I didn't even try to be what he needed.

I was so averse to the idea, so offended by how he wanted to treat me, that I never really gave it a chance.

I couldn't lie to myself about that.

But I still didn't want to do it. I loved how aggressive and authoritative he could be sometimes, but I didn't want a whip to my back or a slap to my ass. I didn't want to be treated as inferior when I worked so hard to be respected.

But this was a deal-breaker for him.

I went through the motions during the week, going to work and then going straight to my room when I got home. I spent a lot of time reading because it was the only thing strong enough to steal my focus. When I wasn't actively doing something, my thoughts constantly wandered to Calloway.

I missed him so much.

I didn't see him at work, which was a good thing and a bad thing. The last time I saw him, he left the car and slammed the door behind him. It was a different kind of anger, a ferocity that Calloway rarely showed.

I knew he was truly pissed at me.

Even if I wanted him back, there was a possibility he might not take me.

At the end of the day on Friday, I walked to the elevator and checked a message on my phone.

Christopher texted me. *Wanna get dinner?*

I hardly had an appetite as it was, especially this early in the evening. *How about a walk through the park instead?*

No. You need to eat. I'll meet you at the pizza place.

I shoved my phone in my pocket as I walked into the elevator.

And joined Calloway.

I hadn't even noticed he was there, let alone holding the door open for me.

He pulled his arm back so the doors would close then hit the button for the lobby. His hands were in his pockets, and he stared at the numbers as we descended to the bottom floor. He didn't seem angry or sad. In fact, he seemed indifferent.

I didn't feel the usual tension between us, the fiery chemistry that always erupted anytime we were near each other. All I felt was nothing—from him. He didn't glance at me. He didn't make conversation.

He just stood there.

The doors opened, and he walked out first. "Have a

good weekend, Ms. Moretti." He spoke to me like he would to any other employee, like I was someone he would forget about the second he was out of the building.

I was so hurt that I stayed in the elevator. I watched the doors slide closed and felt the elevator move back to the top of the building. More people filed in, and the elevator moved up and down, taking people where they needed to go.

I stood there because I didn't know what to do.

I had nowhere to go.

Christopher was already there with the small pizza in front of him. He hadn't waited for me to arrive before he started. He took a bite, and the cheese stretched between his mouth and the slice that was still in his hand.

I slid into the booth across from him, unable to eat anything even if I had a gun pointed to my head.

Christopher knew there was something seriously wrong the second he looked at me. "Rome, what is it?" He dropped the pizza back onto the plate, the cheese still stuck to his fingers. He quickly wiped his hands with a napkin.

"Nothing."

"Rome, you look like shit. It's not nothing." He pushed the pizza off to the side, along with the plates and the sodas. "Talk to me."

"I just saw Calloway... I've never seen him be so cold."

Christopher knew about my last interaction with Calloway. He didn't have much to say at the time. When it came to my personal life, he didn't express his opinion like he did for everything else. "What did you expect to happen?"

"I don't know...it just hurt."

"Well, that's what people do when they break up. They hate each other and move on with their lives."

"I don't hate Calloway." I never could, even if I wanted to. "And he doesn't hate me either."

"He's probably just tired of everything. Eager to move on."

That was the exact impression I got.

Christopher no longer gave me sympathy the way he used to. "Rome, this is the moment of truth. You've got to do something now, or let him walk away for good. Is losing him really worth your stubbornness?"

"I'm not stubborn—"

"Yes, you are," he said coldly. "Either do something about Calloway, or move on with your life. I'm not trying to be an ass here. But you can't keep moping around over this guy if you're the reason you aren't together. He already tried to make it work, but it was too difficult. Now it's your turn."

"You make it sound so easy."

"Because it is easy," he snapped. "You love the guy, or what?"

"Of course…" I would never love another man the way I loved him.

"Then you really need to think about your next move. You're running out of time. Honestly, you probably are out of time."

"You think…?"

He nodded. "I'm sure he went back to his old ways the second he got out of the car. I would have done the same."

I hated picturing Calloway with other women. It wasn't about jealousy, only heartbreak. He was the man I loved, and even after everything we'd been through, I still felt exactly the same way.

Christopher shook his head slightly as he stared at me.

"What?"

"Nothing." He pulled the pizza back to the center of the table and handed me my drink. "Looks like there's nothing else to talk about."

C alloway
I didn't think about Rome anymore.
Because I wouldn't allow myself to.
I was moving on, going back to what I did best.
Fucking. Drinking. And dominating.

I ordered a scotch at the bar and surveyed the talent inside Ruin. I was surprised Isabella hadn't chased me down after she threw me under the bus. Maybe she was worried I was livid with her, that I would never speak to her again.

In reality, I didn't care at all.

The place was full of beautiful women, exotic and mysterious in the darkness. I loved being with a woman without knowing anything about her. I didn't need to have dinner with someone and ask them about their childhood because we had incredible sex. I didn't even need to know her name.

I locked eyes with a pretty blonde on the other side of the room. I usually preferred brunettes, but I wasn't picky enough to ignore a beautiful woman who wanted me. She wore a collar around her neck, the chain grasped in her hand. She sat at a table alone, her drink sitting right in front of her.

I continued to stare at her, noticing her long legs underneath the table. She wasn't as curvy as I liked, but again, I wasn't picky. She continued to stare at me like I was exactly what she was looking for.

I was the Dom she was looking for.

She slid off the chair and sauntered toward me in high heels and a short black dress. Her hair was thick and curled, and her makeup was so dark she nearly looked gothic. When she reached me, she placed the leash in my hand and wrapped my fingers around it. "Good evening, Master."

I gripped the leather in my hand, feeling my entire body come to life. "Look at the ground."

She did as I commanded, immediately obeying me without a fight.

I tested the chain, feeling it tug on her neck slightly. She was exactly what I was looking for, a woman with experience in obedience. She was hungry for me, desperate for my brutality. And I would give it to her.

"Come." I held the leash and pulled her along, heading to the stairs.

A woman crossed my path, someone who looked familiar.

She had bright green eyes that shone brighter than the stars on a cloudless night. She had curves no other woman could compete with. With brown hair that reached her shoulders, framing her beautiful face. In black stockings, black shorts, and a dark corset, she was by far the sexiest woman in the room.

Every man had his eyes on her.

She locked eyes with me, her lips ruby red and her eyes dark with heavy makeup. She looked like an enchantress, the queen of this entire club. A chain was held in both of her hands, a collar on one side and the leash on the other.

She walked right up to me with more confidence than I'd ever seen before. She grabbed the leash in my hand and tossed it on the floor before holding out the collar to me. It was open and ready to be secured around her neck.

I forgot about the blonde.

I forgot about everyone in the room.

All I could think about was the woman standing in front of me, asking me to make her mine in a way she never had before.

"Make me your sub, Calloway."

I'd never been so hard in my life. I'd never felt this kind of thrill, this kind of euphoria. It was better than any dream. It was better than the fantasy I touched myself to. This was real. Rome was standing in front of me, ready to kneel the second I asked her to.

I took the collar from her hands and secured it around her neck. I locked it in place, seeing the metal shine in the dim lighting.

She opened my hand and placed the leash in my grasp. "I am yours."

I squeezed the leash so hard my knuckles almost popped. I could hardly keep myself steady because this moment was too incredible, too powerful. Like the blonde had never crossed my mind at all, I left her behind and pulled Rome by the leash.

And took her to my playroom.

I locked the door behind us with the leash still held in my hand. "Face forward."

Rome hesitated before she did as I asked. She faced the opposite direction, to where the king bed lay, the red comforter contrasting against the black walls.

I came up behind her until my chest almost touched her back. I took the time to study her, to watch her body's reaction to me and this room. The metal collar still sat on her collarbone, locked in place so she couldn't get away.

My hand grazed up her arm, my fingertips lightly touching her skin. With those shorts and corset, she blended right in with everyone else Ruin. At first glance, anyone would say she belonged there. I moved up to her elbow, noticing the way her chest rose and fell at a quicker pace. "Are you sure you want to do this, Rome?" I was going to give her an out just in case she had cold feet.

"Yes."

"Yes, Sir," I corrected her.

"Yes, *Sir*," she repeated, her voice noticeably weak.

I craned my neck and pressed a kiss to her bare shoulder, tasting the skin that drove me wild. I moved up her neck and to her ear, kissing the shell as I breathed into her canal. My hand tightened on the leash, and I gave her a slight tug. "Why are you doing this? I know this isn't what you want."

"May I turn around?" she whispered.

"No." We did things my way when we were in my playroom. She didn't have a voice as far as I was concerned.

"I don't want to lose you, Calloway... I love you."

I pressed my face against the back of her head, treasuring the confession she just made. I stood my ground and walked away from her, and now she was the one chasing me. I used to dream about this moment, but I stopped the second I got out of that car.

But now it came true.

"You trust me, sweetheart?" I wrapped my arms across her chest, holding her against me with the leash still held in my hand. The moment was hard to grasp because it was too good. I needed to pinch myself to make sure this wasn't a dream, to make sure it was real.

"Yes..."

"Yes, *Sir*. Don't make me tell you again."

"Yes, Sir," she said quickly.

I unlocked the collar and tossed it on the floor. It fell with a loud clank once it hit the wooden floorboards. I walked around her until we were face-to-face. Her cheeks were flushed with both fear and arousal. I could see her emotions on the surface of her eyes. "You do as I say. No questions asked."

She kept her arms to her sides, her face straight ahead, and her eyes shifted up to look at me. "Yes, Sir."

Jesus Christ, I was hard. My cock was pressed firmly against the inside of my zipper. I couldn't wait to bury myself in that tight pussy. It'd been so long since I had her. And I'd never had her like this before.

"You do not speak to another man inside Ruin."

Rome wasn't the type of woman to take orders from anyone, especially jealous requests. This would test her commitment, to see if she really could give me what I wanted.

The battle took place on her face. She didn't deny me, but she didn't agree with me either.

I waited, losing my patience.

"Yes, Sir."

My spine tightened at her response. I could feel my muscles tense and coil in satisfaction. My dick twitched in my pants, and I almost came then and there. "You're to look at the floor anytime you're in another man's presence."

She struggled with this too. She closed her mouth and pressed her lips tightly together, swallowing whatever smartass remark sat on the tip of her tongue. Somehow, she found the restraint to swallow it. "Yes, sir."

Damn, this was really happening.

"You will do as I instruct until I release you. I will push you as hard as I want. I will hurt you as much as I want. Your life, your destiny, is completely in my hands. Do you accept those terms?"

Her eyes shifted to the floor.

I raised my voice. "Eyes on me."

They flicked up again, and she swallowed hard.

"Do you accept those terms? I won't repeat myself."

"Yes, Sir."

Now my heart was racing, pumping blood to every

muscle in my body. I felt the sweat collect on the back of my neck even though I was standing absolutely still. My heart ached in my chest, full of excitement and longing. "I'm in charge. I issue the commands, and you obey. You don't need to think while you're in here—just listen. But you do have all the power, Rome."

"I do?" she whispered.

"If you want me to stop, all you need to do is say the safe word. I'll stop everything I'm doing and walk away. I'll move to the other side of the room and kneel until you give me permission to move."

"What's the safe word?"

I looked into her eyes and knew exactly what it would be. I'd always been obsessed with those deep emerald eyes, the only jewelry that I possessed. It was the opposite of the typical safe words I used, but I thought it fit us better. "Green. Repeat it."

"Green..."

"Remember it. If you tell me to stop, I'm not going to stop. I'll only cease what I'm doing if you say the safe word. Do you understand me?"

"Yes, sir."

"Explain what I just said to you."

"Calloway, I understand—"

"It's Sir only."

She shut her mouth at her mistake.

"And do as I asked." I suspected there would be

bumps along the way. Rome had such a strong backbone that it was difficult for her to blindly listen to anyone. But that made breaking her all that much more satisfying.

She hesitated before she spoke. "If it becomes too much for me, all I need to do is say green. Asking you to stop won't work. Only the word green will be effective."

"Good." Now that I knew she understood exactly what I said, we could move on. "Kneel."

Her head tilted to the ground as she absorbed my words.

"Eyes still on me," I snapped.

She locked her gaze with mine once more.

"Now, kneel. Don't make me ask you again."

She slowly lowered herself to the ground, moving to one knee and then the other. She kept her eyes on me the entire time she moved, using her hands for balance so she wouldn't fall.

Fuck.

I ran my hand through my hair and released the breath I was holding. That was the single most erotic thing I'd ever seen. I asked Rome to obey me—and she did. This fearless woman carried out my commands just like a soldier. She allowed me to break her, to let me be the only man to break her.

My cock actually hurt because it was so hard.

I yanked my shirt over my head and tossed it on the

floor. I watched Rome's eyes move across my body, taking in the impressive muscles she used to touch every night. I undid my jeans and boxers and pushed them to my ankles.

My enormous dick popped out, already dripping with pre-come. "Suck me off. Now."

That was one order she didn't struggle to obey. She opened her mouth wide and wrapped her lips around my cock. "Yes, Sir." She pushed her mouth all the way to the base then back to the head, moving slowly as if she was trying to stretch her throat out. Her eyes stayed on mine the entire time, sucking my dick as she watched my reaction.

I gathered her hair in a single hand and pushed and pulled her mouth onto my length, dictating exactly how I wanted her to suck me off. I didn't go easy on her like I used to. I fucked her mouth like I owned it. I thrust my hips and penetrated her hard every time, making saliva spill over her mouth and drip to her knees. Tears bubbled in the corners of her eyes and began to stream down her face.

That turned me on more.

I grabbed her head with both of my hands and fucked her mouth with little sensitivity. I hoped she wouldn't say the safe word because I would be forced to stop. And stopping was the last thing I wanted to do at the moment.

She gagged when I shoved my cock too far inside, but I didn't give her more than a few seconds to recover. I shoved my cock back inside and pushed my head down the back of her throat. She kept her tongue flat and her mouth gaping, but that couldn't overcome my girth.

I fucked her relentlessly until I reached the precipice of a powerful orgasm. I was forced to pull out of her mouth before the fun ended prematurely. My cock was soaked in her saliva, and she inhaled a large gulp of air the second her mouth was free.

More tears had fallen in the meantime, stuck against her cheeks.

I cupped her face with my hand and wiped a tear away with the pad of my thumb. "You doing okay, sweetheart?"

"Yes, Sir." She licked the head of my cock and placed a gentle kiss against on the tip.

I closed my eyes as I savored the magnificent touch. Her mouth was the best I'd ever fucked. "Up."

She rose to her feet, still in the tall heels she hadn't removed.

I grabbed the back of her neck and guided her to the foot of the bed. "Bend over."

She lowered her body until her stomach and chest were against the bed, with her ass slightly in the air.

I took my time getting her bottoms off, removing the

shorts then peeling off the stockings. I pushed everything to her ankles then kneeled in front of her ass. Like I'd hoped, her sex was glistening with desire. I could see the moisture leaking from her entrance. I didn't even need to eat her out to get her wet.

I blew gently on her entrance before I pressed my face into her folds, falling into heaven. I loved Rome's pussy as much as the rest of her body. It was absolutely beautiful, stunning. I loved the way she tasted, loved the way she smelled.

My tongue explored her body like it was the first time, becoming reacquainted with the shrine I once worshiped. She moaned quietly from the bed, gripping and tugging on the comforter as she enjoyed my tongue.

"Spread your cheeks, sweetheart."

She grabbed her ass with her hands and pulled them apart, giving me more room to devour her.

I stuck my thumb inside her soaked pussy and let my skin absorb the moisture. It didn't take long for it to become pruned with her arousal. I inserted my thumb in her asshole then continued to eat her delicious pussy, listening to her moans change in intensity. She loved everything my mouth was doing to her, but her ass tightened around my thumb when the sensation felt too foreign.

She better get used to it because my dick was coming next.

My cock thickened painfully, desperate to feel those tight holes he was obsessed with. I rose to my feet and walked to the stands on the left side of the room. "Don't move." I grabbed a purple butt plug and some lube before I returned to her.

"What are you doing?"

I spanked her hard, leaving a handprint right on her cheek.

She cried out in pain, not expecting the punishment.

"Did I give you permission to ask questions?"

"No, Sir..." She breathed through the pain, her ass flushed and red.

I squirted lube directly into her ass then coated the butt plug. I slowly inserted it into her ass, but her body wouldn't cooperate. "Relax, sweetheart. It'll feel good, I promise."

She relaxed her body into the mattress, and within a few seconds, her body was able to take the thick butt plug.

I stared at the jewel that sparkled under the low lighting of the room. Her ass was stunning, especially with the hand mark to complement it. My balls were blue, and my cock was so hard it ached from receiving too much blood. "Knees on the bed." I lifted her lower body with my strong arms and positioned her on the mattress, her stomach still pressed to the sheets. Her feet slightly dangled over the edge, and her back was arched at a tremendous angle as she held her shoulders up.

I couldn't wait any longer. I had to fuck her.

I grabbed myself by the base and pointed at my head at her gushing entrance. She was so slick I slid in with without having to force myself inside, which was a first. She could pretend she didn't like this, but her soaked pussy couldn't lie.

She loved it.

I shoved myself inside then placed my right foot on the mattress, getting into optimal position to hit her cervix every time I thrust inside her. I sank farther into her, filling up her wet pussy with my raging hard-on. "Jesus Christ..." I gripped each of her cheeks in my hand, my eyes concentrated on the jewel staring back at me.

She moaned quietly as she clenched the sheets.

"Missed this cock, sweetheart?" I gave her a gentle smack with my palm.

"Yes, Sir..."

"Look at me." I wanted her to watch me fuck her, watch me claim her as mine again.

She arched her body and gazed at me over her shoulder.

I squeezed her ass before I began to thrust. Every time I pulled my cock out, it was slathered in her creaminess. White and soft, it lubed up my length all the way to my balls. It collected at the head of my cock, softening it as I rammed my length deep inside her.

I hadn't fucked her in so long, I had no control. I pressed my arm against the mattress on either side of her and fucked her so hard she began to cry out. The mattress squeaked, and the headboard crashed against the wall, tapping with my movements. I fucked her exactly how I wanted, how I dreamed, and I waited for her to say the safe word.

But she never did.

Every time I thrust into her, her clit rubbed against the mattress, giving her some extra friction—not that she needed it.

"You don't come until I say so." I wanted to make her wait until the very last moment, letting it build even more. The longer I made her wait, the better it would feel.

"Calloway…"

I smacked her ass hard, leaving another handprint. "Address me as Sir or Master." I spanked her again just to drill in the message.

She cried out and closed her eyes, feeling all the sensations at once.

"You'll come when I tell you to. Got it?"

"Yes, Master."

I liked Master even more than Sir. My cock thickened to a dangerous level, and I couldn't keep my come inside my balls. I wouldn't last much longer at this rate. Rome lowered my threshold significantly. "Now."

She grabbed my wrist and held on just as the climax hit her hard. She came from deep in the back of her throat, screaming louder than I'd ever heard her before. Her nails dug into my skin, and I hoped I would bleed. Her pussy became so tight it nearly bruised my length. "Oh god…"

I continued to fuck her hard and kept my own orgasm at bay. I wanted her to finish before I moved on to my next desire. She deserved to come after all the time we'd been apart. That one was just for her.

I stopped rocking and pulled the butt plug out of her ass. Her hole stayed wide open because it was used to the stretching and she was finally relaxed. I transferred my cock from her pussy to her asshole and slid right in.

She immediately stiffened as my length entered her, stretching out her tight asshole. Her natural instinct was to tug on her cheek to make the opening bigger, but nothing could relieve the pressure of my ridiculously big cock.

I closed my eyes as I held myself on top of her, enjoying how tight and warm she was. I leaned over her and pressed a kiss to her shoulder, comforting her even though nothing could reduce the thickness of my cock.

"Look at me."

She turned her gaze over her shoulder again, her breathing haywire with her discomfort.

I kissed her hard on the mouth, giving her my tongue. I was buried deep inside her ass in my playroom. It was better than my imagination. My lips moved to her ear, and I kissed the shell. "You know the safe word." I wanted to push her as far as possible, but she didn't need to prove anything to me. She was in my playroom, and she was giving her best effort. I couldn't ask for anything more.

I pulled out my cock until only my tip was inside her. Then I thrust hard, penetrating her with aggression.

She rocked forward and moaned.

I fucked her harder than I ever had before, pounding into her ass with my huge dick. The lube was enough to keep the movements smooth, but I could feel her walls clench around me. I knew I wouldn't last long, but that wasn't the point. This was the finale.

Rome squeezed my wrist harder as tears leaked from her eyes. She didn't cry, but the pain was enough to make her eyes smart and tears drip down her cheeks. Sometimes she moaned, and other times she whimpered with pain.

But she didn't say the safe word.

"Here it comes, sweetheart..." I never called my other submissives by such an endearing name, but Rome had a special place in my heart. No matter how dominant I was in the playroom, I would always be different with her.

She moaned through the final thrusts, her ass taking a serious pounding.

I inserted myself so far my balls tapped against her pussy. I came with a loud grunt, filling her tight little asshole with my seed. My climax was powerful, the most exhilarating one I'd ever had. It seemed to stretch on forever, never-ending. "Rome...fuck." I rested my forehead against the back of her head and closed my eyes. I didn't realize my chest was covered in sweat until I finally stopped to take a breath. My hair was damp from my sweaty scalp. My cock slowly softened inside her, mixed with my come and the lube.

I never wanted to pull out of her.

I wanted to stay just like this forever.

I kissed the back of her neck then wrapped my arms around her shoulders. Now that my darker side was satisfied, I felt the other version of myself come to the surface. I felt Rome underneath me, and I was full of so much joy just from holding her. I buried my face in her hair and enjoyed her smell.

I'd missed her.

I kissed her hairline before I got off her, slowly pulling out my cock to ease the discomfort. Like the gentleman I was, I attended to her with a towel and cleaned her up, kissing her spine as I moved.

I cleaned myself up before I lay on the bed beside her, my hands moving into her hair so I could get a good look at her face. The tears had stopped, but the drops were stained on her cheeks where her makeup had been.

"Are you okay, sweetheart?"

"Yes, Sir," she whispered.

My need for domination had been satisfied. She must have realized the change in my demeanor but chose to play it safe to avoid another smack. "You can speak freely." I leaned in and gave her a gentle kiss on the lips.

I tasted the salt from her tears, and that gave me a twisted sense of satisfaction. "This is what I've always wanted..." I brushed my nose against hers before I pulled away. My hand continued to move through her hair, caressing her with the gentleness she deserved. I enjoyed taking her so roughly, but once we were done, I wanted to take care of her. It was such a contrast I couldn't wrap my mind around it.

Her eyes began to dry even though her makeup was smeared. Her fingers wrapped around my wrist and touched me gently. Her eyes hadn't met mine yet. They stared at the comforter like she was searching for something.

"Sweetheart?"

"Hmm?"

My fingers moved under her chin and lifted her gaze to meet mine. "Talk to me."

"I don't know what to say, Calloway. What do you say after that?"

I had been so caught up in the moment that I hadn't truly thought about how she felt. I told her to save the safe word to rid myself of any guilt. Now that I was myself again, I could think more clearly. "Now you know the other side of me. I hope you don't think he's too harsh."

"I'm not sure what I was expecting."

"Did you enjoy it?" My question was more complicated than the way I phrased it. Obviously, she enjoyed it. There was no way her pussy would have been that wet if she didn't.

"Yes…but it was difficult."

"Difficult, how?"

"I'm just not used to letting someone talk to me that way."

"But you overcame it. You fell into the moment with me, and we had something special."

"I guess," she whispered. "But where do we go from here?"

I hadn't had a chance to think about it. An hour ago, I thought Rome was officially out of my life. "Wherever you want to go." I ran my hand down her smooth back, feeling the stickiness from her previous sweat. "I want to be with you, Rome. I want to have exactly what we had before—including this."

"I want to be with you too. But I can't do that all the time. I just can't." She pulled her hair over one shoulder, beginning to fidget at the topic. "It's hard for me. I know you don't understand, and you never will."

"Fifty-fifty."

She lifted her gaze and looked at me.

"We split it down the middle. I'll be everything you need me to be. And you'll be everything I need. That's more than a fair compromise."

Rome considered the offer, her fingers still in her hair.

"Sweetheart, it'll get easier. Continue to trust me, and I'll make amazing things happen."

She nodded but didn't seem to agree.

"You always have the safe word. If there anything you don't want to do, use it."

"But I want to be a good sub…"

I cupped her face and forced her gaze on me. "There's no such thing as a good or bad sub. You're here with me, living in this moment with me. That's all I want. If you ever say something is too much, I'll never think less of you. All I've ever wanted is for you to try. We can work together on this and make it work. There's gonna be things you love and other things you hate. That's normal."

"I guess that makes me feel a little better. I've missed you so much, and I can't bear it anymore. I miss sleeping with you every night. I miss cooking dinner for you. I miss…everything." Her voice caught in her throat, breaking with emotion that was audible to my ears.

"I've missed you too." I pulled her to my chest and cuddled with her on the comforter, keeping her warm now that our activities had ceased. I grabbed the comforter and dragged and flipped it over onto her body in an attempt to make her comfortable. Instead of lying on this bed, I wanted to go home with her. I wanted us to both get some sleep for once. "You were the last thing I expected to see at Ruin tonight. But I'm so glad you were here. I don't want anyone else, Rome. I meant that when I said it. You're the only person in the world that I want to do this with."

She didn't ask any questions about the blonde or ask if I'd been with other women during the week. She seemed to take my words to heart, her lids growing heavy with warmth. "I know, Calloway."

14

Rome

The sheets were soft against my skin, comfortable because they smelled exactly like the man I loved. Featherlight and silky, they felt like home. My old bed at Christopher's place felt hard and uncomfortable since I hadn't slept in it for so long. Calloway's house had never been mine, but it sure felt that way.

Calloway lay beside me in bed, his arms wrapped around my body in the exact position he always held me. One arm was draped over my waist, while the other rested in the crook of my neck. He spooned me from behind, his cock in perfect position to press against me in the morning.

I was tired, but I couldn't fall asleep. Everything

about this moment was perfect. I was in the bed I once considered my own with the man I adored. After all the sleepless nights of the past month, it was nice to finally feel at peace.

Calloway must have known I was awake because he spoke, the rough hair from his beard moving against my shoulder. "Why aren't you asleep?"

"I could ask you the same thing."

"Because I have a beautiful woman right in front of me. What's your excuse?"

My arm slid over his. "Because I have the love of my life behind me."

He pressed a kiss to my ear, a layer of my hair in the way.

Being his sub wasn't entirely what I was expecting. I knew he would issue orders and expect me to obey them without question. I knew he would be in charge, the ruler of the room. But I didn't realize how hard it would be to lay down my pride and do as he asked.

It was very difficult.

But once I kneeled on the floor, finally submitting to him, I felt relieved. It was nice to give up my control and allow him to take charge. It was nice not to think or worry. I had no voice, so there was no point in predicting situations before they arose.

All I had to do was listen.

When he struck me, I wasn't expecting it. When he

fucked my mouth so aggressively, I wasn't sure if I could handle it. And when he took me on the bed like I was a prisoner rather than a woman, I nearly broke.

But I held on.

A part of me enjoyed Calloway behaving like a dictator. He was strong and authoritative, and that turned me on somehow. But it also reminded me of the men who tried to do the same, who'd tried to rule me into submission.

I had to keep reminding myself that the situations weren't the same.

There was one thing I knew for sure. Being hurt by Calloway in the playroom was far less painful than losing him. I couldn't handle any more lonely nights. I couldn't handle the possibility of him being with someone else. I couldn't handle another cold goodbye from him.

I just couldn't.

This was the lesser of two evils. Calloway said we could split our needs right down the middle so I wouldn't be in his playroom every night. I would get what I needed, get to enjoy the man I'd fallen so deeply in love with. I just had to make a compromise to keep him.

"Sweetheart?" he whispered.

"Hmm?"

"I want you to know I haven't been with anyone." He

was explaining his interaction with the blonde, the woman who'd asked him to dominate her for the night and handed over her leash.

I watched their encounter from the other side of the room and learned a few things. Women spotted Calloway and willingly wanted him to rule them. They strutted over there and point-blank asked for what they wanted. The blonde wasn't the only one interested. I noticed lots of others looking his way.

If I didn't want to be his sub, he really could find a replacement instantly.

He continued. "As in, I haven't touched anyone."

When I saw him with that blonde, I feared what happened earlier in the week while I deliberated with myself. Even if I hadn't changed my mind in time and he had been with someone else, I couldn't hold it against him. I didn't want to think about it either. But his confession made my body relax in a way it never had before. The air left my lungs, and I suddenly felt even more comfortable in that bed.

He kissed the back of my neck. "Just you, sweetheart."

"Thank you."

"We'll go by Christopher's apartment in the morning and grab your things. My house is too empty without your knickknacks."

I wanted to be back home, but trepidation was in my

heart. "Maybe we should give it some time first..." I wasn't ignorant enough to believe that session was as bad as it was going to get. I was sure Calloway intended to do much worse. Maybe I wouldn't be able to handle it in the end.

"We'll make it work, Rome. All we need is communication."

It didn't matter how much we talked. I might just get sick of being whipped all the time. "I don't want to rush into anything...see how it goes first. I've left your place so many times now. I don't have the strength to do it again."

This time, Calloway didn't push me. "Okay, I understand."

I tightened his arm around me, feeling his pulse through his skin.

"We'll talk about hard limits in the morning. I'm sure that will make you feel better."

"Hard limits?"

"Things you're unwilling to do."

"I didn't realize I had a choice."

"Of course you do." His deep voice came from behind me, deep and powerful. "I said you had all the power because you do. You tell me what you can and can't handle, and I'll work around that. As time goes on, you'll probably lower your hard limits. This is why I wanted you to have an open mind in the beginning. It's about pleasure, not pain. It's something we can work out together, as a team."

"So, I can make requests?"

"Yes. Do you have one?"

"Actually, yes..."

"I'm listening." He propped himself on his elbow and looked down at me.

"I don't want to go to Ruin again."

He continued to stare at me like he expected me to say something else.

"It makes me feel like one of the many. If I'm special to you, then I don't want to be screwed on the same bed where you whipped the others. I don't want to be tied to the same headboard. I want to be different." I looked into his dark eyes, hoping to find understanding rather than annoyance.

"That's fair."

Earlier that evening, he smacked me when I didn't address him properly. Then he smacked me again for good measure. He was authoritative and borderline brutal. He was a completely different man from the one I spoke to in that moment. I was in love with the man, but I feared the beast. "It is?"

"I'll construct a playroom here. We don't have to leave the house."

Now I didn't have to look at the other women and wonder if they'd been in the same playroom that I had. I could have something none of the others had. "Thank you."

He turned my head toward him so he could lean down and kiss me on the lips. The kiss was soft and affectionate, containing the love of the man I preferred. He was there with me in that moment, exactly what I wanted him to be. "Let's get some sleep. I've gotta be up in…" His eyes moved to the clock on the nightstand. "In two hours." A quiet sigh escaped his lips followed by a quick chuckle. "Damn."

It felt like a normal day.

Calloway and I went to work together, our hands joined together on his thigh as we sat in the back seat. He walked me to my office once we were in the building, and as usual, he kissed me before he walked away.

Despite being sleep-deprived, I was able to get more work done than I had been lately because I wasn't distracted. My heart wasn't broken in two, and my breaths weren't heavy with despair. I was actually happy for the first time in a month.

At the end of the day, Calloway picked me up at my office. He leaned against the door and typed a quick email on his phone, his large fingers almost too big for the screen. His tailored suit highlighted all the exquisite parts of his body, his powerful arms and broad shoulders.

A feeling of both sadness and joy flooded through me. The routine was something I took for granted, the silent understanding that we would leave once Calloway was finished in his office. He worked harder than anyone else there, so he was usually one of the last people to walk out.

I missed the little things like this. "Ready to go?"

He shoved his phone into his pocket. "Yes. Is my woman ready?"

I loved being his woman. "Yes." I grabbed my purse and walked out with him.

His arm circled my waist, where it remained until we reached the door. Tom immediately drove us to his house.

I hated to interrupt such a great afternoon, but I had somewhere else to be. "I'm gonna go home for a few hours." I hadn't said anything to Christopher about what was going on. He was probably worried about me even if he wouldn't admit it.

Calloway hid his disappointment well. He hit the intercom button. "Change of course, Tom. Let's head to Rome's apartment."

"Of course, sir."

Calloway kept his fingers interlocked with mine for the rest of the car ride, his eyes out the window.

Tom pulled up to the curb a moment later and opened the back door.

Calloway got out then gave me a hand so I could get to the sidewalk without tripping in my black stilettos.

I gripped his arms for balance as I stood on my tiptoes and kissed his now shaven face. His lips were soft despite his obvious ruggedness, and now I wished I hadn't decided to stop by my apartment. "I'll see you later."

"See me later?" he asked. "I'm coming with you." He turned to Tom. "I'll call you when I need you." He raised his hand in the form of a wave then pulled me along.

"Why are you coming with me?" I didn't mean to blurt it out and sound so harsh, but I was sure he had other things to do.

"I just got you back, sweetheart. You think I'm gonna let you run off for a few hours?"

We entered my apartment a moment later and found Christopher sitting on the couch working. His laptop was on the coffee table, and he had folders spread out everywhere. He was probably working on a portfolio for a high-end client. He sipped his coffee and looked up, nearly doing a double take when he saw the two of us walk in together. "Packing up your things again?" He left the couch and shook Calloway's hand.

"No," Calloway answered. "She's staying put for now. But between you and me, I hope she's not here very long."

"Between you and me," Christopher responded. "Me too." Christopher turned to me and put his hands in his pockets, obviously wanting to ask me about Calloway but unable to since he was standing right there. "Wanna get dinner or something?"

"That sounds good," I said. "I'm starving."

"Good," Christopher said. "Since you haven't eaten in a month, I'm not surprised."

My bag over his shoulder, we walked into Calloway's house and headed upstairs to his bedroom on the third floor.

Calloway stripped off his jacket and yanked off his tie the second we were in the bedroom. "Tell me what you want, sweetheart." He came up behind me and yanked my purse off my shoulder, pressing his hard cock against my ass.

"You."

"Be more specific." He wrapped his arms over my chest, pressing right against my frantically beating heart.

I turned my face into his neck, smelling his cologne and masculine scent.

"Anything you want, I'll give it to you. Any fantasy you want, I'll fulfill it."

"Just the way I fulfill yours?"

He pressed his lips to my ear. "Yes."

Now I could have anything I wanted. I did exactly what he asked, and now it was his turn to obey me. The scenarios weren't the same, but now I was the one with the power for a change. "I want you to make love to me."

"Yes, sweetheart." He kissed my neck as his hands groped my body, feeling my tits through my dress.

"I want it to be slow."

"Yes, sweetheart." He gave my tits a squeeze before he unzipped the back of my dress.

"I want you to look me in the eye and tell me you love me."

"Yes, sweetheart." He unclasped my bra and let it fall to the ground.

I grew excited by his obedience. I was getting everything I'd wanted since the beginning of our relationship. Now it was happening. Really happening. "I want you on top of me. I want my legs wrapped around your waist."

He kneeled and pressed a kiss to my ass as his hands gripped my thong and pulled it down my legs. He kissed the back of my thigh, moving inward and back up to my cheeks. Slowly, he inched closer until his lips found the throbbing area between my legs.

I pressed my hand to the wall and gasped the second his tongue met my clit. When it came to Calloway pressing his face between my legs, I lost my mind. His caresses were incredible, skilled with experience and mixed with passion.

Calloway kissed me for several more minutes before he stood up and undressed himself, dropping his slacks and collared shirt. His shoes were kicked off, and his warm cock pushed between my cheeks.

I remembered the way he fucked me in the ass the night before. My body suddenly flushed with heat.

Calloway guided me to the bed until I was on my back with my head on the pillows. He moved over me, his chest a solid wall of strength. His waist led to V at his hips, his core hard and defined with powerful abs. He was all man, all fantasy.

His pinned his arms behind my knees and separated my thighs, exposing my pussy to his anxious cock. He tilted his hips and pressed the head inside my channel, slowly pushing in and feeling the slick lubrication my body produced just for him.

He slowly sank into me, moving inch by inch until he was sheathed deep inside me.

"Calloway..." My arms wrapped around his neck as my legs hugged his waist. He stretched me until the pain started, but it was nothing compared to how wonderful he felt. He made me feel full, like every woman should feel.

He began to rock into me, taking me with a gentleness he hardly ever showed.

Giving him what he needed was worth it. Now I had exactly what I wanted, had exactly what I dreamed about. My fingers moved into his hair, and I kissed him slowly, feeling his large dick move inside me over and over. I already wanted to come, but I wanted to let it build up even more. When Calloway had forced me to wait last night, I had the biggest explosion of my life.

He moved his lips with mine without slowing his pace. He rocked into me with long and even strokes, his balls tapping against my ass every time he fit completely inside me. He breathed into my mouth with longing, feeling the same erotic satisfaction that I did.

I didn't think I could hold myself back much longer. My body was tightening in anticipation, squeezing his dick as the sensation began to sweep over me.

Calloway broke his lips from mine and looked me in the eye. "I love you." Sincerity was obvious in his tone, powerful in his expression. I could feel all of his love through those three little words. He didn't just say those words because I asked. He said them because he felt them—in his heart.

"I love—" I couldn't finish because the orgasm hit me hard, striking me across every inch of my body. My core tightened, and the fire erupted in my veins, the erotic flames searing my skin. My hands dragged down his neck to his shoulders, and my nails buried deep inside his skin. I came all over his dick, my come gushing down his entire length.

He moaned as he watched me come. "You look so beautiful when you come."

I gripped his ass and pulled him deep inside me, enjoying how thick his cock was. It always hardened just a little more before he released inside me, so I knew his release was fast approaching. "Come inside me, Calloway."

He pressed his forehead to mine as he shoved himself deep inside me, gushing inside my pussy and filling me up. His come moved past his length and dripped down my ass, hitting the sheets underneath me. "Jesus Christ... this pussy." He kissed my neck then the corner of my mouth, reeling from the intensity we both felt. Then he slowly began to pull out.

I grabbed his ass and dragged him back inside, keeping him deep within me. He was slowly softening, but I didn't care. "More."

His eyes were dark with pleasure, but the corner of his mouth rose in a smile. "Yes, sweetheart."

When I woke up the next morning, I immediately noticed something different about Calloway.

He was wearing his ring.

He took it off after he got out of the car on that god-awful night. I never saw him wear it again. When he stood beside me in the elevator, I could see the faint tan line of where it'd been sitting before he removed it.

It stuck out to me, dark against his fair skin.

Calloway was ready earlier than he usually was, getting up about twenty minutes before his alarm clock went off. He asked me to get ready quickly so we could leave the house with extra time to spare.

"Why?"

"Because we need to go by your apartment on the way."

I had everything I needed. "Why?"

He showed me his dark expression, the dominant side of him that didn't like to be questioned. Last night, I was in the presence of the man I adored. And today, the beast had returned. "Because I said so."

Tom drove us to my apartment, and we walked inside. Christopher was just about to walk out when we opened the front door. "I'm running late," he said as he walked past us. "I'll see you guys later." He shut the door behind him, and his footsteps faded away.

"What are we here for?"

Calloway walked into my bedroom and examined

my nightstand like he was looking for something. He opened the drawer then rifled through the contents.

"Excuse me?" I snapped. "What are you doing?"

He found the small box he'd given to me and popped the lid, exposing the black diamond he'd given me. "Put this on." He tossed the box back inside and grabbed my right hand. He slipped the ring back onto my finger until it hit the knuckle. "And don't take it off again."

The ring felt right, like it hadn't been removed in the first place. I'd grown attached to the ring ever since he gave it to me, and I'd cried my eyes out the night I took it off. But now it meant more to me than it did before— because I was his submissive. "Same applies to you."

He pushed me back on the bed then undid his belt, the metal sliding along the leather. He pushed his slacks down along with his boxers, revealing his enormous cock with a drop of pre-come at the end. "I didn't want to take it off in the first place."

15

C alloway

The ring had been returned to its rightful place, and I felt whole once more. Being monogamous had never been important to me, but being with Rome was the only thing I truly wanted. Now I had her the way I wanted her—as my sub.

And the love of my life.

I finally got what I wanted, got to do sinister things to Rome because she would allow it. Our first visit to the playroom had been amateur, but I had no doubt she could handle all the things I had in mind. Her love for me was strong enough to combat her past traumas. I knew she enjoyed it, so in time, she would forget about the past transgressions against her altogether.

It would work.

I hired a good friend to construct the playroom for me. I didn't have the time or the interest to do it myself. The walls needed to be redone, the furniture needed to be removed, and all the sinister toys I loved had to be properly placed in their display boxes. They said it would take a week to complete.

A week was nothing in comparison to a lifetime.

Rome and I had dinner just the way we used to. We sat across the table from one another and split a bottle of wine. She picked at her food and ate her laughable portion while I scraped everything off my plate like a real man.

We read together in front of the fire for a few hours, sitting in companionable silence as we enjoy each other's company. I needed to whip her, to hurt her, but it was obvious I needed this as well. This lovely companionship gave me a new sense of joy, something I didn't realize I was missing until Rome came into my life.

We retired upstairs at the end of the night. We usually made love then went to sleep. I was eager for sex, but not the sweet and gentle kind she got off to. No, I had very different plans in mind.

"Kneel." I pulled my shirt over my head and tossed it on the floor. When I turned around, I saw her standing there in the dress she wore to work. Her hair was still pulled back in the sleek ponytail that kept her hair away from her face.

It took her a second to absorb the command. But once it sank in, she lowered herself to her knees. The bedroom was carpeted, so it wasn't as painful on her body as it was in the playroom. We agreed to a fifty-fifty relationship, so half of the time I would get what I wanted. She got the other half.

"Eyes on the ground."

"Yes, Sir." She lowered her gaze.

I stared down at her and enjoyed the sight, loving the fact that I finally conquered my greatest challenge. Rome was an unbreakable woman, but I got her to yield to me, to allow me to become the only man and Dom to possess her.

I removed my jeans and my boxers, taking my time getting undressed so I could make her squirm. She was both excited and afraid, two conflicting emotions that made her uneasy. I knew exactly what I wanted to do with her. "You're to call me Master this evening."

"Yes, Master."

The same chill ran down my spine that I felt the other night. Her obedience was the most arousing thing on the damn planet. I'd never wanted a woman more. I'd never felt like more of a man when she submitted to me. "You've pissed me off a lot over the past year."

She swayed on the spot slightly, not expecting me to start the evening by saying that.

"You didn't move out of your apartment when I asked you to. You didn't tell me about Hank when he was clearly a problem." My hand moved to the base of my cock, and I stroked myself gently, thinking about what I was about to do to her. "You've talked back to me more times than I can count. And when I first asked you to be my submissive, you said no. Do you disagree with these crimes?" It was a trick question. If she said yes, she would only be punished more. If she said no, she was getting punished anyway.

"No, Master."

I walked up to her, my dick inches from her face. "Lick my balls." I massaged my cock and pointed it at the ceiling, my balls hanging between my legs. "Now."

She tilted her head up and stuck out her tongue. She moved forward until my balls sat right on the flattened surface of her wet and warm tongue, feeling smooth and defined at the exact same time. She lapped at my balls then sucked them into her mouth, making love to my sac with those beautiful lips of hers.

"Eyes on me."

She locked her gaze on me, making out with my balls like she couldn't get enough of them.

I continued to jerk myself, feeling like a king standing over a queen. "Fuck." For an inexperienced woman, she sure knew how to kiss my cock and balls. My free hand dug into her hair, watching her enjoy what she was doing as much as I did.

I was tempted to jerk myself hard and come all over her face.

But that would have to wait for another time.

"Up."

She retracted her tongue and rose to her feet.

"Strip." I released my cock and let it hang forward, pointing right at her stomach like she had a target drawn on her.

She removed her dress and underwear until she stood naked in front of me, her nipples hardening because she wanted my cock in her mouth again—at least, that's what I was going to tell myself.

"On your hands and knees. Ass in the air." I pointed at the bed.

She crawled on top and let her ass hang over the edge, her tight little asshole staring at me. When she looked this sexy, I wasn't sure what I wanted to do. I wanted to fuck her in the ass, the pussy, and the mouth all at the same goddamn time.

I pressed my right palm to her ass, rubbing the decadent skin. I'd smacked her before and had seen my own handprint. But now, it would be different. "I'm going to spank you ten times, sweetheart. You're going to count with me."

She hesitated, a response not forthcoming.

I squeezed her cheek. "Did you hear what I said?"

"Yes, Master."

"You're going to count with me."

"Yes, Master…"

I knew she was scared. I could feel the slight tremble of her body. She tried to cover it up by remaining rigid, but it wasn't fooling me. "You know the safe word. Repeat it."

"Green."

"You can always use it if you ever need to. I'll stop. Do you understand?"

"Yes, Master."

"Alright." I rubbed her ass gently then gripped her left hip, getting a good hold on her. She stared straight ahead and breathed deeply, her emotions obvious to me by the rigid way she held herself.

The violent desires inside my body were now on the surface. As fucked up as it was, I wanted to hurt her. I wanted to mark her skin and turn it red. I wanted to listen to her cry as she continued to allow me to hit her. It was sick and twisted, but nothing would ever change my fetishes.

I pulled my hand back then spanked her, giving her a smack that was borderline gentle. I needed to ease her into it, to get her nerves used to the sensation. "What did I say?"

Rome realized she'd failed to count. "One."

"One, Master. We're doing that one again." I pulled my hand back and hit her harder this time, shifting her forward.

She gasped quietly, either from pain or pleasure. It wasn't obvious which it was. "One, Master…"

"Good." I spanked her again, this time with more force.

"Uh…" She held herself up as her body shifted forward, her ass starting to turn red. "Two, Master…"

I rubbed her cheek and felt the heat from her skin. It was blemished and irritated, the strike of my palm possessing enough force to make her uncomfortable. "Eight more to go, sweetheart." I hit her three more times, being far gentler on her than my other submissives. I wanted Rome to keep an open mind, to know she could get through this.

She continued to count. "Five, Master."

Now we were at the halfway point, and I wasn't going to be as easy on her. I hit her harder than before, creating a loud slapping sound once my palm hit her ass.

She lurched forward, releasing a moan of surprise. She breathed through the pain and winced, struggling to swallow the discomfort.

I waited for her to count, my palm twitching to her hit her again.

"Six…Master."

I closed my eyes and felt my hand form a fist. The adrenaline inside my chest was powerful, unstoppable. I'd officially crossed over into my darker side. I enjoyed the hurt in her voice. I loved the fact that she remained strong and didn't utter the safe word. My spine was rigid, and my cock was painfully hard.

I slapped her hard, hitting her with enough force to make anyone cringe.

"Ah..." She pressed her face to the mattress as she gripped the sheets around her. The sound of tears filled the air. "Seven...Master." She sniffed the tears away as she kept her ass in the air.

Jesus Christ.

This was so good.

I felt like a monster for enjoying this. But it felt so erotically wonderful. I didn't want it to end. I hit her again and again. I wanted to hit her until she began to sob. My cock twitched at the idea. I yanked my hand back and smacked her hard again, making a definitive clap fill the air.

She cried out in pain, this time her tears loud. She cried with her face against the mattress, her back rising and falling as she tried to breathe through the agony. "Nine...Master."

"One more, sweetheart." My cock had never wanted to be inside that pussy more than it did now. My jaw was clenched tight as I ground my teeth together. I was eager to fuck her, but I also wanted to slow down, to savor the final smack I was about to give her.

She tensed in anticipation of the final blow.

I hit her harder than I ever did before, using all the momentum my body could muster. I landed my palm hard against her cheek, making it bright red and irritated. The second my palm collided with her skin, she cried out in pain—louder than she ever had before.

My cock couldn't handle it.

She cried quietly into the sheets, the tears making the mattress damp as they soaked through the fabric.

I listened to her cry and only felt hotter.

I positioned myself at her entrance and shoved my cock inside her, greeted by the moisture I'd expected to find. She might be crying, but she obviously liked it. Her mind could betray her, convincing her she shouldn't enjoy what just happened, but her body could never lie. I slid through her warm pussy and owned it. I grabbed her hair and yanked her head up, wanting to see the arch in her back as I rammed inside her.

Once our bodies started to move together, her tears stopped. She rocked back into me harder, taking my length just as hard as I gave it to her. Her grunts turned to moans, and her tears disappeared altogether.

I grabbed her shoulder and held on as I thrust my hips and buried myself inside her, making this pussy mine forever. Her ass was red from all the violent slaps, and I loved staring at it as much as staring at the rest of her gorgeous body.

I placed one foot on the bed to get a steady position. My hand wrapped around her waist and found her clit, and I rubbed it with my forefinger, bringing her to the verge of a climax. I needed her to come immediately because I couldn't last long. I'd spanked her so fiercely that my cock needed a quick release.

Her body reacted to the touch, and she came around my dick, squeezing and constricting until the come gushed around it. She was in the process of screaming when I finally allowed myself to come, to fill her with my all my seed.

Fuck yes.

I gave her my entire load before I pulled out and watched the seed drip from her opening. I loved feeling my woman with my come. It gave me the greatest sense of satisfaction, that I truly owned her.

I grabbed a towel and some cream from the bathroom and returned to her, seeing her in the exact same position as before.

"Come here." I grabbed the pillow and placed it under her head. Then I pushed her hips down so she would lie flat on her stomach. She closed her eyes immediately because she was exhausted. I placed a blanket over the top of half of her body so she wouldn't get cold. Then I attended to her, my dominance disappearing the instant was I satisfied. Now all I cared about was taking care of her, making sure she had everything she needed.

I cleaned her up then rubbed the cream into both of her cheeks, doing my best to minimalize the swelling and the redness. It would be painful until she woke up in the morning, but at least this would help her sleep.

I didn't feel any pity when I looked at her skin—just arousal.

It was my handiwork. That was my handprint. This was my woman.

"Sweetheart?" I finished with the cream then ran my fingers through her hair. Her eyes were closed, but I suspected she wasn't asleep.

"Why do you enjoy hurting me so much...?" She shut her eyes tighter, as if looking at me would be too painful.

I lay beside her and looked into her face, seeing the tearstains imprinted on her cheeks. "Because I'm a fucked-up asshole. That's why." My fingers grazed against her cheek on the way to her hairline. "I'm not gonna make excuses because I don't have any. I enjoy hurting you. I enjoy listening to you cry. I just do."

She finally opened her eyes, a film of moisture on the surface. "But, why? Is it because your father used to hurt you?"

I held her gaze even though I didn't want to answer

that question. "Probably. And probably because I used to watch him do the same thing to other women. It's been programmed in my brain ever since."

She took her gaze off me, staring at the bedding instead.

"I know you enjoyed it, sweetheart."

"I did…but it hurt toward the end."

"But when you came, how did it feel?"

"Good…"

"Better than usual?"

She nodded.

"Being in pain triggers our other senses. It heightens other feelings and experiences. You'll see what I mean as we go along."

She held herself up and looked over her shoulder, staring at her blood-red ass. She rubbed her fingers across the surface then winced when she touched it the wrong way.

"It'll be back to normal tomorrow," I whispered.

She lay back on the pillow and pulled the blanket over her entire body.

"Is there anything I can get you?"

She shook her head. "No, thanks."

I leaned in and kissed her softly on the mouth. "You know, you can always use the safe word, sweetheart. It's there for a reason."

"I know, Calloway."

I kissed her forehead and felt her searing skin against my mouth. "I need to go to Ruin tonight. You'll be okay here on your own?"

The second she knew I was leaving, her posture changed. She was no longer relaxed and tired. "Why are you going there?"

"Jackson gave me back the company, said he couldn't handle it. I just need to take care of business."

"Just business, right?"

I was hurt by the question, but I knew she had every right to ask. "Just business." I held my hand where my ring sat. "You're my sub. I don't need another." I kissed her on the cheek and left the bed. "I'll be back in a few hours."

"Okay."

I pulled on my jeans and t-shirt and headed to the door.

"I love you…" The words were so quiet I could hardly hear them.

I faced her from my position by the door, seeing the beautiful woman lying on my bed. "I love you too."

When Jackson spotted me from his place at the bar, he grinned from ear to ear. "Here's the lucky man…"

I snatched his scotch from the counter and took a

drink. "A very lucky man, indeed."

"Rome changed her mind, huh?"

"How'd you know?"

"Everyone's been talking about it. They said you had a sub already in tow when some brunette that no one had ever seen before snatched you. I assumed that could only be one person..."

Rome was the only woman who had my entire focus. "Your assumption was right."

"I'm glad she finally kneeled. I didn't think she had it in her."

"Oh, she does." I couldn't believe I left the house with her still on my bed, her ass beet-red. "I'm here to resume my duties as the head honcho of this place. Anything specific I need to take care of?"

He shrugged. "Everything. I haven't been doing shit."

"I should have known better." I clapped him on the shoulder then walked to the stairs. I intended to get out of here as quickly as possible when I had my woman waiting for me at home. I didn't want to sit in that leather chair when I could be naked in bed, my arms wrapped around the sexiest woman on the planet.

I made it to the second landing when Isabella emerged out of the shadows like a spider from the corner. "There you are." Her hands were on her hips, and she was dressed entirely in black—except the shoes. Her heels were bright red, just like her lipstick.

"Good evening, Isabella."

She blocked my way down the hallway to the office door, doing her best to put on a good attitude. The hurt was in her eyes—no matter how much she tried to hide it. "You gave her my ring?"

I assumed she would start off the conversation differently. This woman never failed to surprise me. "It was never yours. You just wore it for a period of time."

"No, it was mine."

"I took it back, in case you've forgotten."

She looked like she was seriously considering slapping me across the face. "You think that whore can handle you? She's gonna snap like a twig, and you know it."

I resisted the urge to grab her by the neck. "Call her that again, and see what happens." I took a step forward, crowding her in the most threatening way possible. I wouldn't raise a hand to a woman, but that didn't mean I wouldn't give her a good scare.

Isabella knew I wasn't messing around. "She's gonna break, Calloway. We both know it."

"She's doing a damn fine job. We're very happy." I stepped around her. "Now, if you'll excuse me."

She snatched me by the arm with her petite hands. "Calloway—"

"Don't touch me." I moved out of her grasp, officially ticked off. "I'm not yours to touch."

She dropped her hand and didn't move any closer. "I don't understand. She didn't give you what you wanted, so you came back to me." The earlier hostility quickly faded away, replaced by her raw vulnerability. "And she didn't care that you betrayed her?"

"She was hurt—deeply. But she understood why I did it."

"And now you're throwing me away all over again?"

My anger disappeared when I felt the hurt emanating from her. I shouldn't have gotten involved with her again in the first place. This was my fault. Isabella was getting better, and I dragged her back down. "I explained the circumstances very clearly. I never misled you about my intentions. But I am sorry for hurting you. You're a beautiful woman, and you can do much better than me."

"You're the only one I want, Calloway." Tears formed in her eyes. "Then you gave her my ring. I wore that for a whole year—day and night. And then you just hand it off to someone else...it's like our time together never happened."

I bowed my head, feeling like a jerk. "All I can do is tell you I'm sorry. But that's it."

"Sorry, what?" she hissed. "For treating me like shit?"

"In a nutshell, yeah."

She poked her finger in my chest, hitting right between the pecs. "You'll get what's coming to you, asshole. I can promise you that." With tears streaming down her face, along with a nightmare expression, she stormed off.

My pride wanted to tell her off for touching me again, but the logical part of me said I should let it go. Isabella was a loose cannon, and she wasn't thinking clearly right now. It was best to let her storm off with the last word. Maybe it would inflate her ego and make her feel a little better.

I walked into the office and locked the door behind me, making sure there wouldn't be any surprises. Even though Jackson had been occupying the office for months, it felt exactly the same. The desk was organized the same, and the leather chair was adjusted to my preference. It was dark, the art lights along the ceiling set to the lowest brightness.

It was perfect.

I sat in the chair and felt my back relax against the leather. Like no time had passed at all, I felt like a king in my own universe. My black ring felt heavy on my right ring finger, symbolizing my complete commitment to one woman.

Everything felt the same, but it felt different as well.

I finally had everything I wanted.

I was the strongest and cruelest Dom I'd ever known.

And I was a man very much in love.

16

R ome

The bed shifted when Calloway's weight hit the mattress. He was as thick as a horse and as muscular as a bull. He couldn't enter a room without making the floorboards creak or sit on a cushion without causing it to sink.

Without opening my eyes, I reached out and touched his bare chest, feeling the muscle underneath that warm skin. I scooted closer to him, eager to be beside the man I couldn't live without.

His lips found my temple, and he kissed me. "I tried not to wake you."

"I'm never truly asleep unless you're beside me anyway." My arm circled his waist, and I rested my face on top of his chest.

"How are you feeling?"

After a few hours, the sting had faded away. My ass cheeks were almost as pale as they'd been before he spanked me. "Good. That cream helped."

"Tomorrow, you won't even know I was there."

"That's a shame…"

He chuckled in my ear. "Be careful what you say, sweetheart. You're talking to the man right now, but the beast can rise at any moment."

I hooked my leg around his. "I'm too tired for the beast. I just want Calloway right now."

"Alright, you can have him." He set his alarm on his phone before he placed it back on the nightstand.

"How was Ruin?" I wanted to ask him how work was, but was it really work? He owned a business where people went to fuck. It was a strange way to make a living, but now that I was his sub, I really had no right to judge.

"Good." His tone suddenly became clipped.

Paranoia sat in my heart now that Calloway had betrayed me. Anytime he was there, I wondered if he gave in to the temptation of the atmosphere and wound up with a sub in one of the playrooms. The accusation was offensive, so I didn't dare ask.

Calloway picked up on my slight change in attitude. He was in tune with my moods in the same way I was in tune with his. "I just went to the office then left.

Nothing else happened. Nothing else will ever happen."

Even though he broke my trust, I believed him.

"But I did run into Isabella... She was a peach."

"What did she say?"

"She's upset we got back together. She feels used. She feels hurt."

"I can imagine." If I'd lost Calloway and watched him commit to another woman, I'd be heartbroken too. When I saw that blonde sign her soul over to him, I was devastated. I knew I had to act quickly to get him back.

"She'll move on eventually. Just hope it's sooner rather than later."

"She's a pretty woman. She'll find someone." We had distinctly different features. She looked like she was born out of Ruin, a creature of the dark. With that jet-black hair and confidence, she appeared to be the perfect partner for a Dom/sub relationship. I was ordinary, a regular woman you would see on the street. With one look at me, you would have no idea that I ever set foot inside a place like Ruin.

"I have no doubt she'll find someone. I just hope it's the right someone." His lips brushed over my shoulder, warm and full of affection. "After running into her, my night was pretty boring. I'm trying to clean up Jackson's negligence. I'm surprised employees were even paid while I was gone."

"I'm sure the place would have shut down if they weren't."

"I just don't get Jackson. He says he wants the responsibility, but then he neglects everything. It's not that hard. If he kept his dick in his pants for just one hour a day, he could take care of the basics."

"Does he get paid from Ruin?"

"Yeah."

"So he gets paid to do nothing?"

"I wouldn't say that," he said quietly. "He really affects the tone of Ruin. He's like the unofficial publicist for the place. He connects with members and makes sure they have a good time. He's a people person. It's nice because I'm not a people person at all."

"You don't say…" I teased.

He chuckled next to my ear and held me against his body. "You know you're the only person in the world I actually like."

"Like?" I questioned.

"You know exactly how I feel about you, sweetheart."

We ended the conversation there, and both slipped away into our dreams, our bodies still locked tightly around one another. I didn't have a single nightmare now that Calloway was there to chase away my bad dreams. He was my guardian, my protector from everything.

Work was the same as usual. I had a project with Chad and Denise, and we worked together in the conference room for the rest of the day. It seemed like all my colleagues had officially accepted me back on to the team despite my personal relationship with Calloway. Perhaps Calloway's speech made them realize they were being ridiculous. Or maybe they just took their boss seriously when he said he would fire them all.

It'd been a pleasant working environment ever since.

At the end of the day, Calloway and I went home. We sat in the back seat of the car together, but Calloway didn't take my hand like he usually did. He stayed on his side, his eyes glued out the window and his brooding nature filling the back seat.

I knew exactly what that meant.

I hadn't returned to my apartment and brought my things over because I wanted to take things slow, but that didn't stop me from being with him every hour of the day. When I returned to my apartment to grab new clothes, I was slowly bringing everything back to his house. So, in a way, I was pretty much moving back in anyway—just at a slow pace.

We walked into the house, and the second the front door was shut and locked, I knew which version of Calloway I was with.

The beast.

"Strip." He loosened his tie and dropped his jacket on the floor. He slid his shoes off with his feet, never breaking eye contact with me.

My eyes moved to the ground, and I did ask he asked, peeling off my dress, underwear, and heels. I was used to standing naked in front of him on a daily basis, watching his eyes stare at my tits appreciatively. The look always made my skin burn white-hot, feeling his attraction to me without him having to do or say anything.

"Follow me." He walked upstairs as he unbuttoned his shirt. It fell off his shoulders and onto the floor just before he walked into the new playroom. It'd been under construction for a week.

That must have meant it was finished.

The second I stepped inside, I noticed how different it was. The old guest bedroom had been transformed into Calloway's playground. The window that overlooked the front door had been covered with a new wall, making it impossible for anyone to see what we were doing inside. The previously gray walls had been covered with maroon wallpaper, making it feel royal and mysterious at the same time.

Cases were placed against the walls, housing the same types of toys that I witnessed at Ruin. There was an assortment of whips, various chains, and cable ties within the glass cases. The ceiling had been constructed of a wooden platform that possessed a suspension system, along with a thick length of rope.

I couldn't believe this place was officially in his house.

The playroom still made me tense and uncomfortable. When we were at Ruin, I felt out of my element. I only sucked it up and did it because losing Calloway was the worst thing that ever happened to me. Doing this somewhere I felt comfortable made the experience much more tolerable. There was no one else here—just the two of us.

"Stand here." Calloway tapped his foot against the floor at the center of the room. "Now."

I stood where his foot had been and returned my gaze to the ground. I could hear the clanking sound of his belt as his pulled it out of the loops and dropped his slacks. His boxers came next, adding to the pile of clothes.

"Safe word?" He walked up to me with his black belt in his hands.

"Green."

He secured my wrists to the fastener in the rope, his eyes glued to mine the entire time. His intensity was arousing but also terrifying. Whatever he was about to do to me would deeply please him. That gave me a thrill of excitement, but also a spasm of stress.

He pulled on the suspension until my feet hung a few inches off the ground. I swayed gently as my body shifted, slowing coming to a standstill.

I wanted to ask what he was going to do, but I knew better than to ask questions.

He stepped back and surveyed my position, the black belt still in his right hand as he stood completely naked. His impressive cock was happy to see me. It was thick and long, eager to be buried inside me.

And I wanted him buried inside me.

He slowly walked around me and lifted the belt, the leather gliding over my skin gently. It was rough to the touch, the individual grooves feeling like bumps against my skin. It started at my tummy then glided around to my ass as he reached the rear. "I'm gonna whip you, sweetheart. And you're gonna count—just like last time."

He was going to whip me with the belt…?

"Do you understand?" His powerful voice echoed in the room even though he didn't raise his voice.

"Yes, Master." He usually preferred Master over Sir, so I chose that title.

He gave me a playful tap on the ass. "Good. To ten." He moved behind me, his bare feet tapping against the hardwood floor.

I knew it was coming, so I immediately tensed as I hung from the rope. My back and ass were burning even though no contact had been made. I dreaded the pain before it even arrived, thinking of the way he'd spanked me with his palm.

With no warning, Calloway slapped the belt over my left cheek. The touch wasn't as bad as the final slaps he gave me earlier in the week, but it was enough to make my nerve endings fire off. I rocked with the momentum and swayed from the ceiling.

I almost forgot to count. "One, Master."

He struck the belt against his palm, making a loud slapping noise that reverberated against the walls. It was an audible warning of what was coming next. "Good, sweetheart." He struck again, hitting me a little harder than last time.

"Two, Master." I bit my bottom lip as I swung forward, enjoying the pain but also afraid of it. The most arousing thing about allowing Calloway to dominate me was how much he enjoyed it. When he came into his element, he was a very erotic man. The muscles of his arms bulged and his core was tight. He was frightening, but utterly delicious.

He hit me three more times until we reached the halfway mark.

I knew it was going to get rougher from here on out. "Five, Master."

He circled to the front then stood directly in front of me. His lips found my belly, and he slathered the skin with kisses, his tongue gliding along the small abs of my core. He moved down as he took a knee.

I inhaled when I knew what was coming next.

He hooked my legs over his shoulders and kissed me where I was most tender, ravishing the area with scorching kisses. My head tilted back, and I closed my eyes, savoring the feeling of his tongue as it circled my throbbing clit.

Like the gentleman he was, he brought me to orgasm within minutes, listening to my screams for more. He sucked my clit harder and even gave it a gentle bite, making my hips buck against his face.

"Master…"

He gave me a few final kisses before he rose to his full height. My arousal was smeared across his lips, a bright shine that made me want to kiss him just to taste myself. "Good girl." He walked behind me and smacked the belt against his hand. "Ready, sweetheart?"

"Yes, Master."

He struck me across both cheeks, the bite of the metal digging hard into my skin. It was harder than he'd ever hit me before.

I swung forward and gasped at the pain, not expecting it because I was too focused on the remains of the orgasm that still thudded between my legs. My head dipped forward, and my hair hung down my chest. "Six, Master…"

He struck me again, hardly giving me a chance to recover. He hit me hard, with far more aggression than the way he'd spanked me last week.

Tears pooled in my eyes, immediately bubbling and breaking the surface. It hurt more than any other strike he'd given me. The pain started on the surface of the skin then burned deep into the muscle. The stinging in my eyes increased until the tears escaped. "Seven, Master..." I didn't want any more. In the beginning, the pain was tolerable and Calloway's desire was a turn-on, but now it was becoming unbearable.

He slapped his belt against me again, using nearly all of his strength to strike me.

This time, I sobbed out loud, feeling the pain drill right into the bone. "Ahh..." I shut my eyes closed and felt the hot tears pour down my face. I felt the strain of the rope at my wrists and tried to loosen the hold by grabbing on to the rope with my fingers. I actually considered saying the safe word because I couldn't take any more of this.

"You didn't count," Calloway barked. "And you'll be punished for that." He smacked me twice in a row, hitting me with the leather of the belt and making me cry out in pain. "We'll start at five again."

I could barely make it to ten in the first place. There was no way I could start over. "Calloway."

He slapped me again. "It's Master. For that, we're starting back at one."

I didn't want this anymore. Now it wasn't fun. It was just painful and degrading. Maybe his other subs could handle this kind of torture, but I couldn't. If that made me weak, so be it. If Calloway couldn't compromise, then—

Calloway struck me again, harder than ever before.

That's when I broke. "Green…"

The belt hit the floor, and Calloway dashed for the suspension cables. With a quick movement of his hands, he lowered me to the floor and got the rope free. My wrists came apart, and I could barely hold my weight steady on the ground.

Calloway moved to the other side of the room and kneeled, his head tilted to the ground. He kept his eyes down and didn't utter a single word. His chest rose and fell with his heavy breathing, the sweat dripping down his back and chest. He looked like a statue, a hero carved out of marble.

I moved to the ground and lay on my side because my ass was too sore. It was hot and inflamed from the bite of the leather. I pulled my arms to my chest and let the tears continue to streak to the floor. I wasn't crying because the worst was over, but I was trying to manage the pain in my silence. That cream Calloway had would probably help. "Get me that cream you used last time…"

Calloway did as I asked and dashed out of the room. He was only gone for thirty seconds before he returned to the room with the jar. He placed it on the ground then stepped back again, being careful not to touch me or come too close to me.

"You can touch me, Calloway."

He stared down at me, remorse obvious in his eyes. "Are you sure?"

"Yes…"

He kneeled beside me and rubbed the cream into my bright red skin. He was as gentle as he could be, showing none of the aggression he possessed just an instant ago. He applied his fingertips to the damaged areas with a tenderness I'd never seen before.

I lay there on the hardwood floor, still naked and now a little cold.

He placed the cap back on the jar then carried me from the playroom into the bedroom. He got me under the sheets and tucked me in like it was time to go to sleep. It was only six thirty, and we hadn't even had dinner yet. "I'm gonna make some dinner. I'll be back in fifteen minutes." He moved his hand through my hair, his eyes no longer hot with unfulfilled desire. Now he looked at me just the way he did when he told me he loved me, with beautiful sensitivity. He kissed me on the forehead before he left.

Calloway set the bed tray in front of me, pot roast with a side salad. He gave me a tiny portion because he knew I wouldn't have much of an appetite. There was a glass of ice water and wine as well.

He sat at the edge of the bed and stared at me.

I sat up and looked at the food. "It looks good..." I wasn't hungry because I was in too much pain. The cream helped, but only time would heal the abrasions on my skin. "Are you going to eat too?"

"Not hungry."

I ate just to be polite, appreciating the gesture he'd made. He turned into an animal when he had me as his sub, but once the moment was over, he was a man again.

Calloway stared at his hands, moving his palms across one another before he faced me once more. "Are you going to leave me?" His voice remained steady, but he couldn't stop the fear from entering his eyes.

I lowered the fork, stunned by the question. "No, Calloway. Never."

He took a deep breath and stared at his hands again, the relief obvious in the way his shoulders relaxed. His square jaw stiffened too. "I'm sorry...for hurting you."

"It's okay." It was hard to understand how he truly meant those words. After all, he got off on hurting women. Maybe there were different levels, and our experience was too extreme. "I hope I didn't disappoint you."

"Never." His hand reached for mine on the bed. "As long as you try, that's good enough for me." He brought my hand to his lips and placed a kiss over my knuckles. "Thank you for using the safe word. I only wished you used it sooner."

"Thought I could handle it…"

"It's something we have to learn together, your hard limits."

"Yeah…"

He pulled his hand away so I could keep eating. "Is there anything I can get for you?"

"No, I'm okay."

He stared at the ground again, remaining silent as I finished my dinner. His thoughts were a mystery, but his mood was obvious. He was angry, but I knew he wasn't angry with me. He probably hated himself for taking me so far when I was still a beginner.

"Calloway?"

"Hmm?" He wouldn't look at me, focused on his mood.

"It's really okay."

He shook his head, his jaw clenched. "I enjoy hurting you. I love listening to you cry. My cock has never been harder as it was in there. That makes me a sick son of a bitch, and I know that. The second you said the safe word and I knew you were really in pain...I felt lower than I ever have. I didn't feel any pleasure. I just hated myself."

I hadn't finished my food, but I decided I would eat it later. The conversation seemed too heavy for dinner.

"Rome, I wish I were different. I wish I could be a normal guy. I wish I didn't need this..."

"I know." I believed his sincerity with all my heart.

"I've never cared about pushing the others until their breaking points. I've never cared about their well-being. But I love you...and it hurts when I hurt you. I can't explain it. I love hurting you as a Dom, but I hate myself for it later."

I placed the bed tray to the side and pulled my knees to my chest.

"I wish I could change. But I tried once before, and it completely backfired. I don't think I can be different..."

"That's fine, Calloway."

He turned to me, anger mixed with surprise. "How can you say that? After all your hesitation for the last six months?"

"Neither one of us is ever going to change," I explained. "But we can certainly compromise with one another. Now I know I never want to do that again, at least at that intensity. But we can do other things instead."

He shook his head with a new look in his eyes.

"You're incredible…you're brave. If you told me you wanted to leave, I wouldn't have had the audacity to stop you."

"But I don't want to leave because I love you." Our love didn't make sense on a logical level. Half of Calloway's essence was exactly what I wanted in a man. He was generous, kind, and selfless. But the other half was a man I feared. "I'm glad that I came back to you and gave this another try. I was closed-minded and scared, but once I fell into the moment with you, I began to understand. I do enjoy it, Calloway. I do enjoy the way you hurt me and then fuck me afterward."

The previous remorse slowly drained from his face, replaced by a fire of longing.

"I just can only tolerate so much. You don't need to change, Calloway. We just need to give each other what we need. That's all."

He nodded in agreement. "You're an incredible woman. I've always thought that, but now I think it even more." He scooted closer to me on the bed until his thigh touched my hip. He looked at me with his beautiful blue eye and his messy hair. He was still shirtless, but now he wore sweatpants. "Thanks for not running."

"You're the last person I want to run away from." I cupped his face and kissed him slowly on the mouth, feeling my heart love this man even more. I should be upset and offended by the events that had happened in his playroom, but seeing him love me and worship me so fiercely made everything worth it.

His hands wrapped around my wrists, and he kissed me harder, his tongue moving with mine. It wasn't long before he was moaning into my mouth, enticed by the feel of my lips against his. "Can I make love to you, sweetheart?"

I ignored the discomfort still on my cheeks because my body and heart craved the man staring back at me. I wanted more of those kisses, more of those touches. My hands fell to his shoulders, and I dug my nails into his skin. "Please."

17

Calloway

"What are you doing in here?" I walked into my office at Ruin and spotted Jackson behind the desk.

"I left some condoms in here…" He searched through the drawer and shoved pens and notepads aside. "Can't find them anywhere."

"You probably used them all."

"I don't think so…" He opened another drawer until he found the foil packets. "Ah…here we go." He hit the drawer shut and stood up. "I'm going to get some good use out of these bad boys." He waved them in my face as he walked past. "But have fun doing paperwork and shit."

"I don't have to use condoms with my woman." I

took his place in the chair. "And I already had my fun before I came over here."

"So she's still a good sub?" He sat in one of the armchairs facing my desk.

"Don't you have somewhere to be?"

"She can wait." He shoved the packets into his pocket. "Things are still good?"

I wasn't going to tell him how I'd mistreated her. It would make me look like an ass. My brother already thought the worst of me, but I didn't want to broadcast it. "We're happy, yeah."

"Well, Isabella just turned in her membership yesterday, so I guess she's long gone."

That was the best news I'd heard all week. I leaned back in the chair and didn't bother hiding my sigh. "That's great news. I'm tired of her whiny bullshit."

"She was a big attraction here for the other Doms. You would know. You were obsessed with her at one point."

It seemed like a lifetime ago now. "That was a mistake. I never should have gotten involved with her on such a serious level. Lesson learned."

"And yet...you're doing the same thing with Rome."

"Not the same thing," I argued. "I love her."

Jackson raised an eyebrow. "I don't think I've ever heard you say that before."

I didn't feel an ounce of shame. Jackson could tease

me all he wanted. I didn't give a shit.

To my surprise, he didn't make a smartass comment. "About time you fessed up to it. It's been written on your face all year." He hopped out of the seat and patted the pocket where he kept his condoms. "Well, I'm off to do what I do best. Give my future sister-in-law my best." He opened the door but didn't walk out. He looked at me over his shoulder, his eyebrow raised.

I had no idea what the look meant. "Yes?"

"I thought you tell me to fuck off or something at that last comment."

"Why? It wasn't offensive."

Jackson walked back inside and shut the door. "Are you saying what I think you're saying?"

"I don't know, Jackson. I have no idea what you're saying to begin with."

"You're thinking about marrying her?"

"I'm not thinking about it," I said. "I know I want to marry her. I just don't know when."

"Whoa, hold on." He raised a hand in the air like I needed to hit the brakes. "You're for real right now?"

"The woman lives with me, in case you haven't noticed. She's my sub as well as my lover. Marriage is the next step, isn't it?"

"Yeah, but...wow."

I rolled my eyes because this conversation was getting old. "Get out, Jackson."

"No, I'm happy for you. You know I really like Rome. I just…I honestly never pictured you getting married."

"Things change." Rome had made the biggest compromise to be with me, and I didn't take that lightly. Every bone in her body was against the arrangement, but she did it because she didn't want to lose me. I knew Rome wanted romance, marriage, and kids. If she gave me that, I could give her this. "But I'm not marrying her tomorrow, so there's no reason to get excited about it."

"Too bad. I already am."

I let Senator Swanson drone on over the phone about the donor banner he would like to have presented at the veterans' dinner. He was so specific about how he wanted it to look that I wasn't sure why he didn't just take care of it himself.

And kiss his own ass while he was at it.

Once I got off the phone, my assistant spoke into the intercom. "Mr. Owens, Isabella is here to see you."

I was just about to open an email when I stiffened in agitation. Just when I thought that pain in the ass was gone, she turned up again. She told Jackson she was leaving Ruin, but perhaps that was just a ploy for some attention.

Jesus Christ, she was annoying.

I never should have been monogamous with her. I never should have decided to commit to her even under the understanding it wasn't forever.

Because she obviously felt otherwise.

I couldn't ignore her and let her stay in the lobby. Isabella would either wait until the end of the day, or she would make a big scene in front of all my employees.

I hit the button. "Send her in."

Isabella walked in a moment later, a sneer of anger on her face. She wore skintight jeans and a black top, looking like she'd stepped out of Ruin mere minutes ago. Her hair was long and straight, just the way she usually wore it.

I wanted to strangle her.

Choke her to death.

I fucking hated her.

She was a damn bug that wouldn't disappear. "Can I help you, Isabella?"

She crossed her arms over her chest, looking like the devil's mistress. "Nope."

I rested my hands together on the desk and kept my cool even though I had no idea what was going on. She was awfully confident after being rejected by me so many times. She seemed to think she owned this office —owned me.

What was I missing?

"Is there something you wanted to discuss?"

"Nope." She didn't move.

Now I was really freaked out. Isabella didn't come here to talk. She didn't have any purpose for being here at all. So what was she up to?

Something evil, no doubt.

I rose out of my chair so I could grab her by the arm and escort her out.

Isabella reached into her purse and pulled out a gun, pointing it right at me. Her hand didn't shake as she aimed the barrel right at the center of my chest.

I stopped in my tracks, eyeing the madwoman with a gun pointed directly at me.

"Sit down, Calloway." She pointed with the gun toward the chair before she trained it on me again. "I don't want to shoot you, but I will."

Even though a loaded gun was pointed right at me, it didn't scare me. What I was truly frightened of was the circumstance. She obviously didn't come here to kill me. If that was her intention, she would have done it already. Her goal was to keep me in that chair.

She stepped forward and brought the gun closer. "Sit."

I slowly lowered myself into the chair, never blinking because I needed to witness her every move. I placed my arms on the armrests and gripped the wooden edges, wishing I had the gun so I could shoot her between the eyes. "Isabella, what are you doing?" If she thought she could intimidate me, she was wrong.

"Just sit and be quiet." Her hand didn't shake as she pointed the gun at my forehead. "Do what I say, and you'll get out of this alive."

"Get out of what?" I demanded. "What the hell is going on, Isabella?"

"What did I just say?" She stepped closer to the desk, bringing the gun even closer to my head.

"You gave that cunt my ring." Now the gun began to shake, not out of fear but heartbreak. "It was mine! I wore it for a year, and you just handed it off to someone else. It's like I never meant anything to you."

Normally, I would insult her, but she had a gun pointed at my head. I was stubborn but not stupid. "Isabella, let's just calm down for a second..."

"No! How could you prefer her over me? What does she have that I don't?"

"Nothing." I wasn't inflating her ego. That answer was true. "She doesn't have anything over you, Isabella. My heart chose her. I can't explain it better than that. It doesn't mean you weren't good enough."

"Sure seems that way."

I raised my hands gently. "Isabella, let's put the gun down and talk like adults, alright?"

"No." Her finger tightened over the trigger.

I glanced at the phone beside me. There was no way I

could call 9-1-1 before she popped five bullets into me. I wasn't sure if she would really kill me, but her hand hadn't shaken the whole time. And if she was crazy enough to come into my office and point a gun at me, who knew what else she was capable of. "Tell me what's going on."

"You don't need to worry about it."

Isabella didn't need money, so I doubted this was some kind of robbery. She was obviously trying to keep me in the office and away from the rest of the staff. She was cornering me away from the rest of the herd, but she didn't want to kill me. So what did she want?

And then it hit me.

"Rome." I jumped to my feet. "What the fuck are doing to her?" I moved around the desk, knowing Isabella was just a distraction. Someone else was getting to Rome while I sat on my ass at my desk. She was in far more danger than I was, even with a gun pointed at me.

Isabella maneuvered into my way and pointed the gun right at my heart. "Don't call my bluff, Calloway. I don't want to hurt you, but I certainly will." She shoved the gun into my chest, letting the metal strike me right in the muscle. "Now shut the hell up and sit down."

I eyed the door, trying to think of a way I could escape.

Isabella shook her head. "You're probably already too late, Calloway. No use being killed over it."

18

Rome

I had a packed schedule for the afternoon. I needed to head downtown to the mayor's office to discuss opening a new homeless shelter at the edge of Fifth and Broadway, and then I needed to go down to City Hall for approval. In addition to that, I still had a report to write, finish up a project with Chad, and I hadn't even touched my inbox.

Even though it was exhausting, I loved being busy.

I loved feeling like I was doing something.

My ass didn't hurt anymore because the inflammation had gone down, and the color returned to its normal fair tone. There was no evidence that Calloway had whipped me at all. Around the house, Calloway was a lot more affectionate than he usually was. The beast didn't come by for another visit. It was only the man.

I should compare him to Hank, but I never did. The situations were completely different. When Calloway understood he was really hurting me, pushing me to a boundary where I received no enjoyment, he didn't want to keep going. He didn't want to keep hurting me.

He wasn't a monster.

I grabbed my purse from under my desk and prepared to leave when a hand closed over my mouth. The palm pushed hard into my face while another arm wrapped around my chest and kept me still.

I screamed into his palm, but nothing came out but muffled noises.

I didn't need to see the man's face to know exactly who it was. He might be bigger and stronger, but I wasn't going to give up. I threw my arm back without having any idea where I was aiming and hit him right on the ear.

"Bitch." He contracted his hold and pinned my arms down.

I raised my legs and kicked against the desk, sending my chair flying back and directly into him.

He smacked into the other wall and momentarily released me.

I flew out of the chair and dashed to the phone, needing to call the police. I let out a scream at the same time, wanting my colleagues to hear me. There were a lot of men in the office, men strong enough to get Hank off me.

Hank punched me in the back of the head and sent me to the floor. "Plenty more where that came from." He dragged me to my feet and hooked his arm around my waist. "Make a commotion and see what happens." A barrel was pointed into the side of my stomach, an uncomfortable pinch from where the gun edged into my side. "Understand?"

I nodded because I couldn't speak. Now I was truly terrified. Calloway was in his office on the other side of the floor. Unless he happened to be in the break room or speaking to someone on the main floor, he would never know I was being taken.

"Good." He pushed me out of the office door and kept the gun hidden inside his jacket. "Make a sound, and I'm gonna shoot you right here." He pressed the gun farther into me. "And you can bleed out and die right here on the floor. So let's go."

He walked me down the hallway, keeping me close to his body as we passed the doors on either side. I was hoping to cross paths with someone from the office—anyone. But everyone was either at lunch or inside their offices.

My heart wouldn't stop racing.

Calloway wouldn't know I was missing until the end

of the workday when he noticed my purse still on my desk with my phone inside. He was smart and would put two and two together quickly, but I would be long gone by then.

Fuck.

Hank got me inside the elevator and hit the button for the lobby.

I stopped my body from shaking and tried to remain calm. The only way I was getting out of this was if I figured out a plan. I needed to find an escape route. I needed to do whatever it took to get away without getting a bullet inside me.

And I couldn't let Hank touch me.

The elevator ride to the bottom floor was quick, not buying me any time to figure out my next move. I'd hoped people would join us inside the elevator. Maybe I could have silently communicated to them that I was in danger, that I was being kidnapped.

But I didn't have any such luck.

The doors opened, and we walked through the lobby, passing workers dressed in suits and dresses. I tried to make eye contact with someone, but everyone was too busy on their phones.

No.

Hank got me through the door and pulled me to a black car up ahead. A driver was in the front seat, but the back was completely tinted. Hank got the back door open. "Get in."

I had no idea where he was taking me, but wherever it was, it wasn't good. Ignoring the gun, I remained on the sidewalk and tried not to hyperventilate. If I got into that car, I had a feeling I would never escape.

Hank pressed his lips to my ear. "You think I won't shoot you? Because I will. And I'll still fuck you anyway." He shoved me inside the car, and I fell across the backseat. He pushed my legs away then moved to the seat beside me.

The driver didn't wait for us to get our safety belts on. He immediately pulled away from the curb and joined the swarm of other cars stuck in Manhattan traffic. Hank rested his arm on his leg with the gun still trained on me.

Shit, what was I going to do?

C alloway

Isabella kept her gun trained on me as she glanced at her phone. She was obviously waiting for some kind of signal that whatever plan was set in motion had officially come to an end.

I couldn't sit here any longer, not when Rome was in danger. I had no idea how Isabella constructed this ridiculous plan or how she convinced anyone to help her, but I had to put an end to it now. "Isabella, you don't want to do this."

"You have no idea what I want."

"Making Rome go away isn't going to get me back." I had to keep my voice steady, even though I was terrified inside. I wasn't scared of being shot. I was scared of something terrible happening to the woman I loved.

"She ruined everything. She ruined us."

"We were going to end eventually anyway."

"You don't know that." The gun began to shake, tears bubbling in her eyes.

"I do know that. And it had nothing to do with you, Isabella. There's nothing wrong with you." I slowly rose to a stand, my hands raised. "You're perfect just the way you are. It was nothing personal."

The gun shook harder. "Sit down."

"No." I held my ground. "You aren't going to shoot me." I slowly walked around the desk, my eyes trained on her the entire time.

"You bet your ass, I will."

"No, you won't. You wanna know why?" I made it around the desk, and I was still in one piece. "Because you love me, Isabella. Would you really shoot the man you love?" That was a cheap shot, but I didn't have time to be noble. Every moment I was still in that office was putting Rome's life further in danger.

Isabella used her other hand to hold the gun up, the weight of her decision suddenly growing heavy. Tears emerged from the corners of her eyes, small and reflective of the fluorescent lights. "I can't have you, so it doesn't matter."

"Isabella, we can always be friends. When we were together, I cared a great deal about you. If anyone ever hurt you, I would have killed them. If anyone caused you any pain, they'd be done for. Maybe I didn't love you the way I love Rome, but you still meant something to me."

"Liar…"

"I'm not lying." I took a step closer. "You need to let me go. Rome doesn't deserve this."

"Stop moving!"

"Isabella—"

She pulled the trigger.

Being shot didn't feel the way I thought it would. It happened so quickly that I could barely process the pain. The bullet pierced my stomach, and the blood soaked my shirt instantly. My hand went to the wound because I couldn't believe this was real.

She fucking shot me.

"No!" Isabella cupped her face and dropped the gun onto the floor. "Oh my god! I didn't mean to."

I suddenly felt weak, so I fell to my knees on the floor, my hand soaked in my own blood.

"It was an accident." She got my jacket off and unbuttoned my shirt quickly, not that it would do anything. "I'll call an ambulance." She snatched the phone from my desk and a pair of scissors. Quickly, she cut a long sleeve of fabric from my suit jacket and tied it around the wound.

"No ambulance." I swatted the phone out of her hand, my pulse noticeably quicker in my ears. My lungs ached for more air because my brain wasn't getting enough.

"Calloway!"

"I need to find Rome. Where is she, Isabella? Who took her?"

She grabbed the phone again. "I need to call an ambulance. You'll bleed out and die if we don't get you help."

I snatched the phone back. "If something happens to Rome, I'm dead anyway. Now tell me, Isabella. And make it quick."

Isabella knew me well enough to know I wasn't kidding. I was intent on saving Rome, not myself. "It was Hank."

"Hank?" How the fuck did they know each other?

"Jackson told me about him, so I went to his office and we worked out a deal. He would take Rome away… and I would have you."

I could kill her.

I could fucking kill her.

"Tell me where he took her, Isabella. I'll forgive you for shooting me if you just give me this answer."

Isabella hesitated, her hands still pressed over the fabric around my wound.

I grabbed her by the elbow and yanked on her hard. "Tell me now. If you love me, you'll do this for me."

The tears streaked down her face as she began to sob. "Okay…okay."

R ome
We were just about to leave the city and head to Connecticut. Whatever his plans were, he didn't want anyone around to witness them. Country fields and large stretches of grass meant it would be easy to hide a body.

Really easy.

I had to escape now. The car was driving over fifty miles an hour, but I had to do something. If I rolled onto the street and got hit by a car, I'd probably die. But at least I wouldn't have to be subjected to his torture.

He was just going to kill me anyway. I was the only witness to his crime. If I stayed alive, I could testify to everything he did. I wasn't even a criminal, and I knew that was his only choice. He knew he couldn't have me the way he wanted me, but he was going to get some of me.

I grabbed the door and thrust into it with my shoulder.

It didn't budge.

Hank grinned from his side of the car. "Child safety locks are great, aren't they?"

Fuck.

"You'd really rather die from rolling out of a car than entertain my fantasies?" He scoffed. "You need to straighten out your priorities. I knew how much you used to love sucking my cock."

I couldn't believe I ever kissed that man—and liked it.

"How about we get started now?" He undid his safety belt and scooted to my side of the car.

I tried not to throw up. "Don't fucking touch me."

"Like this?" He gripped my thigh just below my dress. "How about this?" He moved his hand between my legs and touched the outside of my panties. He gripped the fabric in his hand and tugged.

I pushed him hard. "No."

He bounced back and grabbed my panties again. He pulled until they came apart, ripping right in half. He pulled them to his face and gave a hard sniff. "Incredible."

I couldn't believe this was happening.

This was my worst nightmare playing out right before my eyes.

I actually wanted to cry, but I didn't dare allow it. Hank would only like that more.

He moved his hand back between my legs until he found my entrance.

I squeezed my legs tightly together then punched him hard in the nose.

He faltered back, his eyes smarting as his nerve endings fired off. He fell to the floor with his legs still on the back seat.

This was about survival, and I didn't care what I had to do to get out of there in one piece. I raised my heel then slammed it down right into his gut.

"Fuck." He shoved my leg off and quickly straightened himself because he anticipated another hit.

I raised my other foot and aimed right at his face.

He snatched my ankle then grabbed me by the hair, yanking me down onto the leather cushion. He pulled a rope from under the seat then bound my wrists together.

"Let go of me!" The only person who could tie me up was Calloway. When anyone else did it, it was absolutely terrifying—especially when it was Hank.

"The only reason why I'm not gonna fuck you right now is because I wanna see all of you. I want those tits and ass in my face. But once we get into the house, you're done for." He sat on my legs and kept me still, my hands tied behind my back. "And yes, I'm gonna kill you when I'm finished."

The country house was in the middle of nowhere. It was a two-story white house with blue shutters and a blue door. A large willow tree was outside, along with a wraparound porch. The lawn was well taken care of, and flowers blossomed in the garden.

What the hell was this place?

Hank pushed me forward, guiding me by gripping the rope that bound my hands together. "You like it? This is my vacation home. Do a lot of fishing and fucking during my time off." He got the door unlocked and shoved me inside.

The driver pulled away from the house and got back on the road.

Now I really had no way out. There had to be a car here, but it must be in the garage. And I had no idea where that was. I immediately searched the room for something I could use against him, but since my hands were tied behind my back, I didn't have a lot of options. If only there were a hearth with a roaring fire, I could kick him into it.

"Up." He pushed me toward the stairs. "Come on." He was already unbuttoning his shirt and loosening his tie.

There was no way in hell I was cooperating. My heels were gone, but I tried to kick him anyway, aiming between his legs so I could make the blow really count.

He must have been expecting me to pull that stunt because he caught my leg and yanked on me, causing me to slip and fall on the bottom stair. I hit my head on the wood and tensed at the pain. I wanted to groan, but I wouldn't allow myself to do that. Whatever Hank was about to do to me was far worse than getting a bump on the head.

"You don't wanna walk?" Hank stood over me then scooped me into his arms. "That's fine. I'll carry you."

I knew my fate was inevitable, and I wanted to give up. I could just tune my mind out and slip away. It would be easier for me to forget the terrible things he was about to do to my body. But that would be a disgrace to Calloway. If he could talk to me, he would tell me to fight until Hank killed me.

So I had to fight.

I squirmed in his hold and try to knock him backward. With that kind of fall, he was certain to be injured enough for me to get away.

Hank was too strong. He held me closer against his chest and didn't let my feet touch the opposite wall.

"Fight all you want. It's just more of a turn-on." He leaned in to kiss me.

I spat in his face, making a stream of saliva drip down his cheek.

That pissed him off. He got to the top landing and carried me into the first bedroom that was available. "I was gonna shoot you right between the eyes and give you a quick death. But you know what? Fuck that." He threw me on the bed facedown. "Maybe I'll drown you instead."

I thrust my hips so I could roll off the bed, but he shoved his hand against my lower back, keeping me in place. His hand dragged the zipper at the top of my dress and yanked it down just above my ass.

I felt the panic start in my gut.

I was terrified.

I wanted to give in.

He yanked the dress off until I was just in my bra, my lower body completely vulnerable to his eyes. "Wow... look at that ass." He climbed on top of me and kissed my spine, moving up until he reached my bra.

I closed my eyes even though that wouldn't help anything. The reality of the situation wouldn't stop even if I tried to shut it out. This was really happening. This fiend was licking my skin and kissing it like he owned it.

Scum.

He moved down, over my ass, and then to the folds

between my legs. His tongue lapped at the area, kissing my clit and then sucking it.

I was repulsed, broken. The tears came to the surface of my eyes even though I tried to fight them. After everything I did to help other people, this was how I met my end. I would be raped and then murdered.

I wished Calloway would come to save me.

But I knew I was on my own. He would have no way of figuring out where Hank took me. And even if he did, by the time he figured it out, I'd already be dead.

Hank dropped his pants and boxers then crawled on top of me, his hard dick pressed between my ass cheeks. His arms were positioned on either side of me, and his heavy breaths fell on the back of my neck. "Fuck, I've been waiting for this for a long time." He ground his cock against my ass, a drop of moisture leaking from the head then smearing against my skin.

No, this couldn't be real.

"I've gotta make up for our lost time, sweetheart."

"Don't call me that," I hissed. Only one man called me that.

"Hit a nerve, huh?" He moved his lips to my ear and kissed the shell. "I'll call you sweetheart all I want. For the next twenty-four hours, you're mine. I'm gonna ruin this pussy and this asshole. Make that bitch think twice before slapping me." He grabbed the base of his cock and shoved his head into my entrance.

"Stop!" I lost all sense of calm when I felt him push inside me. "Hank, don't do this. Think about what you're doing right now."

"Oh, I am." He pushed harder.

I felt him slide into me, making my pussy clench hard to keep him out. My body immediately knew his dick didn't belong there. Only Calloway did. I felt the black diamond sit on my right hand, the promise Calloway and I made to one another. It was the only thing that gave me comfort in the most painful moment of my life.

"Get. Off. Her."

I would recognize that voice anywhere. I heard it in my dreams, heard it in my thoughts. I turned to the right and saw Calloway standing there in his suit, red stains all across his white collared shirt. He held a gun, and it was pointed right at Hank. "Calloway..." I gripped the sheets underneath me and nearly burst into tears at the sight of him. I didn't know how he got there, and I didn't care. He was my savior.

Hank tensed on top of me, his cock still hard and pressed against my ass. He suddenly grabbed me by the neck and rolled over, covering his body with mine so Calloway couldn't shoot him. "Leave, or I'll snap her neck."

"Let her go, and I'll let you leave." Calloway stepped

forward with the gun still pointed at Hank. "This offer will expire in five seconds."

Hank stared him down, his hand still tight on my neck. Most of his body was blocked by mine, so there was no way Calloway could get a good shot without risking my safety. "I suggest you—"

Calloway pulled the trigger and hit Hank on the side of the skull. Blood sprayed across the bedding and my skin, his skin and tissues sticking to everything.

Hank immediately went limp and fell back, his body collapsing onto the bed. His arm fell forward, releasing me from my hold.

That was when I started to sob. I couldn't hold it in any longer. I scooted out of the way to get as far away from Hank as I could. When he was alive, he was repulsive. But when he was dead, he was even more grotesque. "Oh my god…"

"Sweetheart, it's okay." Calloway came to the foot of the bed and pulled me into his arms, leaving the gun on the corner of the mattress. "I'm here. He can't hurt you anymore." He wrapped his arms around me, but he didn't hug me nearly as tightly as he should.

That's when I felt the blood from his shirt.

"Calloway…?"

I looked down and saw the bloodstains all over his clothes. He'd had those before he even walked through the door, long before he caught up to Hank and me. "Is this yours...?"

He nodded weakly, his jaw tense. "Isabella...she shot me." He suddenly breathed deeply, like he was slipping away.

"Oh god. Why didn't you go to a hospital?"

His eyes started to become lidded and heavy. "Because...I had to save you." He fell back and closed his eyes, his body growing limp.

"Calloway!" I shook him.

No response.

No, this couldn't be happening.

I stuck my hand in his pockets and pulled out his phone, but I dropped it on the ground because I was shaking so much. I finally got it in my hands again and called the first number that came to mind, 9-1-1.

My hand went to Calloway's neck as I stayed on the line, feeling a distant pulse grow weaker and weaker. "Calloway, stay with me. Please stay with me." Through my tears, I managed to talk to the operator and have them pinpoint my address.

And they were there in three minutes.

"Rome." Christopher found me in the waiting room and

took the seat beside me. His hand automatically went to mine. "Rome?"

I was in shock, my heart beating so fast and so slow at the same time. I was caked in blood, Calloway's and Hank's. I'd put my dress back on but felt disgusting wearing it since Hank had removed it in the first place. I'd cried so much that my body couldn't handle it anymore. Now I'd hit rock bottom, feeling absolutely nothing but pure despair.

"Where's Calloway?" Christopher had never held my hand once in our lifetime. It was a rare occasion to get a hug from him. I wasn't sure why he was even down here. I hadn't called him.

"He's in surgery." I got here four hours ago. I rode in the ambulance while the medics did everything they could to keep him alive. I had no other transportation since I'd been taken out there like a captive. Once we were in the hospital, I was pushed off to the side and told I would be given an update when they had one.

So far, I hadn't heard anything.

"What...?" Christopher's eyes narrowed as he squeezed my hand. "What happened? I got a call from Jackson that Hank had taken you... I didn't realize Calloway had been hurt."

That meant Jackson didn't know. I should probably tell him. "I don't really know what happened. He said Isabella shot him...then he passed out. I have no idea why he was with her or what they were doing…then he came to save me." He could have taken himself to the hospital and told the cops where I'd been taken hostage, but he didn't do that.

He risked his life to save mine.

Christopher squeezed my hand again. "I'm sure he'll pull through. This is a great hospital, and he's a strong guy. He can handle it."

I wanted to cry, but I couldn't. I'd already shed all my tears over the past few hours. "If he doesn't make it…"

"He will," he said firmly. "That guy loves you too much to die. Just remember that."

"I hope you're right, Christopher…" I pulled my hand away and set it on my lap. My fingers interlocked together, and the despair crept further into my veins. When it reached my heart, I sighed and felt my eyes water. "I should call Jackson. It slipped my mind…"

"I'll call him. Don't worry about it."

"Okay…"

Christopher patted my thigh before he pulled out his phone and walked away.

I closed my eyes and rested my face in my lap, wanting the darkness my own body provided. Calloway had a deadly wound that was complicated even to a skilled surgeon. Not even the strongest man could combat that. He lost a lot of blood on the drive from

New York to Connecticut. I wasn't even sure how he'd lasted that long.

Another four hours passed until I finally got some news. Calloway had pulled through the surgery without any complications. Now he was resting in ICU. As soon as the doctor said those words, I fell to my knees and sobbed.

Christopher thanked the doctor then kneeled beside me. "I told you he was gonna be okay."

As relieved as I was, I was still terrified. I was terrified this happened at all, that I nearly lost the love of my life. My fingertips became pruned with my own tears because I'd been crying so much over the last four hours.

Christopher was patient with me, but after five minutes, he helped me to my feet. "Let's go see him, huh?"

I nodded and wiped my tears away.

"Any news?" Jackson came from the opposite side of the room where he'd been sitting alone. His mood was dark, just the way Calloway's was from time to time. His jaw was clenched so tightly I could hear his teeth ground together.

Christopher did the talking. "He pulled through. He's

in ICU."

"Thank fucking god." Jackson stepped back with his hands on his hips, his head bowed. He released a loud sigh before he pinched the bridge of his nose. "I was gonna kill him if he died."

"Let's go." Christopher led the way through the hospital until we arrived in ICU. Their visitor rules said only one person could be with Calloway at a time, to reduce the risk of infection. I washed my hands then stepped inside the room. Jackson didn't try to fight me on it. He could have played the family card and won, but he didn't.

When I walked inside, Calloway was lying on his back in the small bed. His feet reached the very end, and he looked too big for the average-size bed. A large tube was down his throat, and a machine breathed for him. An IV was in his arm, along with other tubes and wires.

I hated seeing him like this.

I took the seat at his bedside and refrained from touching him. His gown covered the wound in his stomach. I imagined it stitched up, with a bandage wrapped around his body. He didn't seem as big as he usually was, like he'd lost too much blood. His face was paler than usual too.

He looked so different.

"I'm here..." My hand slid across the bed until I touched his fingers. "If you can hear me...I'm here."

Calloway

The first thing I heard was the sound of the monitor.

Beep. Beep. Beep.

It sounded like a heart rate monitor.

A second later, I felt the blood pressure cuff tighten on my arm until it was uncomfortable.

That's when everything came back to me. I had been barely holding on to consciousness when I pulled the trigger and killed Hank. The only thing that kept me moving was the adrenaline that gave my body the final push to finish my mission.

Save my girl.

I knew when I chose to go after her instead of going to the hospital, I was seriously risking my life. There was a good chance I would have bled out and died before I even got there. But if I went to the hospital and survived, and she didn't...I would have died anyway.

I must be in a hospital.

That must mean Rome got me here. And my gut feeling told me she would be sitting right beside me when I opened my eyes.

I was right. Her face was the very first thing I looked at. With an exhausted expression and the same clothes I'd last seen her in, she was sitting in the chair at my bedside. Her eyes were sunken in, and she looked just as weak as I felt. Her eyes were glued to my hand, where her fingers were interlocked with mine. She didn't notice my stare.

"Sweetheart..."

Her eyes immediately darted to my face, and right on cue, the tears started. "Calloway..." She rushed to stand up and moved to wrap her arms around me, but she suddenly jerked back, taking her affection away. "I shouldn't touch you..." She eyed my abdomen.

"No, I need you to touch me." I wrapped one arm around her waist and brought her against my chest. I didn't hug her the way I wanted because of the IV in my other arm. But I could still feel her warmth, smell her hair, and savor the feeling of my woman in my arms.

She cried into my shoulder, her tears soaking

through the gown and to my bare skin. "Calloway...I was so scared."

"I'm okay. We're okay."

"You could have died, Calloway."

"So be it." When I saw Hank on top of her, about to take something that didn't belong to him, I knew I'd made the right decision. If I'd gotten there just a minute later, he would have raped her.

Raped my woman.

I'd die before I let that happen.

She pulled away, looking at me with reflective tears. "I can't believe you did that..."

"You're the most important thing in my life, sweetheart. You know that."

"I know...you always show it."

I moved my hand to her cheek and touched her smooth skin. She felt warm to my touch, and I wiped away a fallen tear with the pad of my thumb.

"What happened? I still don't understand."

I told her Isabella's role in the kidnapping.

"I can't believe her—and she shot you!"

"She said it was an accident."

"Bullshit," she hissed. "We're putting her away for life, Calloway."

I wasn't eager to turn her over to the police. "If she hadn't shot me, she wouldn't have told me where to find you."

"How so?"

"She felt so guilty for what she did that she told me everything...it was necessary."

She ran her hands up my arm, feeling my skin like she hadn't touched me in years. "I can't believe all of this happened. I went to work that morning like it was a normal day."

"I know. But at least it's over. Hank is dead."

"Yeah...he's dead." She nodded before a small smile stretched on her lips. "He's gone."

I loved seeing that relief on her face. Now she could live her life without looking over her shoulder anymore. She deserved that freedom. "I just hope you continue to live with me even though you don't need my protection anymore."

"I'll always need your protection, Calloway. You're the only man I'll allow to protect me."

Those words meant the world to me. She'd submitted to me in more ways than one, and now she was officially mine. I possessed her in every way possible. She'd given herself to me in every capacity. "I'll protect you with my life—for the rest of my life."

I was stuck at the hospital for five days before they finally discharged me.

For five days, I couldn't get naked with my woman. I couldn't fuck my woman. I had to lie in a bed while she sat in a chair.

Couldn't handle that shit much longer.

I wouldn't allow myself to be pushed in a wheelchair, and I walked myself out in new clothes Jackson picked up for me. My hand was held tightly in Rome's as we made it to the car, and Tom drove us home.

It was nice to be back at the house. It smelled like Rome and me combined together. My shoes were by the door exactly where I left them, and my hoodie was on the coatrack from the last time I went for a jog.

It felt so good to be back.

"Wanna take a seat?" Rome asked, the concern in her voice.

"I'm okay." Actually, I did feel weak. This bullet wound would take some time to get better; that was obvious. I shouldn't put up a front when I didn't need to prove anything, but remaining strong for my woman was important.

Jackson walked in behind us and examined the house like he'd never been here before. "Looks the same as the last time I was here."

"Yeah, I didn't change much."

Rome guided me to the couch and gently pushed on my shoulders so I would sit down. "I'm gonna cook some dinner. You must be sick of hospital food."

"Yeah, I miss your cooking."

She smiled before she turned to Jackson. "Make him realize, okay?"

"I'm on it." He gave her a thumbs-up before she walked into the kitchen. "Got any scotch?"

"No drinking," Rome called from the kitchen.

"What?" Jackson asked as he sat beside me. "What's the point of being a hero and taking a bullet if you can't drink?"

"It's temporary." I sat back and cringed slightly as my core felt strained.

Jackson watched me. "Need anything? A pillow or something?"

"I'm fine," I answered.

Jackson grabbed the remote and turned on the TV. He found a basketball game and let it play in the background. My brother and I hadn't talked much since I'd been shot. He'd visited me at the hospital, but we didn't get much time together because Rome wanted to be at my side nearly all the time. "Glad you're alright, man."

"I know."

"I'm sorry about Isabella. Never should have mentioned Hank."

It was a stupid thing to do, and I had every right to be pissed at him. "You weren't being malicious, so don't worry about it."

"I had no idea she would get that psycho."

"Sometimes you never know…"

"I can handle Ruin while you recover."

"You mean, run it into the ground?" I teased.

"No," he said with a laugh. "I'll do good this time."

Rome came into the living room and handed us both glasses of water.

Jackson eyed the glass like he didn't know what it was. "Please tell me this is vodka."

She tapped him on the nose then walked back into the kitchen.

"She's something, huh?" he asked before he took a drink of his water.

"Yeah…she's pretty great."

"What are you going to do about Hank?"

Hank was dead, and I'd confessed to the police that I was the one who shot him. They interviewed me at the hospital and conducted an investigation at my office. Rome had lots of evidence to prove that he'd been stalking her for some time, and Christopher corroborated her story. I wasn't sure what was gonna happen with that, but I wasn't worried about it. "I don't know. He's dead, and that's all I care about."

"Yeah, that guy is rotting in hell now."

"I hope so." I'd never forget what I saw when I walked through that door. His cock was pressed against her, and she was on the verge of tears. He should be grateful I gave him a quick death. If I'd had more time, I would have tortured him.

Jackson moved his hand to my shoulder and gave me a gentle pat. The affection was awkward since Jackson didn't have a heart. "I love you, man. I know that's a pussy thing to say, but I never say it. And...I was pretty scared I was gonna lose you. You're my big brother...all I have left."

I patted him on the shoulder in return. "I love you too, man. I'm gonna be around for a long time, so expect to be picked on for a few more decades."

He chuckled. "I look forward to it."

I turned back to the TV, feeling a new connection to Jackson that wasn't there before. We spent a lot of time together because of Ruin, but we didn't have serious conversations too often. We pretended to hardly even like each other. It was just one bullshit talk after the next. But now it seemed real.

"Have you seen Mom lately?" he asked.

I shook my head. "No. Not since that day we were all there together."

Jackson sighed. "Too difficult?"

Rome and I were both disheartened when my mother showed no improvement. We both started to believe that there was no hope, that it was all just depressive torture. But I knew I couldn't abandon my mother like that. "We'll go back. We just needed a break. What about you?"

He shrugged then drank his water.

I couldn't tell Jackson what to do in this matter. He should be there for our mother, but I also understood how difficult it was. To have the same conversation with your mother and see the emptiness in her eyes was heartbreaking. If she knew who I was, I knew she would wrap her arms around me and never let go. I remembered the way our mother loved both of us. She was a great mom, always doing her best to give us what we needed. What happened to her wasn't fair—at all.

I didn't go to work for the next two weeks. The doctor said I needed ample time to recover. I had a serious wound, and while it was healing properly with no signs of infection, it was best to take it easy.

Rome didn't go to in to work either, working from home instead and sticking to my side like a sexy nurse who gave me sponge baths. She did a good job of taking care of me, but sometimes the sadness would creep into her features. She did her best to hide it, but when her lips pressed tightly together and her eyes crinkled, I knew exactly what she was thinking about.

By the end of the first week, I was finally able to take

a shower. After being deprived of such a regular luxury, I realized how much I took it for granted. I stepped under the water and closed my eyes as the comfort washed over me.

Rome joined me, constantly terrified I would slip and fall or I would be too weak to hold myself up.

The bandage and wrap still covered the injury in my lower abdomen. To make sure it stayed clean, Rome and I had to change it every morning. With every passing day, the wound improved. The purple color faded, and the scar tissue began to form. It wasn't a pretty sight, but at least I'd survived the ordeal.

Rome looked unbelievable sexy under the water. Her tits were firm and her nipples were hard. Her slender waistline led to beautiful legs that I loved having wrapped around my waist. Her hair was slicked back down her neck and past her shoulders.

I hadn't made a move because I knew it would be inappropriate. Hank hadn't been successful, but what he put her through was scarring. Unless I was absolutely certain she was ready to be physical, I wasn't going to do anything. The most I ever did was kiss her, and even that was PG-13. I was in no shape for rough sex, but I'd certainly like some action.

Once my thoughts wandered, I became hard. My cock sprang to life and extended outward, the running water washing away the drop of pre-come that formed on the tip of my cock. There was nothing I could do about my body's reaction to her naked body, so I didn't feel guilty. I was only a man, after all.

She squirted shampoo into her hand then wrapped her fingers around my length.

The second she touched me, my cock twitched. It pushed back into her palm, wanting more of her soft hand around its length.

She moved closer to me, her lips just inches from mine.

I naturally shifted my hips, moving my length through her fingers. I wanted to come all over her tits and watch it drip down to her stomach. But my arousal was only in charge for so long. The guilt and concern emerged a moment later. If this were another woman, I wouldn't care. But since this was Rome, it made all the difference in the world. I grabbed her wrist and steadied my hand even though I was desperate for her friction. "You don't have to do anything you don't want to do." I held her gaze with mine, seeing the beautiful green eyes that made me weak in the knees.

"But I do want to." She moved her hand up and down and brushed my head with her thumb.

My cock twitched again, wishing her hand was her warm pussy. "You've been through a lot, Rome." She didn't need to do this for me. I had been shot, but she experienced something far worse. My wound would close, and I would move on with my life. But the kinds of memories she had never faded away. It was why she still had nightmares.

"I don't think about him when I'm with you. When I touch you, I feel safe. When I kiss you, I feel happy. When I make love to you...it feels wonderful." She moved her hand up and down my length. "So don't worry about that, Calloway. I touch you because I want to touch you." She moved into me and rose on her tiptoes so she could press her mouth to mine. Her lips slowly kissed mine before she gave me her small tongue. I immediately fell into the moment, and my hand moved to her tit. I gripped it firmly and let my thumb flick across her nipple.

I could already tell my orgasm was going to be phenomenal.

My other hand moved between her legs, and I felt that sexy clit I hadn't tasted in so long.

She moaned into my mouth and jerked me harder, constricting her fingers around my length and giving me a good rubdown.

It was a step down from sex, but I would gladly take it. It felt good to touch each other like this, to get each other off and satisfy our desires. I wanted to make love to my woman and feel her come around my dick, but I would still be able to feel her orgasm with my fingers inside her pussy.

She continued to kiss me and moaned into my mouth, her hand still jerking my length.

I wasn't going to last long, and I was relieved I didn't have to. After over a week with no sex, I could come just from watching Rome suck my finger. I rubbed her clit harder and panted into her mouth, feeling my cock thicken in her hand. I looked at her tits and imagined my come landing on the swell of that gorgeous skin.

"Fuck."

Rome jerked me into the finish line, giving me the final pumps I needed to come with a groan.

I shot up on her tits and shoved my fingers deep inside her, imagining feeling that pussy with my dick instead of my fingers. The orgasm rocked through me and almost made me weak because it felt so good. I sprayed an impressive load on those gorgeous tits, enough that my ego inflated even more.

I kept my mouth pressed to hers, but I couldn't kiss her. I recovered from the overwhelming sensation that swept through my body. Rome was the only woman who could make me come like that just by using her hand.

Now I had to return the favor. I worked her clit with my thumb and pulsed my fingers deep inside her. My mouth started to work again, so I kissed her the way she liked, nice and slow. My tongue danced with hers, and I felt her sticky tits press against my chest.

Damn, I loved this woman.

I worked her clit harder when I felt her breathing hitch. Sometimes she stopped kissing me altogether as she gripped my arms for balance. She panted and moaned, her nails digging into me as she enjoyed everything I was doing to her.

The only thing I loved more than coming myself was watching her come.

She hit her threshold, and her pussy clenched around my fingers, her voice rising a few octaves as she screamed in the shower. Her cries were amplified by the tile like a speaker system had been installed in the shower. Her lips trembled against mine as she finished, her screams fading away to quiet whimpers.

I kept my fingers inside her because I loved how wet she was. I was the reason she was soaked—no one else. Honestly, that made me feel like a king.

She always made me feel like a king.

After staying home for three weeks, I was finally cleared to return to work.

Thank god. I was sick of sitting on my ass all the time.

We got ready for work like usual and walked outside where Tom was waiting for us. Rome eyed the car then glanced at the sidewalk, her bag over her shoulder and her stilettos on her feet.

"What is it, sweetheart?" Maybe she didn't think I was ready to return to work. If that was the case, I would have to override her with my doctor's note. If I sat around and did nothing any longer, I would turn into a huge pain in the ass.

"I think I'm gonna walk today." She eyed the sidewalk before she turned back to me, a slight smile on her face. "Alone."

It only took me a second to understand her motives. Now that Hank was gone, she felt independent again. She could walk up the street without worry of him getting in her way. She didn't have to look over her shoulder in fear anymore. She didn't need me as her personal bodyguard.

She was finally free.

I would never take this moment away from her, even if I wasn't thrilled about the idea. Hank was no longer a problem, but anything else could happen. She was a beautiful woman in a huge city full of criminals. But I held my tongue because being supportive was more important right now. "I'll meet you there." I wrapped my arm around her and gave her a quick kiss on the lips.

She moved her lips to my ear. "Thank you."

"My woman can have whatever she wants."

R ome
I tried to stay in my office and get my work done, but my mind kept wandering to Calloway. The doctor cleared him for work and other activities, but I still worried about him. He still wore the gauze around his midsection because he hadn't officially healed all the way, so I always feared the worst.

By midday, I needed to see him. I needed to see that his skin was still tinted with a slight blush of red, and his flesh wasn't turning white with illness. I needed to know he wasn't in pain even though the doctor weaned him off the painkillers he'd prescribed. This man was my world, and I needed to know he was perfectly okay.

I didn't check in with his assistant and just walked inside exactly the way he told me to. He was behind his desk talking on the phone, looking healthy and vibrant. I knew this was the place where he'd been shot, but I didn't spot any signs of violence. The hardwood floor looked as good as new, as well as the rest of the furniture in the office.

Calloway acknowledged me with a nod before he hung up the phone. "Hey, sweetheart. Need something?" He sat back in his chair, looking like a president with his crisp suit and tie.

"Just wanted to check on you."

He propped his elbow on the armrest and rested his fingertips over his mouth. He looked sexy no matter what he did, but he looked particularly sexy with a freshly shaven jaw and a haircut. With the new energy and life that had entered his body, he looked like a brand-new man. I loved this version of him, not the weak one that struggled to combat the pain every single day. "I'm doing great, sweetheart. You really don't need to worry."

"I'll always worry." I sat on the edge of his desk and let my legs hang over the floor.

"The doctor said he's taking the stitches out tomorrow. I'll be back to new. And I'm sure you can guess exactly what I want once that time comes." He gave me a charming wink, his arrogance cute rather than obnoxious.

"That sounds nice."

"We'll go somewhere nice for dinner, and then we'll spend the night in bed together."

"Depends," I said. "Who am I having this dinner with?" I hadn't seen the beast in a long time, so I suspected he was on the mend. After my ordeal with Hank, I didn't think I wanted to see the beast for a while. But when I remembered that Calloway was still the man underneath, I knew I could handle it.

"Me," he said quietly. "Just me."

"You know, the beast can come back—"

"He's not interested in coming back for a while. So let's not worry about it." His eyes darkened in anger, reliving the nightmare behind the privacy of his eyes. After what he witnessed, he probably didn't want to go down that road for a while.

That was fine with me. "Okay."

"As much as I would love to sit here and talk with you, I should get back to work. I haven't even made a dent in my inbox yet."

"I should get back to work too." I slipped off the desk even though I ached to be close to him. Over the past few weeks, all I'd been doing was tending to him around the clock, but even a few minutes apart was too much for me.

"We'll be home in a few hours." He left his chair and walked around the desk until he was in front of me. His arms circled my waist, and he pressed his forehead to mine. Instead of a kiss, we shared something far deeper. "I love you, sweetheart."

I loved it when he called me by something so sweet. It contrasted against the fierce way he spanked me and bossed me around. That was how I knew it was true, that his affection was sincere. "I love you too, Calloway."

He kissed my cheek the way a husband kissed his wife. "I'll see you later."

The doctor removed Calloway's stitches and sent us on our way. There was prominent scarring in the area, but most of his muscle remained intact. Various lines in his flesh were now permanent, and he didn't have the flawless skin that he once possessed.

But he was still beautiful.

We went home and changed for dinner then arrived at the restaurant Calloway selected. It was a fancy French bistro right in the middle of the vibrant life of Manhattan. The place usually possessed a six-month waiting list, but Calloway somehow managed to get us in with just a few hours of notice.

We took our seats in a private booth near the window and ordered our drinks and appetizers. Calloway had had a new suit delivered to the house for the occasion. It was midnight black with a beautiful custom fit. It was tight on his impressive shoulders and stretched across the prominent muscles of his back.

He looked delicious.

He hadn't shaved since that morning, so his five-o'clock shadow was coming in strong. The stubble contrasted against the fair skin of his jaw, giving him the features of a movie star. His blue eyes stood out against the dark colors he wore. He was a very handsome man.

And he was my man.

The black ring sat on his right hand, the dark band thick with the commitment he made to me. I loved imagining that ring on the other hand, giving our relationship a whole new meaning altogether.

I selected a scallop from the center plate and took a few bites.

Calloway did the same, his eyes glued to my face. "You look beautiful tonight."

"Thanks, Calloway." He was an honest man who only said things he meant. It wasn't just a line to manipulate me into doing what he wanted. That was why I took his compliments so easily, knowing they weren't meaningless. "That suit looks great on you."

"Everything looks great on me." He wore a slight smile. "But I look even better in nothing."

"I can attest to that." I sipped the wine he'd picked out, noting that it went well with the bread and the appetizers.

"You know what I think you look the sexiest in?"

"Hmm?" I swallowed, feeling the tension rise between us.

"In your panties and my t-shirt." He drank his wine as his eyes remained glued to mine. "You don't even need lingerie."

"That's good. Your shirts are a lot more comfortable."

He ripped off a piece of bread and dipped it in the olive oil in the center of the table. Then he brought it to my lips and fed it to me, his fingertips brushing against my mouth.

I took it one step further and sucked his fingertip into my mouth, brushing my tongue across the pad of his fingers. I slowly pulled them out of my mouth then kissed each one, adoring the man who changed my life.

He watched me with concentrated eyes, glued to the sight in front on him.

When I pulled his hand away, I wasn't sure how we were going to get through the rest of dinner. We hadn't made love in nearly a month because of his condition, and we were both anxious to be reunited. We fooled around in other ways to get off, but nothing compared to having that huge dick inside me.

Calloway took a deep breath, swallowing his anxiousness by taking a large drink of his wine and finishing his glass.

I wasn't sure why he wanted to go to dinner at all. If

we went home and fucked, that would have been fine by me.

Calloway searched for the waiter then turned his eyes back to mine. "I'm tempted to get the food to go."

"Not a bad idea."

"I wanted to have a date with you. I was trying to be romantic."

"Calloway, you're romantic every single day." He didn't need to take me to a fancy dinner to prove anything. He didn't need to do a damn thing to prove anything to me. Just a look from him was all I needed.

"Yeah?" he asked. "Didn't realize I was."

"You are." I ran my fingertips across his hand, feeling the prominent knuckles. They were mountains. This man was willing to give up his life to save mine. There was no greater sacrifice than that. I shouldn't be surprised because I would have done the same for him. That was real love. Maybe he needed to dominate me sometimes. Maybe he needed to punish me, to make me cry. He always made me come hard at the end, so the pain was irrelevant. Maybe our relationship wasn't traditional, but it was still beautiful. "Take me home."

Calloway's hand shot into the air immediately, and he waved the waiter over. "Check, please."

His large hands slipped off my heels one at a time, and then he got my dress off in one quick motion. Calloway was always eager to have me, but tonight, his hands shook with intense longing. Once he got me naked, he pushed me back onto the bed. My back hit the mattress, and I propped myself up on my elbows. I kept my thighs together and my knees bent, wanting to tease him until the final moment he was inside me.

He dropped his expensive jacket on the floor then undid the buttons of his shirt. One by one, he popped them open until the pristine white shirt came loose and revealed the violent scar on his lower abdomen.

I hated looking at it, not because it blemished his gorgeous appearance, but because it reminded me of that horrific day. My eyes moved to other parts of his body, his muscular chest and his powerful shoulders. He was over six feet of all man, the kind of man I would touch myself to if I were alone in my bedroom.

He dropped the shirt then moved to his slacks, taking forever so he could tease me in return. My nipples were hard, and my chest was flushed with heat. I couldn't stop biting my bottom lip because I was eager for this man.

He finally got his pants and boxers off, revealing a hard cock that was red at the top. The blood pumping into his dick made him thicker than I'd ever seen him.

The hair over his balls was trimmed, and he oozed from the tip.

I squeezed my thighs tighter.

He yanked off his shoes and socks until he was finally completely naked, ready for me to devour. He placed his knee on the bed, and his weight immediately made it sink in. Slowly, he moved on top of me until our naked bodies were pressed together.

My hands started at his stomach and slowly moved up his chest, my mouth already open in anticipation. My body had missed that throbbing dick inside me, missed that fullness that only he could provide. He made me so wet that I could take a cock as big as his.

He positioned his arms behind my knees and widened my legs, his lips just inches from mine. He kept his eyes on me, those dreamy eyes that could see right into my soul. He tilted his hips and pressed the head of his cock right against my entrance. His head became moistened from the pool of lubrication that emitted from my pussy.

"Jesus Christ." He breathed into my mouth as he slowly sank inside me.

I sucked his bottom lip as I felt him slide into me, inch after inch of pure man. "Calloway…"

He stopped when he was completely sheathed, his balls resting against my ass. "I jerked off today because I thought it would make me last longer...but fuck, it didn't help at all."

I cupped his face and breathed with him, feeling the waves of chemistry between us. "Fuck me a dozen times, and you'll be back to normal."

He groaned against my mouth as he began to rock into me. Sometimes he kissed me, and sometimes he fisted my hair. My ankles rubbed against his torso as he rocked into me, his thrusts becoming deeper and quicker.

There was nothing I loved more than making love to Calloway.

He looked into my eyes as he made love to me, treated me like I was the only woman that ever mattered. There was no one before me, and there would be no one after me. He grabbed my right hand and pinned it to the mattress, his fingers interlocked with mine.

"Calloway..." I wanted this to last forever because it felt so incredible. Three weeks of no sex was a trial for our relationship. Every time we had the urge, we had to do something else not to risk his stitches ripping. But now we could do exactly what we wanted.

"Sweetheart." He rocked into me on the bed as his lips moved to the corner of my mouth. He kissed me as his fingers played with my ring. Slowly, he pulled it off altogether.

I didn't ask what he was doing because I didn't really care. All I cared about was the connection between us in that moment, the way we moved together. I wanted to do this every night for the rest of my life.

Calloway grabbed my left hand and slipped the ring onto my left ring finger. He stopped rocking into me as he held my gaze.

I felt the ring with my thumb, noting how strange it felt on the opposite hand. I didn't know what he was doing, but once I saw the intensity of his gaze, everything hit me. I knew exactly what he was doing.

I knew exactly what was coming.

"Marry me." All he said were two simple words. He didn't ask me. He just commanded me, like he wasn't giving me the option to say no. "I don't want to go another day wasting our potential. I don't ever want to be with another woman. I want us to be together—and never be apart."

I stared into the face of the man I loved, knowing he'd meant something to me since the first day I saw him. I slapped him in that bar because I was furious. But once he asked me my name, the room turned silent. I'd felt the heat in my body when he asked for my name. When I saw him later at that dinner, I knew I couldn't let him go.

And now we were so much more.

Our relationship was a road of heartache, but we

overcame the bumps. We weren't exactly what I wanted, but I knew I wouldn't have it any other way. I'd only fallen in love one time—and that was with Calloway. I'd only been with one guy, but I didn't need to be with others to know I'd found the right one.

He was the one.

The tears burned in my eyes and quickly dripped down my face. I saw the same emotion in his eyes even if they didn't water. He knew what my answer was without waiting for me to give it. "There's no one else I'd rather spend my life with."

He kissed me as he rocked into me again, making love to me on the same bed where he took my virginity. Now we clung to each other in a different way than we did before, not just out of desperation, but out of love. "Mrs. Calloway Owens…I like it."

"I love it."

"I'm gonna call you that every day."

I grabbed his hips and pulled him farther into me. "You better."

Calloway

"You're engaged?" Jackson asked over the phone. "For real?"

"Yep." I sat in the same office chair I had since the day I opened Humanitarians United. I looked out the window and over the city, knowing this was the very office where I'd been shot. But no bullet was going to keep me from where I belonged. "I asked her last night."

"Wow…you're getting married."

"Yep."

"You know I'm happy for you. I just…I'm surprised. You made it sound like you were gonna wait awhile."

"Yeah, I was going to. Changed my mind…" My black ring still sat on my right hand, but once I was married, I intended to switch it over to my left hand. I didn't want to wear any other ring for the rest of my life. I may have worn it with Isabella, but it meant something completely different with Rome.

"Why?"

"Almost dying changes your perspective on things." I'd always been a selfish and stubborn man. If someone had told me I was going to let me myself bleed out and die to save a woman, I wouldn't have believed it. But Rome was special to me. She was my whole world. "I almost lost her to Hank...almost lost everything. I love her, I want to be with her, and that's all that matters."

"Yeah, I can understand that. Well, congrats."

"Thanks."

"When's the big day? Are you gonna do a huge wedding with every figurehead in New York?"

No. Not my style. "We'll do something small. Something private."

"I'm invited, right?"

"Shut the hell up." I rolled my eyes even though he couldn't see my face.

"So...does that mean I'm invited?"

"Yes, idiot."

"Oh, good. Because I was gonna come regardless."

I eyed my watch and knew I needed to get back to work. "I'll talk to you later, alright? I need to get back to work."

"More like fuck your fiancée in your office." He hung up.

I chuckled then returned the phone to the base. I got to work and focused on my emails, trying not to think about the beautiful woman down the hallway...who was going to be my wife.

Holy shit, I was going to have a wife.

If you'd said that to me a year ago, I wouldn't have believed it.

I was going to be someone's husband.

Damn.

A few minutes later, a light knock sounded on the door before Rome stepped inside. She looked just as beautiful as she did that morning. The ring I gave her sat on her left hand, a black diamond that made an unusual engagement ring. But it fit her—it fit us. "Hey." She tucked her hair behind her ear as she walked up to my desk.

"Hey." I looked her up and down, liking the curves of her body.

"So...this is hard for me to say, so I'm just gonna say it."

That was basically a death sentence. Was she reconsidering marrying me? Did I do something to push her away? Everything seemed perfect, so I had no idea what the problem was. "Okay..."

"My birth name is Lisa. I changed it the day I ran away."

Now that I knew what this was about, I stopped breathing. I knew she had a secret, something she'd never felt comfortable telling me about. But now she was coming clean—without my asking her to.

"The man who adopted Christopher and me was a pedophile. Adoption agencies usually have foolproof techniques to make sure kids are going to great homes, but this guy was too smart for that. When I was sixteen, he started making his moves. He would force me to lie down while he jerked off—"

"I don't want to know." I thought I was prepared for this information, but I would never be prepared for it. I had to walk in on a man trying to rape my woman. I couldn't handle any more of this bullshit. Now that she was mine, she would never have to worry about being treated like that again. "I'm sorry…I can't handle it."

"I understand," she said quietly. "Long story short, he wasn't a good guy. I ran away as soon as I turned eighteen and moved in to an apartment next to the university I'd secretly applied to. I didn't start class for a few months, but that's where I stayed—with Christopher. I changed my name, so my school application was updated. I knew he would try to find me, and changing my name was the only way to ensure my safety."

Now I needed his name—because I was going to kill him. "Has he bothered you ever since?"

"No. Haven't heard anything from him."

Maybe that asshole was already dead.

"So…that's the truth. The only reason why I didn't tell you was because I didn't want to talk about it. I wanted a fresh start. I didn't want to drag my past everywhere I went."

"It's okay, sweetheart." Now that I knew the truth, I felt like a jackass for sticking my nose where it didn't belong. "You don't need to discuss it anymore."

"Okay…I just want to forget about it."

"Absolutely."

"I prefer Rome. So please don't call me Lisa."

That was all I'd ever known her as. I liked her name. "I like it better anyway. What made you pick it?"

She shrugged. "I was eighteen at the time, full of hopes and dreams."

I nodded for her to continue.

"Historians say Rome was the greatest empire in the world. I guess I wanted to be strong like the greatest historical government. It's stupid…but that's what I was thinking."

"No, it's not stupid," I whispered. "It fits you perfectly."

A small smile came onto her lips. "Thanks…"

"Thank you for telling me."

"No secrets between spouses, right?" she asked.

I nodded. "No secrets."

"Well...I'll let you get back to work." She walked to the door, her hips swaying as she moved.

"Sweetheart?"

"Hmm?" She looked at me over her shoulder.

"When do you wanna marry me?"

The mention of the wedding made her smile brighter. "As soon as possible."

"Yeah?" I asked.

"Yeah."

"I was thinking something small, something intimate."

"Me too." She leaned against the door with her hair pulled over one shoulder.

"City Hall?"

She shook her head. "More personal than that."

"Where do you want to get married?"

"There's this church that I love on Fifth..."

I wasn't a big fan of churches, but I wouldn't deny the woman I loved what she wanted. "I'll make some calls."

"Really?" she whispered.

"Whatever you want, sweetheart."

She smiled wide, the love reaching her eyes. "I'm a very lucky woman."

She was the one who saved my life. I was the lucky

one. "I think we're both pretty lucky."

"Cheers." Christopher raised his wineglass, and we clinked our glasses together.

"Cheers." Jackson downed his scotch because he wasn't refined enough for wine.

"I'm happy for my sister." Christopher clinked his glass against hers. "She deserves the best, and I think Calloway is the best." He turned to me next. "Calloway... I think you're making a huge mistake, but I don't think you're gonna listen to my advice."

I chuckled. "Not a chance."

Christopher drank his wine before he set it down. "You're gonna have to tell me what you want for your wedding because I'm not good with gifts."

"You don't need to get us anything," Rome said. "The wedding will be tiny."

"Just the four of us," I said. "Next Saturday."

"What about Mom?" Jackson asked.

Christopher didn't know anything about my mom as far as I knew. I didn't want to discuss it in front of him, but he was bound to find out anyway. There was nothing to be embarrassed of. He'd had a hard life, just the way I did. "What do you mean?"

"Don't you want her there?" Jackson asked.

"I don't think she could handle that since she doesn't remember anything." Even if my mother could come and enjoy the day, she would never remember it. The next morning, it would be like it never happened.

"I think she should be there," Rome said. "I'm sure we can figure out a way to make it work. It would mean a lot to me if she was there."

I locked eyes with Rome, the woman who only wanted the best for me. She'd been by my side since the beginning, going to visit my mom even on days when I didn't want to be there. She was my rock—and she understood my pain.

"So, does this mean I'm the maid of honor?" Christopher asked as he cringed. "Because I'm not really the girly type."

"You just have to stand there," Rome said. "And not say something stupid."

Christopher laughed before he took a drink. "Can't promise anything, sis."

"I'm the best man, right?" Jackson asked.

"I wouldn't want it to be anyone else." I fist-bumped Jackson across the table.

He smiled and fist-bumped me back. "Thanks, man."

"I'm happy for you guys," Christopher said. "You guys have had your ups and downs...a lot of them. But I think this is gonna last forever. I can see that you really love each other. If you ask me, that's all you really need."

"Aw," Rome whispered. "That was sweet, Christopher."

He shrugged. "I'm a big softy. Don't tell anyone."

"We'll keep it between the four of us," I said. "No one else needs to know you're a pussy."

Rome turned her fiery gaze on me. "Calloway."

"Come on, he knows I'm kidding," I said. "We're brothers so I have to tease him."

"He's got a point, Rome," Christopher said. "And as brothers, it's my job to get him back. And I will."

I gave him a slight nod. "Bring it on, bro."

Rome walked inside with her wedding dress covered in a thick plastic bag that blocked my view.

I couldn't wait to see it—and then rip it off. "How'd it go?"

"The woman did some alterations, and now it fits perfectly." She opened the hallway closet and gently placed the dress inside.

"I'm sure it looks stunning on you." I walked to her in the entryway then circled my arms around her. Her hips were a perfect place to rest my arms as I held her petite waist.

"You'd say that if I were just in a thong."

"And I would mean it." I kissed her on the mouth and

felt the heat scorching through my veins. Even a simple kiss, a closed-mouth one, still got me hard. My hands moved to her ass, and I gripped her cheeks. I wanted to fuck her right against the wall, to claim her as my woman for the thousandth time.

Rome pressed her hands to my chest and stepped away. "I think we should wait until tomorrow."

What the hell was she talking about? "Wait for what?"

"You know, wait until after the wedding to have sex."

My eyes narrowed in displeasure.

"It'll make it more special."

"It'll already be special," I said with a growl.

"Come on, Calloway." She moved back into my chest and rested her forehead against mine.

We'd already screwed before marriage, so why did we have to wait now? But if it was important to her, I suppose I could wait one more day. "After we say I do, I'm in charge, alright?"

"Fine by me." She looked up at me, smiling now that she was getting her way.

"And that means lots of sex."

"I'm not gonna argue with you."

"Good. Because we both know you'd lose every argument." I kissed her again, and when the feel of her tongue made me harder, I pulled away. If I couldn't get any action, there was no point in torturing myself.

"So, do you want to go see your mom today?"

I knew it was going to come up at some point. "I don't know...probably just bum me out."

"I think she should be there."

"Even if I talked to her today and tell her who I am, she's not gonna remember tomorrow."

When Rome bowed her head, I knew she agreed with me. If my mother had other problems, we could make it work. But if she never remembered anything from the previous day, no progress would ever be made. "I'll stop by and see her before the wedding. It only takes me five minutes to get ready anyway."

"Yeah...that would be nice. I would go too but—"

"We shouldn't see each other before the wedding." I wasn't a traditional kind of guy, but I understood the basics. "Don't worry about it."

"Are you sure? We could see her afterward."

"I know exactly what I want to do after the wedding —and it's not visit my mother." I placed a kiss on her forehead and stepped away. "We're leaving for our honeymoon, and nothing is getting in the way of that."

Rome couldn't contain her excitement. She pressed her lips tightly together like she was trying to stop herself from letting out a scream. Her eyes were nearly double in size so that was a dead giveaway. "Drinks on the beach and visits to the spa..."

"And lots of lovemaking in our bungalow." I was

taking Rome to the Caribbean, where we would be staying in our private bungalow over the water. The privacy would allow me to stare at her tits while she swam in our own pool.

"It's gonna be amazing." She moved into my body and wrapped her arms around my waist. "I'm so excited."

"Me too." I wasn't just excited for the awesome trip we were about to take. I was excited that I was sharing my life with this incredible woman. When I was old and gray, I wouldn't have to sit on a balcony alone and stare out into the gardens. I would be surrounded by my wife and kids—my world.

Calloway

I walked onto the patio in my suit and tie. My shoes were shiny because they were brand-new, and I'd ordered this custom suit for our special occasion. I wouldn't wear it again after today. Like a woman with her wedding dress, I would hang it up in my closet and keep it for sentimental reasons.

I didn't care if that made me a pussy.

I took a seat with my mom, the same paperback tucked under my arm. She looked exactly the same way she did every other day. Her hair was short and curled, and she'd lengthened her eyelashes to make them thick and long. She wore a white blouse with dark jeans, looking just as classy as she did when she still retained her memory.

I introduced myself for the zillionth time.

She eyed my tie, her eyes focusing on the silk fabric. "You look very handsome, Calloway. A little dressed up to visit an old woman like me."

I smiled. "You don't look old to me, Theresa." One of these days, I would slip up and accidentally call her Mom. I wondered what her reaction would be.

"You're a sweet, man. What's today?"

"Saturday."

"You're dressed like that and spending the day with some woman on a Saturday?" She chuckled. "Boy, you need to get a life."

I chuckled, appreciating my mom's feistiness. She used to put my dad in his place—before he turned into a psychopath. "Actually, I'm getting married today. Just wanted to kill some time, so I thought I would stop by."

"What?" She grabbed my hand, her slender fingers covering my knuckles. "You're getting married today?"

I couldn't remember the last time my mother touched me. I hadn't gotten a hug from her in years. I was a grown man who didn't need anyone for anything, but my mother's affection meant something to me. "Yeah."

"That's wonderful." She clapped her hands and gave me a beaming smile. "Who's the lucky lady?"

"Her name is Rome. And she's my world." That summarized my feelings in a nutshell. She was the center of my universe, the focal point through which I looked at the world.

"That's so romantic. Where are you getting married?"

"St. Thomas Church."

"Not sure where that is, but I'm sure it's beautiful."

I nodded. "It's what she wanted. And my woman gets what she wants."

"I can already tell you're going to make a great husband."

"Thank you." Some days would be more difficult than others, but with Rome's help, I knew I would be okay. We could work through any problems we had.

"I'm surprised you aren't having a drink with your friends to fight off the nerves."

"I'm not nervous." Rome was the woman I wanted to spend my life with. Why should I be nervous?

"You have to admit, spending the day with a stranger is an odd utilization of time," she said with a chuckle.

"You aren't a stranger." I didn't know what motivated me to say that. Since I'd been visiting her for years and having the same conversations over and over, I guess I just didn't want to repeat them again. It was a special day for me, and I wanted something different.

She tilted her head slightly, unsure of my meaning.

"I've been visiting you every week for years," I whispered. "You've lost your memory due to illness, so you don't recall me. But I've been reading to you, keeping you company, and spending time with you for a long time."

Instead of asking a million questions, her face fell in sadness. She watched me with pity, like I was the one who was suffering. "You're right...I can't remember anything. My parents...my friends... I woke up this morning in a place I've never seen."

I held the book in my hands, hating the fact that I was sitting there completely helpless. I couldn't make my mother better. If I could shorten my life so she could fully live hers, I would. "I know it must be scary. Just know that you're in a safe place, and you have people who love you."

She felt her necklace around her throat, a piece of jewelry my father gave her when he wasn't such a monster. He eyes drifted to the wooden floor, her look suddenly sunken with despair.

I hated seeing it.

"Are you one of those people, Calloway?" She lowered her hand from her necklace and looked me in the eye, strength slowly replacing her sadness.

"What people?"

"One of the people who love me?"

I gripped the book before I nodded. "I am."

Her eyes watered like she already knew exactly who I was. Maybe she recognized my eyes because they were identical to her own. Maybe she felt the unspoken connection between us, the bond between mother and son. "You're my son…"

I swallowed hard before I nodded, feeling the pain deep in my throat. I thought I would feel happy the day she knew who I was, but somehow, it made me feel worse. Now she knew she missed out on so much of my life, not because she wasn't there, but because those memories were lost. "Yeah."

"Oh…" She reached for my hand, comforting me when I should be comforting her. "You're such a handsome man… I can't believe you're my son."

I gave her hand a squeeze. "I have your eyes." I looked into hers without blinking, wanting her to see the blue color she carried.

"Yes…you do." She brought my hand to her mouth and kissed it. "I'm so sorry I can't remember… I try but I can't."

"Don't apologize, Mom." Tears burned in my eyes when I finally called her by her rightful name. I hated saying Theresa. It was impersonal and improper. "I remember for the both of us. You were a great mom. The best, actually."

"Yeah?" Tears bubbled in her eyes then fell down her cheeks. "Do you have any siblings?"

"A younger brother. Jackson."

"Aww. Do you two look alike?"

"Yes," I said with a chuckle. "People think we're twins from time to time."

"That's wonderful. I'm glad the two of you have stuck together. And what of your father?"

I wasn't going to tell her that he was an evil psychopath that made the world a better place once he died. "He passed away a long time ago."

"Oh…I see."

"You two loved each other a lot."

"I'm sure we did. So, my son is getting married today?"

I knew she wouldn't remember this conversation in the morning, but it was nice to have this moment with her. It was fleeting, about to disappear as quickly as it came, but that was okay. I was grateful I got to have the experience at all. "Yeah. I'm meeting her at the church in an hour."

"I would love to meet her, Calloway. I'm sure she's lovely."

I'd never taken my mom out of the facility before, but we'd never ventured to this level of honesty either. "Come to the wedding."

"Really?" she asked. "You think that's a good idea?"

Rome and Jackson would be surprised, but they would welcome her with open arms. I couldn't think of anything that would make this day more perfect. "Nothing would make me happier."

R ome
I stood outside the church with
Christopher, listening to the cars pass in the
street just a few feet away. When pedestrians walked by,
they looked at me in my floor-length wedding dress.
There was some pointing and smiling. Some people
waved. I even got a few whistles from both men and
women.

"This is the one and only time I'm gonna say this,"
Christopher said. "So you better not miss it."

"I love you too," I blurted.

"Actually, that's not what I was gonna say. Let's not
get carried away."

"Fine," I said with a laugh. "What were you
gonna say?"

He grabbed both of my shoulders and turned serious. "You look really pretty."

"Yeah?" This was already turning out to be a great day.

"Yeah." He squeezed my shoulders before he extended his elbow. "You ready for this?"

"So ready."

"Not nervous?"

"Not even a little bit." Calloway was the only man I wanted to spend my life with. He was exactly what I'd been looking for my whole life. I was excited to change my last name, to become one with him forever.

"Good." He opened the door and walked me inside. Calloway stood at the end of the aisle in front of the empty seats and the pastor. Jackson stood beside him, wearing a dark suit and tie. Music came over the speakers, and even though there was no one there but the four of us, it felt perfect. It was just right—for us.

I loved the way Calloway looked at me. It was the exact same way he'd stared at me every single day of our lives so far. There was need, desperation, and unconditional love in those beautiful blue eyes. I knew he would cherish me every single day, make me strong when I was weak, make me feel beautiful when I was hideous.

He would give me everything I needed.

It seemed to take a lifetime for Christopher to walk

me to the front. We didn't walk with the music, but time seemed to slow down anyway. By the time I finally got there, I didn't even realize I was holding onto Christopher. I didn't feel him beside me at all.

Calloway took my hand and ignored Christopher like he wasn't there. Calloway grabbed my hands and looked me in the eyes, not having a flicker of doubt on his features. He looked like the strong man I'd seen every single day. Calloway wasn't the kind of man to be nervous, and he definitely wasn't nervous then.

The priest began the short ceremony, reading our vows and our promise to love one another. I nearly forgot to repeat the words that were spoken to me because I was concentrating on Calloway's face, on the clean look of his jaw since he shaved that morning. The priest read the vows to Calloway. "Will you take this woman to be your wife, to love and cherish her until death do you part?"

The corner of his mouth rose in a smile. "I'll love you longer than that."

The priest continued. "Do you take this man to be your husband, to love and obey him until death do you part?"

I knew Calloway specifically asked the priest to put that line about obedience in there. But that was a compromise, one of many that we would make together. "I do."

His eyes darkened just the way I liked, the way he looked at me before he possessed me on the bed. He hands gently squeezed mine, and he restrained himself from pulling me into his chest.

"I now pronounce you husband and wife. You may kiss the bride."

Calloway took those words very seriously as his hands cupped my face and he kissed me, giving me that delicious mouth and some of his tongue. He kissed me long and hard, not caring about Jackson and Christopher being forced to watch our ridiculous display of affection.

My hands moved around his wrists, feeling his gently beating pulse under the skin. I could feel forever in that kiss, feel a lifetime of joy. Calloway and I had our problems in the past, but all of that didn't seem to matter anymore.

He pulled away then pressed a kiss to my forehead. "Mrs. Owens. I love the way that sounds."

"Me too, Mr. Owens."

Calloway took my hand and guided me to a seat in the front aisle. A woman I hadn't noticed before was sitting there, dabbing her eyes with a tissue. It took me a second to understand who she was.

"Your mom...?"

Calloway nodded. "I visited her today, and things went well..."

"Then she knows who you are?"

"Yeah."

His mother rose to her feet, her eyes still wet. "You look so beautiful." She pulled me into her arms and hugged me in a way my own mother never did. Her touch was full of affection even though, to her, she'd just met me that day. She didn't know a single thing about me, but she already loved me. "You'll give my son such beautiful children. That makes me so happy." She pulled away and kissed me on the cheek. "So proud of you, Cal." She moved into his side and hugged him.

"Thanks, Mom." Calloway never showed his weak spots to anyone. The only time his shell seemed to soften was when he was with me—and his mother. I loved the fact that he wasn't callused all the time, that he wore his heart on his sleeve sometimes. "Jackson is gonna take you home so Rome and I can head on our trip."

"That's wonderful," she said. "You two have the best time, okay?"

"We will." Calloway grabbed my hand and guided me to the large church doors I'd entered through in the beginning. When we got outside, a white limo was waiting for us, Tom holding the back door for us.

Sunlight hit us hard in the face on that spring afternoon, making Calloway's eyes light up brighter than usual. He rarely smiled, but right now he wore a grin I'd never seen before. It was the kind of happiness that infected all of his features, turned him into a softer version of himself. Sometimes he chuckled when I made a joke, but it wasn't anything compared to this. It was the first time he'd seemed truly happy.

"I like it when you smile like that."

He guided me to the car, but his eyes were on me the entire time. "Smile like what?"

"Smile like you're free."

"I don't feel free," he said. "I've been free my whole life, and that's why I was so miserable. But now...I have something to live for." He took the door from Tom and extended his hand so he could help me inside.

"Now I have something to live for too."

Calloway Mom sat on my left at the table, while Jackson sat on my other side. Rome just finished placing all the dishes on the table and finally sat down to eat. Our wineglasses were full, and the meal smelled incredible.

"So how long have you two been married?" Mom asked.

"A year," I answered. "Our anniversary is next week."

"Oh, that's wonderful," Mom said. "They say the first year is the hardest... I'm not sure how correct that is. Honestly, I can't remember the first year of my marriage. I can't even remember your father."

"That's okay, Mom," I said. "We can always remind you."

"Yeah," Jackson. "Calloway and I look just like him—except we have your eyes."

"And that's not correct," I said. "The first year was a breeze." Rome and I enjoyed our honeymoon and all the fantastic routine of our married life. We worked together every day, used the gym together, came home and had dinner, and of course, the sex was as great as it'd always been—in and out of the playroom.

Rome wore a smile as she sat down. "I've enjoying picking up his dirty socks a lot more than I thought I would."

Mom chuckled. "I just hope they didn't smell too bad."

"I don't smell," I countered. Mom could probably contradict that with stories of my childhood, but fortunately, she didn't remember any of that. When I went to visit her in the nursing home, I reminded her who I was, and she took the revelation well. But there were times when she didn't take the news well at all. She screamed and cried and got so worked up that she demanded I leave and never come back.

"I'm sure they smelled like ass." Jackson dug into his food immediately, shoving large chunks of food into his mouth like a grizzly bear.

"Manners," Mom snapped.

Jackson took his elbows off the table and took

smaller bites of food, eating like a human rather than a wild animal.

Mom took a few bites then turned to Rome. "You have a brother, don't you, sweetheart?"

"I do." Rome sipped her wine before she returned the glass to the table. "His name is Christopher. He works in bonds and mutual funds at a private wealth company in the city. He likes it."

"Delightful. Is he older than you?"

"By a few months."

Mom raised an eyebrow, knowing that didn't add up.

"Rome and Christopher were both adopted," I explained. Mom asked about this many times, but since she could never remember it, we had to repeat.

"Oh, I see," Mom said. "Water is just as strong as blood sometimes."

"I think it's stronger." I shot Jackson a glare.

"Oh, shut up." Jackson picked up a piece of corn and threw it at me. "You love me, and you know it."

"Do not."

"I distinctly remember you saying otherwise." Jackson shoved another pile of food into his mouth.

"Only because you said it first, and I didn't want you to feel like an idiot." After I was shot, Jackson turned soft on me. But now we picked on each other again like I'd never had a near-death experience.

"Shut up, you two," Rome said. "Theresa and I know

you two love each other. So stop pretending that you don't."

"I never said I didn't love him," Jackson argued. "He's the one saying he doesn't love me."

I rolled my eyes. "This is the stupidest argument we've ever had."

"No," Jackson said. "I'm pretty sure we've had worse."

A knock sounded on the door.

"Hmm, I wonder who that is." Rome set her napkin on the table and pushed her chair back.

"No." I rose to my feet and pointed at her chair. "Sit."

Jackson grabbed his fork and knife and started acting like a caveman. "You do this…you do that. Now."

Rome covered her mouth and laughed at his dead-on impersonation.

"You got something to say, punk?" I crossed my arms over my chest and stared him down.

"Me?" He continued to do his caveman act. "Me hungry. Me thirsty."

The knock sounded again.

Rome laughed again, and that's when I gave up. I walked to the front door and checked the peephole before I let Christopher walk inside. "Hey, man. We're just having dinner. You wanna join us?"

"Free food?" he asked. "Hell yeah."

"Then come on in." We walked back into the dining room. Christopher grabbed a plate and sat beside

Rome. Just like Jackson, he shoveled pounds of food onto his plate like he hadn't eaten in days. When he realized my mother was at the table, he introduced himself. He'd met her dozens of times, but he was used to the routine. "Hey, Theresa. I'm Christopher, Rome's brother."

"Oh, we were just talking about you," Mom said. "They were all good things, I promise."

"I'm sure," Christopher said. "Rome thinks the world of me."

"Yeah…" Rome said sarcastically. "I always chat you up."

Christopher grabbed a piece of corn and threw it at Rome just the way Jackson threw a piece at me earlier.

Rome opened her mouth and caught it.

"Wow." Jackson clapped his hands together. "That's good instincts right there."

"That's my woman," I said proudly. "Quick reflexes."

"Hey, I wanted to talk to you about something," Christopher said as he turned on Jackson.

"Yeah?" Jackson asked. "Finances? Women? Style? I've got a great tailor on Fifth—"

"No, it's about that chick, Isabella," Christopher said. "I ran into her at Ruin the other night."

I didn't realize Christopher was a new member. And I certainly didn't know Isabella was back.

"What's her story?" Christopher asked. "She's hot."

Rome kept eating like she didn't want to be part of the conversation.

I assumed that meant Christopher didn't realize that this Isabella and the one who shot me were one and the same.

Jackson clearly didn't know what to say. He eyed me like he wanted me to handle the conversation.

"Isabella and I used to be involved," I explained. "A long time ago."

"Oh…" Christopher leaned back and looked down at his food. "Sorry, man. I didn't know."

"No, it's alright," I said. "And she's the one who, you know." I didn't want to mention the story in front of my mom. She would get upset, and since she wouldn't remember it tomorrow, it was a waste of time.

"Oh…" Christopher stopped chewing, speaking with his full mouth. "Shit, I didn't make that connection."

"She's a good girl," I said. "You should go for it."

Jackson raised an eyebrow. "A good girl? Are you kidding me?"

Rome's mood darkened, her feelings about Isabella obvious. She would never forgive the woman for shooting me, even if it was an accident.

"She made a mistake," I said. "I know she didn't mean to do it."

"But she meant to allow Hank to kidnap me," Rome said darkly.

"She didn't know what he was going to do with you," I said. "She was depressed and out of her mind—"

"Don't defend her," Rome hissed.

Mom kept eating, her head down once the conversation became tense.

I didn't want to get into this with Rome in front of everyone. We didn't talk about Isabella or Hank anymore. Now we just lived our lives—in happiness. "All I'm saying is, if you're looking for a woman from Ruin, she's a good match."

"Well, I'm kinda looking for a wife," Christopher said. "You know, someone who's pretty, got her shit together, and knows how to cook. The basics."

"That's sweet," Mom said. "You'll find someone special if you look hard enough."

"She's definitely not the wife type," Jackson said with a laugh. "She's more of a pit stop on the race track."

"Christopher." Rome's cold voice cut through the conversation. "I don't want you anywhere near her. I don't tell you what to do or who to see. But she's off-limits. There's plenty of other fish in the sea."

That was the worst possible thing Rome could say.

"Now she's forbidden…" He waggled his eyebrows.

"I'm being serious, Christopher," she hissed. "She's not good enough for you—even if it's just for the night."

"Aww." He patted her on the shoulder. "My little sister is protective. Pointless, but cute."

Rome returned her attention to her dinner, finally dropping the conversation.

We were having a great night, so I decided to change the subject to chase away the tension. "Rome and I are taking a trip to Martha's Vineyard for our anniversary. We're gonna have some wine and relax by the pool."

"Geez, that sounds boring," Jackson said. "I'd rather go to Vegas or something."

"For an anniversary?" Christopher asked. "I'm not romantic, but even I know that's not a good choice."

"It's not boring when you're in love." I looked across the table and made eye contact with Rome. She was still angry, her lips pressed tightly together in irritation. She tried to avoid my look because she wanted to stay angry. When she was in a bad mood, she did her best to stay that way.

But under my ruthless stare, she didn't last long. Her heart called the shots, and her eyes obeyed. She looked at me across the table, those pretty emeralds weak against mine. Her lips slowly softened because she easily fell victim to my powerful look.

For our anniversary, we would dine on wine and cheese and make love in the cottage I rented on the vineyard. It would be a great way to celebrate a year of marriage, the best year of my life. Everyone was busy talking about Vegas, so I mouthed to her across the table, "I love you."

That was the final nail in the coffin. Now she was completely vulnerable to me, a meal on a platter. She pressed her lips together firmly as she repressed the smile that wanted to stretch across her mouth. The joy moved into her eyes before she moved it back. "I love you too." Isabella was forgotten. Hank was forgotten. Even everyone at the table was forgotten.

It was just the two of us.

Rome lay on the bed, her head dangling over the edge with her face to the ceiling. Her mouth was wide open, and I was fucking her throat at the foot of the bed. One hand gripped her firm tit while the other gripped the edge for balance.

I rammed my cock inside her warm mouth, hitting her deep in the throat every time. Her saliva dripped down her face and onto the carpet at my feet. "Mrs. Owens...just like that." Anytime I had the opportunity to call her by that name, I did. I didn't care about referring to her as sweetheart anymore.

She kept her tongue flat and only breathed when I gave her the opportunity to. She'd become an experienced submissive, doing the things I enjoyed without hitting her own triggers. We'd come to a good understanding of what the other person could handle.

She didn't fulfill every single desire I had, but she made up for it in other ways.

I was on the verge of coming since I could see my cock press against the inside of her throat. Her skin moved every single time I thrust, and seeing my own definition made me want to squirt down that beautiful throat of hers.

I pulled out then grabbed my belt from the floor. "On your stomach, feet on the ground." I slapped the belt against my hand and made a cracking noise, telling her I meant business.

She turned over and moved to the edge of the bed, but she held herself up on her hands and knees.

"On your stomach."

She shook her ass in my face. "Master, punish me."

I slapped the belt against her ass hard, wanting to punish her for defying me. "Call me Husband. Nothing else." I'd thought Master was the most powerful word in the world, but when she called me Husband, it gave me a new thrill. I loved it.

She gasped when she felt the belt bite her skin.

"On your stomach." I wanted to spank her like a child over my knee.

She still didn't cooperate. "You want to be punished more?" I slapped her with the belt again, making her shift forward. "These aren't part of the ten, just to be clear." I'd give her ten new ones when she was in the right position.

Rome turned over, wearing her black bra and thong. She looked beautiful when she was stripped down to her undergarments, her brown hair soft and curly. Her eyes contrasted against the darkness of the room, completely beautiful. "Calloway."

I slapped the belt against my hand since I couldn't hit her when she faced me like this.

"I don't want to lie on my stomach because..." Her hand moved to her stomach.

I eyed her hand, unsure what was happening. Did she have a stomachache? Did she feel sick? I didn't have a clue. She'd seemed fine a second ago when she was sucking my dick. "What is it, Mrs. Owens?"

She looked down at her stomach, taking her time before she said her next words. "I'm pregnant, Calloway." When she lifted her chin, reluctance was written all over her face. She was scared of my reaction, scared of this unexpected news.

We hadn't been trying. She'd been taking her pills as far as I knew. We hadn't even talked about children yet. I assumed it would happen at some point. I just figured it would happen intentionally.

I had my doubts about being a father since my own was worthless. But Rome would be there with me the entire time. It wasn't like I would be alone. While I had my darker world, being in charge of Humanitarians United still made me a great role model. Or I could just walk away from Ruin altogether.

It was a sacrifice I was willing to make.

But all those questions and discussions could happen at a different time. Right now, she needed my assurance that I was happy, that I would love our baby as much as I would love her. I dropped the belt on the ground then placed my large palms on her slightly distended stomach. I'd noticed she was rounder in that area, but I never cared enough about her physical fitness to pay attention to it. She was perfect, in my ways.

I kneeled down and pressed a kiss to her stomach, my eyes on her. "That's wonderful, Mrs. Owens."

"Really?" That single word escaped her throat with such relief that it filled the entire room. Her hands moved over mine, and her shoulders visibly relaxed. "I know we didn't plan for this and—"

"It'll be alright." I kissed her stomach again and rested my forehead against her belly, unable to believe there was life growing inside her. "I'm happy."

"You are? I was scared what you would think…"

"I'm your husband. How can I not love anything that comes out of you?" My hands slid over her bare stomach to her hips. I rose to my feet then leaned over her, forcing her back to the mattress. I had been intent on fucking her senseless, but now I wasn't interested in something so harsh. I wanted to make love to my wife, to celebrate the beautiful thing we made together. "I'll take good care of you, sweetheart—both of you."

Her hands cupped my face, and she gave me a look of love that had deepened over the years. With every passing day, it grew bigger and stronger. She didn't just look at me as the man she fell in love with, but as the man she wanted to spend her life with. We'd be together every day until time ripped our bodies apart. But our souls would always remain intertwined.

Forever.

ABOUT THE AUTHOR

Keep in touch with Victoria Quinn and get the latest news about upcoming releases at www.VictoriaQuinnBooks.com